WHEN THE DAY OF EVIL COMES

WHEN THE DAY OF
EVIL
COMES

A NOVEL OF SUSPENSE

MELANIE WELLS

Multnomah® Publishers Sisters, Oregon

WHEN THE DAY OF EVIL COMES
published by Multnomah Publishers, Inc.

© 2005 by Melanie Wells
International Standard Book Number: 1-59052-426-8

Cover image by M. Neugebauer/Masterfile
Author photo by Hillsman Jackson

Multnomah is a trademark of Multnomah Publishers, Inc.,
and is registered in the U.S. Patent and Trademark Office.
The colophon is a trademark of Multnomah Publishers, Inc.

Printed in the United States of America

For information:
MULTNOMAH PUBLISHERS, INC.
POST OFFICE BOX 1720
SISTERS, OREGON 97759

Library of Congress Cataloging-in-Publication Data

Wells, Melanie.
    When the day of evil comes : a novel / Melanie Wells.
        p. cm.
    ISBN 1-59052-426-8
    I. Title.
    PS3623.E476W47 2005
    813'.6—dc22

                                        2004029822

05 06 07 08 09 10—10 9 8 7 6 5 4 3 2 1 0

~

For Trish, my sister
and
For Dennis, who has my heart

"Our cause is never more in danger than when a human,
no longer desiring, but still intending, to do our Enemy's will,
looks round upon a universe from which every trace of Him seems
to have vanished, asks why he has been forsaken, and still obeys."

SCREWTAPE TO WORMWOOD IN
THE SCREWTAPE LETTERS BY C. S. LEWIS

ACKNOWLEDGMENTS

~

Writing is a tedious and solitary endeavor. In the glow of the computer screen at 3:00 a.m. on a Tuesday, with a full day of civilian work on the other side of daylight, writing a novel can seem like the most extravagant, irresponsible indulgence.

I offer immense gratitude to those who encouraged me to stick with it.

My parents, Dot and Ron Wells, taught me to color outside the lines. Felicia Brady, singer-songwriter and fellow traveler, has quite literally cheered me on. I have the poster to prove it. Susan Thornberg read every word of an earlier work and always wanted more. Kim Coffin read this manuscript in her usual obsessive manner, noticing details everyone else had missed, as did Elizabeth Emerson. My fellow Wednesday night whiners—the Waah Waah Sisterhood—prayed for me and encouraged me weekly. Trish Murphy, singer-songwriter and best friend, shares the crucible and has fried me lots of chicken. And Dennis Ippolito, who sees with such a clear eye, encouraged me to set a deadline, take some time off work, and finish this book. He then read every word, more than once, through drafts, rewrites, and edits, pen in hand, and offered invaluable insight.

Following the bread-crumb trail to Multnomah…Allen Dorsett of the Sanctuary International pointed me across the room to James Langteaux, who was visiting Vail that evening and had just signed with Multnomah. James read an early work of mine and sent it to his editor, David Kopp, who walked it down the hall to Rod Morris, who liked my voice. A particular, thunderous thanks to Rod, who encouraged me to write this book, continued to check in on me, even during the wasteland years, and when the manuscript finally arrived, uttered the magic words, "I like it. I want to publish it." Rod went to bat for this book and then, with a careful surgical hand, shaved the edges off and left a book that is exactly what I hoped it would be.

All my thanks.

1

~

SOMEONE SAID TO ME THAT DAY, "It's hotter than the eyes of hell out here." I can't remember who. Looking back, I wonder if it meant something, that phrase. Something more than a weather report. But as it was, I let the remark pass without giving it a thought. It was hot. Hotter than the eyes of hell. That was true enough.

If I'd known enough to be afraid, I would have been. But I was a thousand years younger then, it seems, and I didn't know what was out there. To me, it seemed like an ordinary day.

I was making a rare appearance at a faculty event. I hate faculty events. Generally, truth be told, I hate any sort of event. Anything that involves pretending, in a preordained way, to like a bunch of people with whom I have something perfunctory in common. Faculty events fall into this category.

This particular faculty event was a picnic at Barton Springs in Austin. The picnic was the final fling of a faculty retreat—my definition of hell on earth, speaking of hell. They'd all spent the weekend at a retreat center in the hill country of Texas, getting to know each other. Or bonding, as we say in the industry.

Imagine the scene. A dozen puffed-up psychologists (I include myself only in the latter part of this description, for I do admit I'm a psychologist), wallowing in all the clichés. Bonding exercises. Trust falls. Processing groups. Sharing. I could imagine few things more horrific.

I'd begged off the retreat, citing a speaking engagement in San Antonio. A speaking engagement, might I add, that had been carefully calendared a year before, timed precisely to oppose the dreaded faculty retreat.

So I'd spent the weekend in the hill country too. But my gig involved talking to entering master's-degree students about surviving graduate school. A topic on which I considered myself an expert, since I'd done more time in graduate school than 99 percent of the population of this grand country of ours. Hard time, in fact. I'd won my release a few years before by earning my PhD and promising myself I'd never breach the last frontier—the suck-you-in quagmire known as "post-graduate education."

Over the weekend, I'd let those entering students in on my secret—higher education is all about perseverance. It has nothing to do with smarts or creativity or anything else.

It's about cultivating the willingness and stamina for hoop-jumping.

Jump through the hoops, I'd said. Do it well. Do it relentlessly. And in a few years, you can join the elite of the American education system, secure in the knowledge that you too can endure with the best of them.

After sharing this little tidbit, I'd decided to take my own advice and jump through a hoop myself. The aforementioned faculty picnic at Barton Springs.

Barton Springs is a natural spring-fed pool in the heart of Austin, which is in the heart of Texas. And since it was the heart of summer, the water would be sixty-eight degrees of heaven on a hundred-degree day.

I like picnics, generally. And anything that involves water is a good thing in my eyes. I'd started swimming competitively once I figured out that swimming is like graduate school. Perseverance is the thing. And I'm pretty good at that.

So I drove to the picnic that day with a fairly good attitude, for me, considering this was a herd event for professional hoop-jumpers.

I parked my truck in the shade, saying a quick prayer of thanks for the shady spot. I don't know why I do things like that, pray over a parking spot, as though the Lord Himself is concerned about which parking space I get. Surely He has more important things on His mind. But I said the prayer anyway, parked my truck, grabbed my swim bag, and set out to find my colleagues.

They were bunched up in a good spot: near a group of picnic tables, under a live oak tree, and next to one of my favorite things in life. A rope swing. What could be more fun, I ask you? Rope swings are childhood for grown-ups.

I said my hellos and settled in at one of the tables next to my department head, Helene Levine. I liked the name. It had a swingy, rhymie sort of rhythm to it. One of the matriarchs, as she liked to describe herself, referring to her Jewish heritage.

Helene is indeed matriarchal. She's an imposing woman, with a big battle-axe bosom and a manner that is simultaneously threatening and nurturing. I don't know how she pulls that off, but I love her. And she loves me. For some reason, as different as we are, we hit it off from the beginning. I signed up as daughter to her nurturing side.

This day, she was in threatening mode, at least with everyone else. Foul-tempered in the heat, I guess. And probably sick of babysitting her faculty charges. In any case, she brightened when she saw me, handed me a plate of fried chicken and potato salad, and poured me a cold soda. I settled in to eat.

The food was good. Few things in the world sing to my heart like picnic food. Especially good fried chicken, and I knew Helene had fried this chicken herself. I ate a breast and a wing, two helpings of potato salad, and a huge fudge brownie, all washed down with the national drink of Texas, Dr. Pepper. A meal of champions.

Then the rope swing beckoned.

Since most PhD'd folks spend lots and lots of time bent over books or lecturing halls full of students, they don't get outside much. Hence, they tend to be white and lumpy. They are also not very much fun.

I am not terribly lumpy by nature and try to grasp at any fun that is to be had, being determined as I am not to sacrifice my life on the altar of academe. So while everyone else stayed safely dressed and sheltered on the shore, I availed myself of the dressing room, changed into my bikini, and jumped in the pool.

For a while, I was self-conscious, with all those psychologists watching me frolic by myself. Surely there was something Freudian in my behavior that would get me duly diagnosed and labeled. I kept at it, though, and eventually they lost interest in me and returned to their conversations.

After some diligent practice with the rope swing, I discovered that if I timed it just right, letting go at the very zenith of the arc as I swung out over the spring, I could hit a deep well in the pool, falling into cool, dark water that seemed to take me somewhere safe and almost otherworldly. I did that over and over, sloughing off my stress from the weekend (I had been working, after all) and leaving it on the cold smooth slabs of limestone at the bottom of the pool.

After several minutes of this, I climbed onto the shore, ready for another go, and discovered that someone was competing for my toy. A man stood there, holding the swing tentatively. I found everything about him unsettling.

His skin was chalk-white and he was hairless as a cue ball. He looked like a cancer victim. Not a survivor, which conjures up sinewy visions of strength and triumph, but a victim. Someone weak and bony and sickly, just this side of death. Next to me, with my against-dermatologist's-advice summer tan, he looked like death itself.

I'm not shy, so I walked up next to him. "You want a turn?" I asked.

"What do you do?" His voice was strong and deep, incongruous against his appearance.

I wasn't sure if he was asking what I did for a living or what you do with a rope swing. Since I don't like to tell people what I do for a living, I opted for the rope swing question. "You just grab on and swing out," I said. "And then let go as far out as you can. I'll show you."

I took the rope from him and walked backward to the rock I'd been jumping off of, then made a run for it, landing again in my favorite spot.

When I came up for air, he was in the water right next to me. I suddenly felt uncomfortable.

I fell back on a lame old line.

"Come here often?" I asked.

"Never," he said. "I'm not from Austin."

"Where are you from?"

"I live in Houston now."

Which made sense, since that's where the big cancer center is. Maybe he was just there for treatment or something. I felt sorry for him, but something about him wasn't sitting right with me. I have pretty good instincts about people. I decided to listen to myself and end the encounter.

"The cold water's starting to get to me," I said. "I think I'm going to get out. Nice meeting you."

"We didn't actually meet," he said. "I'm Peter Terry."

I gave him a little nod and said, "nice meeting you" again. "I'm Dylan," I said, and immediately regretted it.

"Nice meeting you," he said.

Okay. Done meeting this guy. I swam for the shore and climbed out onto the bank, making a point to look back at him and wave after I got on solid ground.

I felt my stomach clench as he turned to swim away. His back had a big gash in it, red and unspeakably violent against all that pasty white skin.

I strained to see it clearly. The wound was jagged and severe, brutal enough to be fatal, it looked like to me, in my quick view of it. It ran horizontally, between his shoulders, blade to blade. It was red and ugly, shredded, pulpy flesh pulled back from a scarlet strip of bleeding muscle.

My mind started casting about for a better explanation, needing to make some sense of what I was seeing. Surely it wasn't a real gash. No one with a wound like that would be walking around.

I finally decided it could be a tattoo. In fact, it must be a tattoo. That was the only logical conclusion. Which just confirmed my impression that something was off with this guy. Anyone with a tattoo like that had some issues, in my professional opinion. Good riddance.

I toweled off and walked back to my group, glad to be with the lumpy whities. Suddenly they looked pretty good to me. I sat down next to Helene and reached into my swim bag.

I found a surprise. A box, ribboned and wrapped.

I held it up. "Hey, what's this?"

Helene looked over. "I have no idea. I got one too. I thought it was from you."

The others started looking into purses and bags. Eventually, each person came up with a box, all identically wrapped.

We opened them together, accusing one another of being the thoughtful culprit behind such a fun surprise. No one copped to it, though.

Each box contained something different, but they were all personal gifts. Expensive personal gifts. No one at that picnic could afford such extravagance on faculty salaries. Even those of us who were in private practice wouldn't have spent that kind of money. We didn't like each other that much.

Someone must have a secret, I assumed. Someone who was equally wealthy and codependent. And slightly manipulative.

I didn't really care. I like presents.

My gift was a black leather cord necklace with one big, rough black stone trimmed in silver. It was beautiful and very funky. Perfect for me, since I'm sort of a hippie and like strange jewelry. Whoever picked it out knew me pretty well.

We accused each other for a while longer, until it became obvious that no one was going to confess. Finally, we packed up our stuff and called it a weekend, the faculty retreat officially over. I suspected everyone would show up Monday morning wearing or using their gifts. John would mark his appointments in his new leather Day-timer. Helene would be using her fountain pen. And you bet I'd be wearing that nifty necklace.

I said my good-byes and walked to my old, worn-out pickup truck—a '72 Ford I'd purchased for seven hundred dollars—yanking the door open and promising myself once again I was going to buy a can of WD-40. That door was stubborn as a donkey and twice as loud.

I threw my bag in and started to scoot onto the seat when something caught my eye.

It was another package, wrapped just like the necklace had been. Identically.

I picked it up, examining this one more closely. The paper was expensive. Not the kind of wrapping paper you get at the drugstore. The kind you buy from specialty stores that sell handmade journals and twenty-dollar soap. The ribbon was fresh, unwrinkled satin. Off-white paper, off-white ribbon. Lovely and tasteful.

Warily I pulled one end of the ribbon and eased the paper away from the box. The box was generic, as the others had been. Thick pressed white cardboard, expensively made. But no store logo on it. Nothing that would identify where it came from.

I tilted open the lid, took a peek, and dropped the box. Inside was an engagement ring. It was platinum, an antique setting, with a beautiful 1.2-carat diamond set among a few dainty smaller stones.

The reason I knew the weight of the diamond is that I knew the ring. Intimately. It was my mother's ring. And it was supposed to be on her finger, six feet under at the cemetery outside her hometown.

I'd decided to bury her with it instead of keeping it for myself. I'd seen it on her finger before they closed the lid. That was two years ago last March.

I fished my new necklace out of my purse, opening that box carefully, suspiciously. The necklace was still there, funky and chunky. I took it out of the box and closed my fingers around it in a fist.

I got out of the truck, slammed that noisy door, and marched back to the water's edge. I stood on my launching rock and wound up, throwing that necklace as far as I could into the spring. It was a good, long throw, reminiscent of years of childhood lessons from my brother. The necklace hit with barely a plop and sank to the bottom.

I sat down on the rock for a minute. Queasy and green with emotion.

I waited there until my head stopped spinning, then walked out to the parking lot and got in my truck. It started with its usual rumble, reminding me that I needed a new muffler too. But it got me home, which is where I wanted to be.

I pulled up in my driveway in Dallas four hours later, relieved at the impending comfort of my house and looking forward to a warm, soapy bath. I unloaded my gear, tucking the box with the ring in it carefully into my swim bag, and hauled all my stuff to the front door.

And there, hanging on my front doorknob, was that necklace, still dripping with the cold water of Barton Springs.

2

I HAD A TIME DECIDING what to do with that necklace overnight. I didn't want it in the house. That I was certain of. But I was afraid that if I tried to dispose of it, it would keep following me around, as ridiculous as that seemed.

What if I threw it in the dumpster, only to find it on my bedside table when I crawled out from under the covers the next morning? I couldn't stand the thought. It was just too creepy.

I felt somehow that the solution was to satisfy the ghost. Or whatever it was that had brought the necklace back to me.

Now let me say here that I do not believe in ghosts. And though I am a Christian person and consider myself to be fairly serious about my faith, I am not one to see a demon under every rock. The supernatural is not something I think a lot about.

But this experience had me rocked. Ghost. Demon. Weirdo Peter Terry. Whatever or whoever had retrieved that necklace from the bottom of the Springs and hung it on my doorknob had my attention. I intended to play the odds.

So I took the necklace and the ring, put them both in a little velvet bag that had held some other jewelry at one time, and locked them in the buffet cabinet in my living room.

The cabinet was old, a hand-me-down from my mother.

The connection to Mother seemed to have an appropriate vibe to it. Maybe she wanted me to have both gifts or something, as weird as that sounded. I trusted her furniture to hold the jewelry for me overnight.

I locked it in there, said a long prayer for safety, and went to bed. Slept like a stone, believe it or not.

Somehow I always manage to run late the first day of the semester. Some subconscious resistance on my part to working, no doubt, since I'm truly lazy by nature. I overslept that day and had to get myself ready for work in a hurry.

But I made it to class on time, with about four seconds to spare, and found myself standing in front of thirty-seven freshmen, all of whom had signed up for my Intro to Psychology class at Southern Methodist University.

I should say a few things about SMU. Though the "M" stands for "Methodist," SMU is a liberal arts school. Not a church school like some other universities that have churchy words in their names. No theology or religion classes are required, and you can get through your entire academic career on campus and never hear a word about God or the Methodist church, either one.

That worked for me. It is an atmosphere for free thinkers (unless you are a Democrat, but that's another conversation), and I like to keep my theology and religion to myself, thank you very much.

And where my colleagues at other churchy-named schools are regularly getting themselves called before boards to defend their beliefs (or lack thereof), my superiors are happy if I can get my students to use their actual brains and get myself published on a regular basis. I am rigorously faithful to both of these tasks. Faculty events, thankfully, are optional.

I like to start the semester off, especially when I have nice fresh, green minds in the seats, with an exercise in the psychology of assumptions. It throws the students a curve, gets the semester started out right.

I stood in front of the class and tried to look authoritative, which is a stretch for me, since I don't look much older than my students do.

"Everyone look at me," I said sternly. I am not terribly stern, in actuality, but they didn't know that yet.

They all looked up at me like they were in trouble.

"Keep your eyes on me," I said, "and clear your desks. Do not look down at what you're doing. No pens and paper allowed on your desks."

They shuffled around with their stuff, trying to maintain eye contact with me, but dying to look at one another. They wanted to pass the question around the room with their eyes—"What's up with this psycho?"

After a minute or two, the desks were clear. I took out a tennis ball and held it up for everyone to look at, as though it had some sort of cosmic importance.

Without saying a word, I tossed the ball to a kid in the first row. He caught it, and I said, "Name, please?"

"Jeremy," he said, and tossed the ball back to me.

I tossed it to another kid and raised my eyebrows, as though I were asking him a question.

"Darin," he said without prompting, and threw the ball back to me.

I repeated the exercise until everyone had caught the ball, recited his or her first name, and thrown the ball back to me. It happened, like magic, thirty-seven times.

"Now," I said, "what did you learn?" I looked over the faces. "Lauren." I called on a girl in the second row. By the look on her face you'd have thought I'd punched her in the gut.

She turned to her left and right. "This is Stephanie," she said. "And that's Chris."

"Anything else?" I asked.

"I don't remember any of the others."

I looked disappointed and called on another kid. He remembered six or seven names. I asked around the class, prodding them all to tell me what they'd learned. One after another, they listed all the names they could remember.

Finally one kid sitting near the back raised his hand.

I called on him.

"I learned something," he offered.

I liked the look of him. He was scruffy and seemed slightly disreputable. He had an ankh on a leather rope around his neck and earrings in both ears. His hair was bleached yellow-white and his clothes could have been purchased at an Army surplus store. Or stolen from one, maybe.

"And what might that be?" I searched my memory for his name. "Gavin?"

"We're all a bunch of sheep."

People turned around to look at him.

I grinned. "Go on."

"You never told us to say our names."

"Are you sure?" I asked.

"Positive. You asked the first guy what his name was, then everyone else just went along. We all assumed that's what you wanted. But you never said that at all."

"Good observation. Anything else?"

"Yeah. Come to think of it, you never asked us to throw the ball back either. We just did it. Every last one of us. Like sheep."

"Gavin, you are a genius." I threw him a bite-size Snickers bar, my standard reward for creative thinking. "You get the first candy of the semester."

I turned to the class and began clapping. Everyone clapped along.

"See?" Gavin said, when the clapping had died down. "Sheep. Everyone clapped. Just because you did."

"Good point."

I threw him another Snickers bar. He opened it up with a rattle and popped it into his mouth, staring at me while he chewed.

I spent the rest of the hour leading a discussion about perception versus reality. How we all make subtle, unspoken assumptions, sometimes in unison, and allow those assumptions to govern our thinking and our behavior. By the end of the hour, I'd knocked some holes in their concrete brains and, I hope, planted a few seeds for nonconformity and creative thought.

I could tell it would be a good semester. I began to feel myself being drawn into the school year, and remembered once again how much I love teaching. It happens every fall, usually after I've spent the entire summer thinking about changing jobs.

I left to grab an early lunch at my favorite sub sandwich place across the street, spent a little time sitting outside working on my skin cancer, and then did my afternoon lecture.

As the students got up to leave, I was surprised to see Gavin walk into the classroom and stand by my desk.

"Good work this morning," I said to him. "Is this your first semester at SMU?"

"Yep." He picked up my book bag to carry it for me. My hands were full with my mug and a stack of notebooks, so I was grateful for the help. "You have another class now?" he asked.

I shook my head. "Office hours." I looked up at the clock on the wall. It was 3:35. My office was two floors up and I was supposed to be there five minutes ago. I started up the stairs, Gavin tagging along.

"Mind if I follow you to your office?" he asked.

"Of course not. Are you one of my advisees this semester? I give lousy advice. Scheduling conflicts are complete nightmares for me."

He shook his head. "I don't need that kind of advice."

We wove through student traffic and found our way to my office. I unlocked the door and shoved it open with my hip, dropping the stack of notebooks onto a chair and clearing another one for him to sit in.

I like my faculty office. It's full of things that inspire me. Rocks I brought back from a mission trip to Guatemala. Pictures of my grandparents when they were still optimistic. Shelves and shelves of books written by my favorite smart people—Eudora Welty and Francis Schaeffer and C.S. Lewis. People like that.

The office is tiny, since I have no status at all in a fairly weighty department. But it has a window and it's cozy and it's mine. It's a good place to settle in and think.

I fixed myself another cup of tea—the last cup of a half-gallon this day, it seemed, and offered Gavin one. He declined.

He looked nervous, so I settled in behind my desk and asked him what was on his mind.

"I read your bio," he said.

"My bio? I have a bio?"

"On the Internet. The university has a website and each department has faculty bios and pictures."

"Tell me there's not a picture." This could be bad. I'm always the one with the eyes closed and the mouth open.

"It's a pretty good one," he said. "You look a little drunk, is all."

"Well, I probably wasn't, but I might want to be after I take a look at the picture." We had a laugh. "Anyway, you were saying?"

"The bio. It said you have a theology degree."

I nodded. "Guilty as charged. A master's in systematic theology, actually. I went to school here in Dallas."

"Yeah, I saw that." He shifted around. "Why'd you do that?"

"What? Go to grad school in Dallas or get a theology degree?"

"The theology part. Are you really religious or something?"

"Actually, no. The theology degree was personal. I wanted to learn some things."

"What brand of religion are you? Methodist?"

I laughed and followed his metaphor. "Generic. The kind that comes in the plain black and white box."

My mind zoomed back to the boxed gifts from the day before. I'd forgotten about them for a few hours.

"Why? Are you Methodist?" I asked.

"No, I'm not anything, really. But something weird happened to me yesterday. I wanted to talk to you about it."

I resisted the temptation to compete over weird yesterdays. I was certain I would win. Instead, I sat back and picked up my cup, waiting for him to tell me. It's my therapist posture. I do it automatically when I'm listening to someone. I can't seem to have a clear thought in session without a mug of tea in my hand.

"I have this friend who's pretty religious," he began. "I've known him for a long time. You remind me of him a little bit. Something about you...he thinks like you do, I guess it is. He always challenges me to think about things differently."

"He sounds like a fabulous human being," I said, grinning.

"He is. But yesterday he gave me a Bible. A real nice blue leather Bible with my name stamped on it. Probably cost sixty or seventy bucks."

"What's wrong with that?"

"It made me mad, for one thing. We'd never talked about him getting me a Bible. I thought it was sort of pushy. So I'm like, 'Hey, thanks for the book. Looks real nice and expensive, and I hope this doesn't offend you, but I'm not into it. I'll probably never read one word.'"

"What did your friend say?"

"He said fine. He just wanted me to have it. I mean, where does he get off, doing that? I never asked him to save me."

"Sounds to me like he meant it as a good thing. Not an insult."

Gavin nodded. "I know. But I was still mad. It was like he backed me into a corner or something. I took the Bible—I didn't want to hurt his feelings—but I threw it in the backseat of my car and drove home."

"So what's the problem?" I asked, stirring my tea. That's the other thing I do. I stir. Slowly. Like I'm trying to mingle my thoughts together and come up with something cohesive. "Sounds like he was a sport about it."

"The problem is, I got scared."

"Of what?"

"I don't know, just scared. And not ordinary scared. It started out ordinary, when I was driving home. But then I got to my dorm and parked my car, and by the time I got to my room I was shaking. I could barely put my key in the lock."

"Go on," I said. Stupid, therapist cliché. I hate it when things like that pop out of my mouth in civilian conversations.

"I'm talking about terror, at this point. Like, serious terror. I climbed straight into my bed and crawled under the covers. I was afraid to even leave my foot hanging over the edge of the bed. Like something was going to grab it from underneath. Monsters under the bed or something, like I'm a little kid.

"My roommate comes home and I'm lying there shaking

and sweating with my teeth practically chattering. He asked me what was wrong and I told him I had food poisoning. He left to go to some party and I stayed there the rest of the night afraid to move. Literally. Afraid to move." He looked up at me. "I think there was something in the room with me."

"Like what?" I asked.

"Do you believe in demons?"

I stirred my tea again. It was getting cold. "Do you?" I set the cup down.

"I do now. I think it was a demon."

"What makes you think that?"

"I had a dream last night."

Now we were in familiar territory. I could probably gain some insight from the dream.

"Tell me about the dream." Another psychology cliché. Oh-for-two.

"I was at a lake. Some lake. I don't know what lake, but a lake. Sort of a rocky lake. And there was this guy. He was white. Sick white. Like he had cancer or something."

I felt my skin begin to prickle.

"He was bald," he continued. "And made me really nervous for some reason. He got into the water with me. And when I told him to go away, he just stood up where he was. On the water. I swam to the shore and got out of the lake. Someone handed me my new Bible. I picked it up and threw it at him, and he screamed and turned around and ran."

"Go on." I knew there was more. I knew what it would be.

"He had a big cut on his back."

"Up and down or side to side?" I asked.

He looked surprised. "Side to side. Why?"

I bluffed. "It makes a difference in the interpretation. What happened next?"

"I woke up. I was sopping wet from sweat. I was shaking. I was too afraid to move. So I prayed."

"What did you pray?"

"I said that I didn't know if God was real, but that if He was there, I wanted Him to come and protect me from evil. I didn't want to be afraid anymore."

"And?"

"And I felt it go away. Immediately. All that fear just evaporated. And I felt peace. I fell asleep. I slept so hard, I barely made it to class this morning."

I leaned forward and put my elbows on the table. He was still holding something back.

"Why are you telling me this? Because of the theology degree?"

He met my eyes. "No. Because you were in the dream."

"Where? It was just you and the bald white guy, right?"

"You were the one who handed me the Bible. The one standing on the shore."

He looked at me with bright eyes. Waiting for my reaction.

"You probably just associated me into the dream because you'd read the bio," I said.

"No." He shook his head emphatically.

"How do you know?"

"Because I'd never seen you before."

"I thought you just said you looked me up on the web."

"I did that today. After class."

I felt myself get cold. Barton Springs cold. "And you'd never seen my face before this morning?"

He shook his head. "Nope. Not once in my whole life."

"How do you explain that?" I asked.

"I think you believe in demons, too," he said.

3

~

I F THIS WERE A MOVIE, my next move would be to visit
a priest. But since this is not a movie, and since I do not
personally know any priests, I called my friend Bob.

Bob Follet teaches at the seminary where I got my master's
degree. It is a conservative school, both theologically and
socially, and I was in trouble most of the time I was there. Which
isn't surprising, given my aversion to herd activities and to
hoop-jumping. Seminaries, even more than other graduate
schools, tend to require a lot of hoop-jumping.

Bob is a rebel too, but is better at conformity than I am, and
thus had managed to stick around long enough to get his
doctorate in theology. He was still sticking around, in fact. He'd
landed himself a spot as an assistant professor in the systematic
theology department.

Bob is a very good egg. Also to his credit, he still has most
of his hair and his sense of humor. Two of my favorite qualities
in a man.

I was relieved when he answered the phone and said he
could meet me after his first class the next day.

I ventured onto the seminary campus the next morning
cautiously, as I always do.

Since I teach in the "secular" world, I get to wear whatever I want. Academics are supposed to be strange and eccentric, and everyone knows psychologists are just this side of the loony bin, so I happily dress the part. I wear jeans with beads on them and funky shirts and hats I buy in thrift shops.

The seminary has a dress code ("professional attire required"), and no one there dresses like I do. But I was determined not to give in to the peer pressure, convinced as I am that if Jesus were walking around today, he would be wearing ratty jeans too.

Bob was not in his office, but the door was standing open, so I let myself in and helped myself to a cup of coffee. I hate coffee. But I was desperate. I needed the caffeine. I poked around his office while I waited for him.

I've always thought you could learn a lot about a person by studying his bookshelves. People who buy their books by the yard, with matching leather bindings, always seem like phonies to me. Like they're trying too hard. But Bob's bookshelves let me into his creative, critical-thinking mind. He had C.S. Lewis and Francis Schaeffer too, along with Langston Hughes, Kierkegaard, and a bunch of people I'd never heard of. Since Bob is my intellectual hero and I want to be like him when I grow up, I got out a pen and paper and copied down a few titles.

"Analyzing my bookshelves again?" Bob's voice startled me.

I turned around, busted.

We hugged and he offered me a seat, settling himself in behind a very tidy desk.

"You look good, Dylan," he said, loosening his tie. "Satan invented neckties, I'm convinced."

"And panty hose," I added.

"How would you know? When was the last time you wore a pair?"

I thought about it. "November '99. My brother's wedding."

"He still married?"

"Guthrie? Oh yeah. They're moving to Seattle."

"Any kids yet?"

"No, they're trying to get it right with the cats first."

"Absolutely." Bob nodded and checked his watch. "You didn't sound too good on the phone."

"Well, I'm not too good, to tell you the truth. I've got some pretty bizarre stuff happening."

I told him my story. Both of them, actually. Weirdo Peter Terry and the jewelry, and then Gavin and his dream.

Bob listened without changing his expression. He raised his eyebrows a couple of times, but that was it. When I was finished, he checked a list beside his phone and dialed an extension.

"Tony?" he said into the phone. "You got a minute? I've got something you might want to hear. Great. In my office."

He hung up the phone and looked at me. "You remember Tony DeStefano?"

"The missions guy with the glasses?"

"No, the other one. The short one with the briefcase."

"I always got those two mixed up."

"Well, Tony doesn't have the briefcase anymore. He's been in Central America for six years. Guy's got cockroach stories like you wouldn't believe."

"Cockroach stories? What does that have to do with—"

He waved my question away. "No, not the cockroaches. He's teaching here for a year while he's on sabbatical from Central America. I forget where he was stationed. Costa Rica, I think."

"Nicaragua," a voice said.

I turned around and laid eyes on Tony DeStefano for the first time in more than a decade. Bob was right, the briefcase was gone. Tony wasn't Mr. Buttoned-Down Seminary Guy anymore. He was worn around the edges. Wrinkled khakis, a little-boy tie clipped to his shirt pocket (I guess in deference to the Seminary's requirement that the men wear ties), and hair that was beginning to gray.

We said our greetings and spent a few minutes catching up. Then Bob asked me to repeat my story.

"What do you think?" Bob asked Tony when I was finished.

Tony shrugged. "I think you got some demonic activity there."

Tony was from New York. I loved his accent. Hearing him talk always made me want to go to a baseball game and order a hot dog.

"You think?" I said. "Seems like there must be some other explanation."

Tony squinted at me. "Why look for one?"

"Because it seems so far-fetched. Demons don't just run around going to picnics and giving people presents and injecting themselves into people's dreams. This is America. Modern times. Cell phones and computerized air-conditioning and skin grafts with synthetic skin. Not first-century Jerusalem."

"What difference does that make?" Tony asked. "Spirits— angels and demons both—are eternal. It's not like they all died off after the New Testament was written. They're still around."

"That's why I called you," Bob said to Tony.

Bob turned to me. "Missionaries see theology happening all around them every day. Americans are so insulated from this stuff, I think. We don't see it. It's all theory for us. But these missions guys have stories you wouldn't believe. Where life is more primitive and primal, theology is very raw and daily. And demonic activity is easy to spot. You see it every day."

"Is that true?" I asked Tony.

"Absolutely." Tony nodded emphatically. "I been in Nicaragua for, what, six years? And Haiti before that. Both cultures, they got these traditions of spiritism. You see some crazy stuff. Stuff you wouldn't believe. When you're not living in the culture, it's easy to dismiss as superstition. You think, these people just aren't sophisticated enough to know any better, see?

"But when you're there, living with them, eating and sleeping and praying with them, you see that it's real. And pragmatically, and scripturally too, there's no reason not to see it for what it is. You see it a lot in these cultures. All the time."

I shifted uncomfortably. I was willing to concede the point. Tony obviously knew what he was talking about.

"Why would I rate a visit?" I said. "It's not like I'm a threat to anyone. I'm not out there holding evangelism crusades, you know? And I'm not out there holding séances either. I'm just going about my tiny little life, doing my tiny little thing."

"Bad theology," Bob interjected.

"Excuse me?" I feigned offense.

"Lousy theology, in point of fact. 'Do not neglect to show hospitality to strangers, for by this some have entertained angels without knowing it.'"

"Hebrews," Tony said. "Thirteen, verse two, I think. New American Standard, right?"

Bob nodded and grinned.

"You guys need some hobbies," I said.

"Demons are angels, Dylan," Bob was saying. "Just fallen ones. The passage says nothing about the person who receives the visit being in any way special. It's the angel that's special."

"Then why show up in my life as opposed to someone else's?" I asked. "It's not like this happens to people every day. Something bizarre is going on."

"I remember something about you," Tony said quietly. "From school. You were always real good about knowing who to pray for.

"I remember you called me out of the blue one time. Just totally out of the blue. Hadn't heard from you since graduation, and this was about six, seven months after. You said I'd been on your mind and you had the feeling you should pray for me. You called to find out how I was. See what was up. You remember that?"

I didn't. I'm always getting some powerful urge about something. It pops up out of nowhere. Sometimes it lingers, and I say a prayer, and then it goes away. Sometimes it sticks around and bugs me. That's when I make a phone call, just to put my mind at ease.

I've always considered myself to be a world-class worrier. If I weren't into swimming, worrying would be my only true sport. It's easily one of my top ten character flaws.

"Well, I remember it like yesterday," Tony said. "I barely knew you in school, and here it was, half a year after graduation and you're calling me up out of nowhere."

"Go on," Bob said. Maybe the clichés weren't limited to psychologists after all.

"I was all in turmoil inside," Tony was saying. "Just going nuts. Trying to decide whether or not to propose to Jenny. I'd been going over and over it in my mind for, what? Months, by then. I knew my parents would never give their blessing 'cause she wasn't Italian. And if you're Italian, you need your parents to approve your marriage."

He said this as though it was obvious to everyone.

"I'd been up all night that night, on my knees, begging for an answer. Around daylight, I finally decided I'd ask her, and I got this terrific feeling of peace. All at once. That was about the time you said you'd gotten out of bed to pray for me. You don't remember that?"

"Vaguely," I said. Jenny had called and thanked me at the time, I think. They'd been married almost ten years now. Three kids.

"I remember thinking at the time that you must be one of those people with the good radar," Tony said.

"Come again?" I said.

"A good radar for spiritual things," Bob said. "I absolutely see that in you. The Apostle Paul was like that, and he warns us to be attuned to spiritual battles. Ephesians."

"Six," Tony said.

I rolled my eyes at him.

"What's been happening in your life lately?" Tony asked. "Anything else unusual going on?"

I thought a minute. "Some strange things have been happening at home, now that you mention it."

"At your apartment? You still in that dump in Lakewood?" Tony asked.

I shook my head. "I've moved three times since then. I'm in Oak Lawn now. In an actual house." Oak Lawn is an old artist neighborhood in Dallas. Creaky houses and interesting people.

"What kind of things?" Bob asked.

"Okay, I thought this was pretty weird. I've had some photos fall off the walls. I have about thirty or so old family photos lining one hallway, and three pictures have fallen off the walls in the last month."

"Old place, right?" Bob asked. "Maybe the house is settling."

"They were all pictures of my mother," I said. "And they fell off the wall without knocking off any of the ones hanging below them. Three separate times. The glass broke each time."

"Didn't you say it was your mother's ring in the package?" Tony asked.

"Yep."

We were all silent for a moment.

"Anything else?" Tony asked.

"Okay, here's something really weird. I'm sort of embarrassed to tell you about it, actually, because it makes me sound like a fruit loop. But two months ago I went to Honduras on a short-term mission trip. It was a medical mission. I went with a group of doctors, and we set up a clinic down there." I got up to fix another cup of coffee. "I bought some masks in the square."

"What kind of masks?" Bob asked.

"I don't know—tribal masks or something."

Tony cut in. "There's Indian tribes down there that still practice their ancient religions. Same as in Nicaragua. Countries are right next door to each other."

I returned to my seat, finding comfort in my coffee and my spoon. "I never found out anything about them. I just knew they were ritual masks, and I thought they were sort of exotic-looking, so I bought them."

"Sounds harmless enough," Bob said.

"I thought so. I had them in a bag with some other stuff I'd bought and just stuck them in a closet in my bedroom till I could decide where to hang them. That same night, I started having these horrible nightmares. Screaming, horrific, terrifying nightmares. Violent. For a solid week.

"I tried everything I could think of to get rid of them. Did all my psychologist tricks. I kept a journal, took some herbal sleep remedies, started reading my Bible before I went to bed, meditating, praying, the whole bit. But they kept on. It was just debilitating. They didn't stop until I threw the masks away. I thought of it on a hunch—even though it sounded completely ridiculous. But that night I slept like a baby. All night long. Haven't had a nightmare since."

"Any theories about the connection to your mom? With the photos and the ring?" Bob asked.

"Not really. My mom's been gone for two years. She wasn't a particularly spiritual woman. I don't even think she was a believer."

"You were close to her, though," Bob said. "I remember when she died, I thought we were going to have to put you away for a while."

"Yeah, it was tough," I said. She'd died of breast cancer. Fifty-five years old. I still had a hard time thinking about it.

"Well," Tony said finally, "the good news is that as a child of the King, you're entitled to protection."

"You don't think Christians are at risk for being harmed by demons?" I asked.

"Sure they are," Bob said. "But you have access to protection. I'll send you back to Ephesians. Chapter six. Why would you need to arm yourself if you were in no danger? Why fight the battle at all, in fact?"

"So what can I expect? What should I be doing? Should I keep the jewelry? Should I…" I couldn't think of where to begin.

"I think you can expect that it will keep up for a while," Tony said. "And I think you should pay attention to that kid's dream. What's his name? Devon?"

"Gavin," I said. "Which part of the dream?"

"The part where he threw the book at old slash-back and he turned tail and ran," Bob said. "'Living and sharper than a two-edged sword,'" he quoted.

"Hebrews chapter four?" I guessed.

"Very good. You're not that rusty," Bob said.

"Too rusty to fight a battle like this one," I said.

Bob got up and went to his bookshelf. "Here's another book for you."

I looked at the title. *Demons and the Christian Heart*. By Tony DeStefano.

"If you want, I'll sign it for you," Tony said. "I've sold at least fifteen of these. Maybe twenty. I'm a celeb now."

"You and me both, man," I said. "It's just that I've apparently caught the attention of a different crowd."

4
~

I WENT BACK TO WORK with neither creativity nor enthusiasm. At the end of the long afternoon, I said good-bye to the last student, started my noisy truck, and drove the hot, congested streets of Dallas to my house.

I locked my front door behind me and went straight to the buffet cabinet, unlocking it and pulling the velvet bag out into the daylight that streamed through the windows. I felt it before I opened it up, probing it with my fingers to see if anything was still in there. The lumps felt like they were supposed to, so I pulled the drawstring and emptied the contents gently onto my kitchen table.

I picked the necklace up first and examined it closely. There was nothing extraordinary or other-worldly about it. There were no freaky markings on it. It didn't twine itself into a 666 pattern when I laid it down. Nothing weird or spooky like that. I guess you could make a case for the black stone being symbolic somehow. But the necklace itself just didn't seem sinister to me at all. It was just a necklace. An odd but beautiful piece of jewelry that I liked. Something I would have bought for myself, had I had the chance.

I undid the clasp and tried it on. I guess I expected it to suddenly get heavy or burn a mark in my skin. Something fantastic that would be…I don't know…obvious. But it just lay there like a normal necklace, perfectly passive and well-behaved. I glanced in the mirror. I liked the way it looked on me. It looked like it belonged there.

The ring sparkled in the light and caught my attention.

I didn't feel nearly as casual picking up the ring as I had the necklace. I almost went to the utensil drawer to get some tongs, as a matter of fact. I couldn't get past the idea that my mom was supposed to be wearing that ring in her grave. But I made myself reach out and put my fingers on it and bring it up to my eye.

It was lovely and delicate. Platinum and small stones woven around a bright, perfect center diamond.

The ring was a copy of one my mother had seen when she and my dad were backpacking through some tiny town in Italy the summer before their senior year at the University of Texas in Austin. My father had it made before he proposed.

My parents were hippies then. They'd lived together in my dad's van after they met in a sophomore philosophy class. I suspected they'd done the drugs that were so common at the time, though they never told me and I never asked. I do know they used to go listen to Janis Joplin at Threadgill's and that they missed Woodstock because my dad was enrolling in med school. I don't think my mother ever forgave him for that.

My brother was born three months after they married, and I came along eleven months later.

I grew up thinking John Lennon was deity. I'm still a huge fan, of course, but realized Jesus was further up in line when I was about nine, the year I became a Christian.

The ring had been purchased with my dad's family money, a concession to the materialism they were supposedly committed to avoiding. But my mom had liked that Italian ring, and my dad had really liked my mom. She hadn't taken that ring off her finger since the day she said yes in 1969. Not when she was washing dishes or bathing my brother in their first crummy med-school apartment, not during their two years in the Peace Corps in Bolivia, not when she was pouring concrete for the foundation of their first house. And not even when they divorced three years ago after thirty-three years of marriage. She wore it even after that. She never told me why.

She did try to give it to me before she died. She really wanted me to have it. But I couldn't deal with the weight of that ring—the burden of their optimism gone.

And when she died, the three of us—my dad, my brother, and I—all agreed wordlessly that she should be buried wearing it. We never even discussed it.

And here I was staring at it, two years after it had gone to her grave with her. I could almost feel her in the room. I put the ring back in the bag and picked up the phone.

My dad, once a Peace Corp volunteer and organic gardener—Mr. Peace, Love, and Macramé himself—had slowly morphed into one of the more successful heart surgeons in the country. He was famous, busy, wealthy, and completely impossible to reach, in spite of the cell phone and two pagers he carried. He taught cardiovascular something-or-other at the University of Texas Medical School in Houston and was always either lecturing people or cutting them open.

I decided to avoid the technological maze and called his secretary.

"Janet," I said. "Dylan."

"Hon, I was just thinking about you."

"You always say that when I call."

"Well, I was," she insisted.

"Is he in?" I asked. I already knew the answer.

She laughed. "Of course not. He's in surgery." I listened while she checked his schedule. "Mitral valve replacement. He went in at three. I'm guessing he'll check in here in about a half hour. Someone else will close for him."

Janet knew my father better than any of us ever had.

"He set a date yet?" I don't know why I asked. Scratching some irritating little itch of curiosity.

"Thanksgiving weekend," she said. "Now don't get mad."

Too late. Leave it to my father to plan his wedding on Thanksgiving weekend. I had no plans to attend anyway. I'd plan a ski trip or something.

"Kellee spending all his money planning it?"

"You know it. On the beach at Cabo San Lucas. They're flying everyone down and putting them up at some spa hotel. Should be quite the shindig."

Kellee-with-two-e's was my dad's scrub nurse. Half his age and silicone-enhanced. I detested her. My dad would never cop to it, but I was certain Kellee had come along before my parents split. The last spark of the long slow scorching of their marriage.

"Maybe it'll rain," I said hopefully.

"It never rains in Cabo," Janet said. "Kellee chants that like a mantra."

I changed the subject. "Hey, I'm hoping you can help me with something."

"Anything," Janet said.

"Do you have any idea where my dad buys jewelry? I'm trying to find out who made my mother's wedding ring. I think he still uses the same guy. Some dude his family's been using forever."

Janet was already flipping through her Rolodex. "Got a pencil?"

I picked up a pen. "Ready," I said, and wrote down the information. It was a Dallas phone number.

"Thanks, Janet. You've been a big help, as always."

"You take care of yourself. Come see me," she said.

I promised I would and hung up the phone.

Tibor Silverstein. No wonder I couldn't remember the name. I dialed the number and got a quick answer.

"Tibor," the man said.

"Uh, Mr. Silverstein?"

"What?" he demanded. Tibor Silverstein, apparently, was not a patient man.

"My name is Dylan Foster. I'm Phil Foster's daughter."

"Aach!" he said. "Why didn't you say so?"

I thought I just had.

"What can I do for you, Phil Foster's daughter?"

I explained that I wanted to talk to him about some jewelry and asked him if I could arrange a time to meet him. I might as well have asked him for one of his toes, pretty please, for the reluctance he displayed in giving up ten minutes for me. But we agreed on four o'clock the following afternoon. I wasn't looking forward to the meeting. I didn't need any more grouchy people in my life.

I hung up and went back to staring at the jewelry.

Actually I was alternating staring at the jewelry and staring out my kitchen window thinking about my mother, when I saw a car pull up. A faded blue Honda Accord. It looked like John Mulvaney's car. John was a colleague of mine at the university.

I checked the Honda's window decal. University of Wisconsin alumni sticker. It was John Mulvaney's car, all right. How odd.

While I watched, John stepped out of the driver's side, reached in and pulled his sport coat out of the backseat, and hunched himself into it. I sighed as he marched to the front door and rang the bell.

I shoved the jewelry into the velvet bag and locked it hastily back in the buffet, and then hustled to answer the door.

I couldn't imagine why in the world John Mulvaney was ringing my doorbell on a Thursday evening. John was sort of a fluffy fellow—a soft, white, extremely lumpy academic—who couldn't make eye contact with a baby bunny. We'd never seen each other, outside of work-related events, in the two years we'd been working together. I wasn't even aware he knew where I lived.

I swung open the door.

"Hey, John," I said. "How's it going?"

John liked to be called Dr. Mulvaney, even by the other PhD's. Some of them complied, throwing him a bone, I think, but he'd never gotten one "Dr. Mulvaney" out of me.

The poor man was sweating bricks. I couldn't tell if it was the heat or the enormous amount of stress he seemed to be experiencing. But he just nodded at me and continued sweating. I thought he might pass out.

I reached for his arm. "Why don't you come inside?" I said. "Let me fix you some iced tea. Or would you prefer a Coke or something?"

He coughed out the word "tea" and nodded.

I turned toward the kitchen, talking over my shoulder to him.

"This is a surprise," I was saying. "I didn't even know you knew my address."

No answer.

I turned around to see that he wasn't behind me. I walked back into the foyer. He was still standing by the front door, stuck to the same spot, staring at the ground.

"John?"

He looked up. "Huh?"

"Why don't you come with me into the kitchen?" I said gently. "Here, let me take your coat. It's a hundred degrees out."

I reached over and helped him take his sport coat off and hung it on the doorknob. I didn't want to send any sort of "welcome guest" message by hanging it in the closet on an actual hanger. I don't know why I bothered with the distinction. John wasn't the type to catch that sort of subtlety.

I led him back into the kitchen and settled him onto a bar stool, then fussed around for a minute to produce the promised glass of iced tea, complete with mint leaves and a slice of lemon. My mother had taught me to be particular about such sundries.

John gulped about half the glass down while I settled in on another bar stool. I kept an empty stool between us. I figured we'd both prefer that.

"What's up, John?"

He put his glass down and made an attempt to look me in the eye. He looked me in the chin instead, which was pretty good for him.

"Nothing in particular," he said.

Thank the Maker John was a research psychologist and made no pretense at having clinical skills. Rarely had I known anyone so profoundly unequipped for personal interaction. He wasn't married, I didn't think. At least, I'd never noticed a wedding ring. Frankly, I couldn't imagine he'd ever had a date. He was that shy.

I tried again. "Well, was there something you wanted to talk to me about?"

Blue eyes staring at my chin. "No, not really. I just…"

"Just what, John?"

"Just…"

"Yes?"

"Thought…"

"You thought what?"

"Thought it was better to be early," he blurted. "I didn't know how long it would take me to get here. With traffic."

I found myself staring dumbly at his forehead. "Early? For what?"

"I thought we might go to The Grape. I hear it's nice."

The Grape is a romantic little spot in a groovy part of town. Fabulous mushroom soup. No way was I going to The Grape with John Mulvaney.

"You thought who might go to The Grape? You and me?"

Finally his eyes found mine. "Yes," he said firmly. "At seven o'clock." Eyes back to the chin.

I looked at the clock on the wall. It was 5:30.

"That's an hour and a half from now." I don't know why I chose to tackle that particular point, there were so many to choose from.

"I thought it was better to be early," he repeated.

"Early for what, John? Is there a faculty dinner tonight or something? I'm not sure what's going on."

"Should I go and then come back at seven?" he asked.

"Go where?" I said.

"Is there a Starbucks?"

Okay, rewind. "John, look at me." His eyes made it up to my nose. "What are you talking about? I don't understand what you're doing here."

"I'm here to pick you up."

"For what?"

"Our date," he said, and looked immediately down at his tea glass.

"Our date?" I tried not to sound aggravated. "We don't have a date, John."

"Is it tomorrow?"

"No," I said. "There is no date. Not tonight and not tomorrow. I'm not sure where you got the idea that we were going out." Maybe he was having a psychotic break or something.

"It was your idea." He was defensive now, and I could tell he was horribly embarrassed.

I softened my tone. "John, I'm sorry about the mix-up. I appreciate the thought. Really I do, but I'm sure we don't have a date tonight. I hope I haven't somehow given you that impression."

"Are you playing a joke on me?"

He looked like he was about to cry. Suddenly I could see his childhood, vividly. Pudgy shy boy, picked on by classmates. Laughed at by girls he admired from a distance. And always, always alone.

"John," I said, "look at me. Look at my eyes." He managed to return my gaze with now-watery eyes. "John, I would never play a joke on you. I promise. This is just some sort of misunderstanding. What gave you the idea that I wanted to go on a date tonight?"

"The Day-timer," he said. "I told you I needed a new one."

I thought back to the day at the lake. John had received a leather Day-timer. It looked expensive. I didn't remember him ever telling me he needed a new one. But all conversations with John were innocuous and centered around minutiae. He could have mentioned it half a dozen times and it wouldn't have made an impression.

"You think the Day-timer was from me?"

"I know it was." His embarrassment was turning to anger.

"Why would you think that?"

He got up and walked to the front door and out to his car, returning a moment later with the Day-timer. He flipped it open to today's date and showed it to me.

There it was, in lavender ink, written in what looked to be my handwriting: "John, thanks for your friendship. Let's get to know each other better. Pick me up at seven. Dylan." A heart was drawn around the words.

I don't own a lavender pen. I don't draw hearts around notes to men. And I do not write flirty notes to John Mulvaney.

"John, I don't know what to say. I didn't write this."

He grabbed the Day-timer from me and stared at the page.

"I promise."

He continued to stare at the page, too humiliated even to meet my chin.

"Hey," I said, "I'm really sorry. It's just a misunderstanding." The drums should have started rolling then, because all my sick, codependent rescuer tendencies kicked in. "Tell you what…I'm not up for The Grape, but why don't we go get a burger at Jack's? I'll buy."

"I don't think so," he said.

"Oh, come on. We've worked together for two years and we've never had a burger together. It'll be fun. Have you ever been to Jack's?"

He looked up at me. "No."

"Greasy burgers, salty fries, and incredible chocolate malts. We can work on your heart attack."

He allowed himself a little grin. "Okay."

And so I spent the evening with John Mulvaney anyway. A mistake with repercussions far beyond a two-thousand calorie meal and one boring Thursday night.

5

~

FRIDAYS ARE NOT BAD DAYS IN ACADEMIA. MWF
classes are usually only an hour long. And by the afternoon, the
no-show rate has reached epidemic proportions. Plus, no one
wants any office time from me after class. Everyone's in too big
a hurry to get home and get on with their weekend.

All that to say, I was able to scoot away in plenty of time to
make my appointment with Tibor Silverstein.

The address Silverstein had given me was in an office
building, tenth floor, which threw me off a bit. Not exactly like
he was going to attract the Zales' crowd with this off-the-beaten-
path location. The door plate said only "Silverstein & Co." No
indication of what kind of business it was. I pushed open the
huge wooden door and stepped into a tomb-like waiting room.

I found myself alone and freezing, with air conditioning
blasting onto my head through the ceiling vents. The carpets
had fresh vacuum tracks in them. Clearly the waiting room
didn't get much traffic. My fanny was inches away from the seat
of an expensive wingback chair when God spoke to me.

It wasn't God, really. But it was a booming voice from above
with an eastern-European Jewish accent. Which was always
what I imagined God would sound like (even though in all the

Charlton Heston movies, everyone has a British accent).

"Yes?" the Almighty said.

I froze in midair, still poised above the cushion.

"I'm here to see Mr. Silverstein," I said.

"Which Mr. Silverstein?" the voice demanded.

"Tibor Silverstein."

"Who are you?"

"Dylan Foster."

There was no answer from above. I heard a loud click as the door at the end of the room opened, apparently by itself.

I looked around the room for the cameras, but I couldn't spot them and didn't want to be obvious. After all, I was being watched.

I stood up and spoke to the ceiling. "Do I—?"

"Through the door and all the way to the end of the hall," the voice said.

I did as I was told. Through the door, which locked itself behind me, and all the way to the end of the hall. I walked past six or seven closed, and I'm sure locked, doors on either side. Not a particularly collegial work environment.

I reached the final door and pushed the button on the outside of the door. I heard a bell ring, and the door clicked open by itself. I stepped through the doorway and walked into the work area of Tibor Silverstein.

He didn't look up when I came in, which gave me a chance to look around.

The space was tiny and dominated by a large, flat work surface—I'd say desk, but it really wasn't a desk. It was more like a workbench, but not so official. It was an old, sort of plywood-looking structure, with tools scattered all over it and drawers half open. A bright worklight ignited little rainbow piles of gems dotting the desk.

Over this workspace bent a man who could have passed for lumberjack, truck driver, or perhaps dictator of a third-world country. He was huge, bearded and rough-handed, and completely uninterested in me.

"Should I—?"

"Sit," he said, still not looking up.

I sat. And waited.

Several minutes passed before Tibor Silverstein looked up from his work.

"Vat do you vant?" he demanded, taking off thick, black-rimmed glasses.

I translated silently to myself: "And what can I do for you, Ms. Foster?"

Out loud I answered, "I don't know if you remember making my mother's wedding ring. My father, Phil Foster, had it made here—"

"Platinum ring, antique setting. 1.2-carat diamond, VVS1 gem quality."

I pulled out the ring and handed it to him. "Is that the same ring?"

Tibor took the ring from me, put his glass up to his eye, and studied the ring.

"Yes," he said, and handed it back to me. He looked at me. Clearly it was my move.

"How can you be positive? Could it be a—"

"No. I made that ring."

"How do you know?"

He handed me the glass. "Look through the loupe," he said. I guess that little glass thingy was called a loupe. "Same stone. And look on the inside, underneath the stone."

I looked. Engraved in the platinum were the initials TS and the numbers 969.

"What do the numbers mean?"

"September 1969." He swiveled in his chair and opened a file drawer, pulling out a thick folder and opening it on the desktop. He placed a pair of wire reading glasses on his nose and squinted through the papers until he found what he wanted.

He handed me a pink sheet of paper.

The print was faded, but clearly legible. It was a mimeograph copy of the original design notes, along with a detailed description of the stone. My father had signed off on the order. It was dated July 15, 1969.

"This says July," I said.

"September is the completion date. I delivered it to him…" he checked the file, "September 8." He looked up. "A Monday."

"You keep good records," I said.

"Yes." He stared at me over his glasses. "Is there anything else?"

I thought a minute, trying to decide what to do. Finally, I said, "Yes, there is. Could you just…give me a minute? This is sort of a strange situation."

"Vat is sort of a strange situation?"

"The original ring," I said, "was buried with my mother. Two years ago. And now it's turned up again, and I am looking for an explanation. You're sure no one else could have made that ring? Maybe even copied the markings?"

He was shaking his head before I finished. "Same stone. And only record of those markings is in these files. And as you can see," he smiled for the first time and gestured toward the door, "I keep a very tight shop."

"Why is that?"

"Aach! You are naive." He poked through one of the piles of stones on the table, picked out a big sparkly diamond and handed it to me. "Look."

I put the loupe up to my eye and was dazzled by the brilliance of what I saw—faceted white light sprayed with rainbow color at the edges.

"Ten thousand dollars," he said. "Wholesale."

I pursed my lips and handed it back to him.

"And the meticulous records?"

"Insurance," he said. "Always they require detailed records."

"Can you think of any way—?"

"A thief," he said simply.

"A thief," I repeated, staring at him. The man was rude *and* insane.

"Yes. A thief."

"You mean someone dug up my mother's grave and stole her ring? I don't think so."

He shook his head impatiently. "Before she was buried. A thief. He slips it off her finger, he puts it in his pocket, and he feeds his family for months. No one ever will find out."

"But I saw it on her finger."

"Did you see them close the lid to the…what do you say, casket? And did you lose sight of this casket between that moment and the moment they closed the grave? Did you ride with this casket in the car to the burial yard? Many, many opportunities for a thief. Many."

I didn't say anything. He had a point.

"It's happened before," he continued. "A few times I have been asked to verify a piece of jewelry that disappeared in the same way."

I stood up. "Thank you for your time, Mr. Silverstein."

"Tibor," he said gruffly. Then he looked at me sideways, his expression softening. "How is your father? Will he marry that woman?"

"Kellee? I'm afraid so."

Tibor shook his head regretfully. "It is a very gaudy ring."

"You're making Kellee's ring?"

He nodded. "Yellow gold. Six-carat yellow diamond, pear-shaped, with two round white diamonds, two carats each, on either side." He shook his head again, his face softening at last. "It is a ring that would choke a farm horse."

I laughed out loud and held out my hand. His hand covered mine completely. I wondered how such huge hands had mastered such delicate work.

"It was good meeting you, Tibor." I turned to go. "I do appreciate your time."

"How do you like the necklace?" he asked.

I froze.

"What necklace?"

"Your father. He ordered you a necklace."

"What does it look like?"

"He hasn't give it to you yet? Ach. I spoiled the surprise."

"What does it look like?" I repeated.

"Small platinum cross, nine-diamond inlay, eighteen-inch chain. Very tasteful."

I felt myself relax, the surge of electric panic dissipating. "I'm sure it's lovely. He hasn't given it to me yet." I winked at him. "I won't tell him you mentioned it."

"Dylan Foster, I hope you solve your mystery," he said.

"Thank you. I do too."

6

I DIDN'T MIND THE HEAT and the smog that hit me
when I left that refrigerator of a building. I felt my goose bumps
go away as I started the truck and drove home. The drive settled
me down. Something about the warm air and the dailiness of
sitting in Dallas traffic.

When I got to my house, I threw my stuff down and
immediately locked the ring back in the buffet with the
necklace. I went back outside and sat on the porch swing with
my cordless phone, a phone book, and a pad of paper.

I'm always tempted to page my dad and claim to be in the
throes of a myocardial infarction, just to get a little immediate
attention out of him. But if I did, I know the answering service
would just tell me to call 911. I left a message for him and
decided to call Guthrie instead.

I looked up my brother's phone number and dialed, hoping
his wife wouldn't answer the phone.

She did, of course.

"Hello Cleo," I said.

"Dylan," she said, faking delight. "How nice to hear from
you."

"Great to talk to you too," I lied. "It's been too long. How's the packing coming?"

"You know your brother," she said.

I didn't, really.

"...leaving everything to me. Only a man has time to play golf two days before a cross-country move."

"So he's not around?"

"He's settling in at the nineteenth hole, I would guess. Why don't you try him on his mobile?"

I reached for the pad. "Do you have the number?"

"You don't know your brother's phone number?" The fake affection had lasted all of twenty seconds.

"Could you just give it to me, please?"

She reeled it off, told me again how delighted she was that I'd called, and asked me if I'd send my brother home when I talked to him.

I assured her I would. As if he'd obey me and race right to her side.

I dialed the number and waited until the fourth ring. I was about to hang up when I heard his voice in front of a crowd.

"Guthrie Foster," he said.

"Hey, big brother."

"Dylan!" he shouted. "Can you hear me?"

"I can hear you fine. Can you hear me?"

"Loud and clear, baby sister."

"How was golf?"

"If I improve every day for the rest of my life, I ought to be a scratch golfer about thirty years after I'm dead. That's how bad I played today. All eighteen holes. It was a thing of beauty, really." I heard him ask the bartender for another gin and tonic. "What's up?"

"Strange request," I said. "You don't happen to remember the name of the funeral home that did mom's funeral, do you?"

"Sutter," he said without hesitating.

"How do you remember that?" I asked in wonder. If I asked him what color my fifth-grade bicycle seat was, he could probably tell me. It was remarkable. He was like a savant or something.

"Sutter Home," he said. "We drank it that night because we thought it was so stupid to name a funeral home after a lousy bottle of wine. A good bottle of wine, maybe. Beringer. Now that's a good bottle of wine. A nice Beringer chardonnay. But Sutter Home?" There was a roar in the bar. Guthrie swore. "Hang onto the ball. What are they paying this moron?"

I guess some guy on TV had dropped a pass.

"Why?" he asked.

"I'm just piecing together some things for a book I'm working on. It's about grieving." That was my third or fourth lie today. No, fifth. In the last fifteen minutes. Not a good ratio. "You don't happen to remember the funeral director's name?"

I heard him rattle the ice in his glass. "Shykovsky. D.A. Shykovsky. Never did find out what the initials stood for. 'Dead Already,' maybe. The man was a ghoul."

"That I do remember. His suit and that awful purple tie. Right out of *The Addams Family*. We started calling him Lurch."

"Lurch Shykovsky. That's the dude. He's probably still there. His dad started the place."

"Shykovsky Funeral Home isn't too catchy," I conceded. "No wonder they went with Sutter."

"Shoulda gone with Beringer," he said. "Big mistake. Anything else going on?"

"Not much. Classes just started. The little darlings are back on campus. Eager young minds, ready to learn. You?"

"I'm about three months away from cutting my own throat. If this transfer doesn't work out, I'm changing careers. I have no passion for assuring the world of unfettered access to digital cell phone technology."

"Maybe you could open the Beringer Chardonnay Funeral Home."

He laughed. My brother has a great sense of humor. I'm always honored when I make him laugh.

"Oh, and Cleo said to hurry right on home. I think she misses you."

He laughed again. "I'm missing her too, right about now. And all those boxes and that packing paper and that sweet, adoring look on her face."

"How are the cats?" I asked. The cat question was the standard wrap-up cue for both of us.

"They have sweet adoring looks on their faces too. Still haven't found the litter box, the little monsters. We've lived in that house three years."

"Maybe they'll improve in Seattle. Cats are so adaptable, you know."

"Just like Cleo. Adaptable. That's the word."

"Good luck on the move," I said. "Let me know how it goes."

"Will do." He clicked off.

I liked my brother. One of these days I'd have to get to know him a little better.

I called the Sutter Funeral Home and had a brief conversation with Lurch. He said I could come by tomorrow and take a look at the records. Apparently funeral homes are open even on Saturdays.

What a treat that would be for us both, I thought.

I went back into the house to start supper. I poured myself a glass of chardonnay and raised my glass to my brother.

The wine had a nice round flavor. Not quite a Beringer, but it was no Sutter Home either.

7

~

MAYBE IT WAS THE WINE. I don't know. I'm not much of a drinker, to be sure, but one glass with supper isn't enough to send me around the bend. But around the bend I went that night. And I did not like what I saw on the other side.

It started with the flies.

I keep a meticulous house. I am rigorously tidy—actually downright obsessive-compulsive. It's practically a disorder with me.

I don't leave dishes in the sink. I don't let spills dry on the countertop. I don't leave laundry in the hamper for more than a day or two. I wash my towels every day.

Tree-hugger that I am, I love chemicals. Bleach and biodegradable surfactants are my dear and intimate companions.

And I never, ever have bugs. Even in bug-infested Dallas in the hot middle of the summer.

My exacting habits make my home a completely inhospitable environment for any living creature other than me. Maybe that's one reason why I've never married, come to think of it. No one else could survive the Pine-Sol fumes.

Imagine my disgust, then, when I saw the first fly alight on the edge of my plate during supper.

And this was no ordinary fly. It was huge. The size of a small Volkswagen. I could have painted daisies on it and sold rides to small children.

Instead, I waved it off my plate and went for the flyswatter. I chased it around the kitchen for a few minutes until it landed on the countertop within my reach. I smashed the sucker, scrubbed the counter with a paper towel and a large dose of Clorox Clean-Up, and emptied my plate into the garbage disposal.

When I switched off the disposal, I heard a buzz. A loud buzz. I turned around to see another Volkswagen buzzing around my kitchen.

Two flies in one evening. Two flies in one year was my usual quota.

Same drill. Chase, kill, clean, though this one was harder to kill. The chase took several minutes.

By now, I'd completely lost my appetite. I threw out the rest of my casserole—on the chance that either fly had landed on it while I wasn't looking—hosed the whole place down, and turned off the kitchen light.

It was time to shake off this day for good, so I began my getting-ready-for-bed ritual. I started myself a bubble bath and flipped on the bedroom's window unit air conditioner (I love a warm bed and a cold room at night). I turned down the bedspread and recoiled.

A big black fly was sitting on my nice, clean white pillowcase. Just sitting there. Staring at me. Like it had been waiting for me.

I waved my hand at it. It didn't move.

I picked up the pillow by a corner and shook it.

I heard the buzz as the fly took off, but lost sight of it immediately. I rushed to the kitchen for the flyswatter and returned, armed for battle.

This was one aggressive bug. It dive-bombed me. It chased me. It landed on me for a split-second and then took off, as if to taunt me. This fly was not going down without a fight.

I won, eventually, but not without a maniacal battle. I must have looked crazed by the end of it. I *was* crazed by the end of it.

By the end of the night, I'd chased and killed a succession of one dozen flies. And by the time I put my Clorox away for the final time that night, I was shaken.

It seems strange to say, but there was something otherworldly about these bugs. Flies don't travel in packs. They buzz inside one at a time.

You spot it, you chase it, you kill it. No more fly.

Yet someone seemed to be sending out a lone soldier to replace each one that went down.

And how did they manage to appear, one by one, just as their predecessors died?

The last one I spotted eluded me. I had to go to bed that night knowing there was a big black fly waiting somewhere in the house. Waiting for what, I didn't know.

Since fly number three had spent time on my pillow, I changed my sheets and threw the dirty ones in the washing machine. Hot water, lots of Tide and Clorox.

I took my bath, tucked myself in, and pulled the sheet over my head. No way was I sleeping with my face exposed.

Sleeping might not be the right word for what took place that night. Tossing and turning doesn't quite do it justice either. More like standing on the edge of some bizarre dream state and not quite walking in.

I've never dreamed a smell before, for instance. But sometime in the center of the night, I caught the distinct, sulfury scent of hard-boiled eggs.

Some people, I'm sure, especially people who like eggs, wouldn't find this smell offensive. I do. I hate eggs. I have them in my refrigerator, but only for baking. Eggs cooked any way—fried, scrambled, or hard-boiled—had never touched any of my plates.

I curled my nose and writhed under the sheets, trying to get away from the smell. Of course it was impossible. A smell is one thing that cannot be gotten away from. Eventually the smell slipped away—or I slipped away from the smell—depending on which world the smell was in. And was replaced with the comforting smell of Downy as I breathed in my clean cotton sheets.

A succession of visitors populated my dreams that night. Gavin, my student, showed up with his leather Bible. He just stood there, in the middle of a creek, looking at me before he turned and splashed away. My brother came, only to be shooed away by Tibor Silverstein. And I was in the middle of a conversation with my mother when the screech of my cell phone jarred me awake.

I whipped the sheet off my face and looked at the clock. 5:15 a.m. It was still dark outside.

I hurled myself out of bed and snatched the phone off its charger, squinting at the little screen through exhausted eyes to see if I could identify the number. It looked familiar, but I couldn't place it exactly. Reluctantly, I pushed the button and said hello.

"Dylan?" a voice said.

"Yes. Who is this?"

"It's Helene."

"Helene? What's going on? Is something wrong?"

"Did I wake you?" she asked.

"Of course you woke me." She knew I didn't get up this

early. No one in academia gets up this early. We're not ambitious enough. And it was Saturday, for crying out loud.

"I'm sorry," she said. "But I just got an emergency call from one of the students at the counseling clinic."

"One of mine?" I asked.

"He says he's yours."

"What's his name?"

"Erik Zocci," she said.

I didn't recognize the name. I would remember a name like that. Maybe this was a patient from a previous school year or something. A one-timer, perhaps. We got lots of those.

"What did he say?" I asked. "And why did he call you instead of me?"

"He called to complain about you," she said. "He said you'd made advances during therapy sessions."

I felt a surge of alarm. "Made advances? Like, sexual advances? He's alleging I'm coming on to him?"

This was every therapist's worst nightmare. Unfounded accusations of impropriety from an unstable client. Once the suggestion is out there, careers can be tainted forever.

"Yes. He was very explicit. Do you want me to tell you what he said?"

I shook my head. "No. It doesn't matter. I don't even recognize the guy's name."

"He said he saw you three or four times this summer. And then quit after you began trying to seduce him."

"Did he sound coherent? Was he lucid?"

"Quite," she said.

I couldn't think of what to say. I sat there and let it sink in.

She paused. "I'm sorry, but I have to ask you this. Is it true?"

"Helene."

"I need to hear it from you. I need to know."

"You do know," I said. "It's not true. Of course it's not true."

"That's what I wanted to hear."

"You doubted me?"

"It's just that you've been acting strangely."

"Strange how?"

"John Mulvaney told me about your date."

"Date? We didn't have a date. The man was delusional. I would never go out with him. You know me better than that."

"He said you asked him out. And that you'd changed your mind at the last minute and tried to humiliate him. And then insisted he go out with you anyway. He was very upset."

"Helene."

"I know. We're talking about John Mulvaney. That's why I didn't give it any credence. I didn't even mention it to you. But now, with this…I don't know, Dylan. It doesn't look good."

"No, it doesn't. What should I do?"

"I have to investigate," she said. "You can't work in the clinic until it's cleared up."

"How long, do you think?"

"Depends on how credible this guy is. I'll go down to the clinic this morning and pull his files. I'll give you a call after I've had a look at them. With any luck, we've got some testing on him already that will confirm some sort of psychosis or something."

"And if we do?"

"That would be enough for me. I won't call the licensing board. We'll try to clear it up internally, and you can go back to the clinic as soon as we've put it to rest. Probably within a week or so."

"And if we don't? What if Erik Whatever-His-Name-Is is a perfectly sane, model student? Or worse yet, an antisocial personality disorder who knows how to lie and beat standardized psych exams?"

"Then you might want to consider a new career."

I felt a sudden urge to roll into a ball and suck my thumb.

"Should I keep teaching?" I asked.

She thought for a minute. "I think so. Just suspend your clinical work and leave your door open for student conferences. I'll keep a lid on this. Hopefully we can clear it up quietly and no one else will have to know."

Helene promised again to call me as soon as she saw the file, warned me to stay away from the clinic and not to go hunting for it myself, and hung up the phone.

Sleep was out of the question at this point. I put on a bathrobe and went to the kitchen to start the tea kettle.

8

~

I SAT THERE AT MY KITCHEN TABLE for a good long while, listening to large chunks of my carefully constructed life slam to the ground around me.

I'd spent nine long and fairly unpleasant years in graduate school. Four in seminary, and then another five to get my PhD. A year doing a clinical internship on a locked inpatient unit at a public hospital, dealing with indigent schizophrenia patients who couldn't tell the difference between Big Bird and Larry Bird, but who believed that both Birds were communicating with them through the mercury fillings in their teeth.

And for my trouble, I had landed my dream job right out of school. Assistant professor at a major university—not known for its psych department, I admit, but still a good school. A good school in a nice city that I didn't mind living in. A good school with a health plan and a 401(k) and convenient faculty parking.

But the best part was that my job afforded me plenty of opportunities for clinical work. I got to teach, which I love, *and* see cases, which meant that I got to sit around and talk to students and help them with their problems. This is rare in the world of academic psychology, believe it or not, since most academia centers around research. In fact, most of the psychology professors I know spend their entire careers trying to avoid dealing with people and their problems. Ironic, I know.

So here I was, with my dream job, thirty-three years old, single, no prospects for marriage. Not that I was looking to get married. But still. I hadn't had a date in a year. And I consider myself to be eminently datable. I'm a smart, reasonably interesting, non-lumpy, fairly athletic woman with my mother's eyes and thick auburn hair that isn't showing any gray yet.

I'm not the kind of girl who begs the John Mulvaneys of the world for dinner companionship.

Yet that was what he was out there saying about me. To my boss.

And even if I were the kind of girl who begged the John Mulvaneys of the world for dinner companionship, I wouldn't be the kind of girl or the kind of psychologist who would hit on a patient.

It was utterly unthinkable. The most heinous of offenses.

Therapy patients trust their therapists with the deep, intimate details of their lives. They make themselves utterly vulnerable to us. They cry in front of us—I go through crates of tissue in my office—they tell us their secrets, they confide their hopes and confess their dismal, most humiliating failures.

To abuse this trust by violating that person sexually would be completely unconscionable to me. Not to mention that it would go against every moral fiber of my being. And it would get me thrown out of my chosen profession in less time than it would take to boil water.

And yet that was what someone was out there saying about me. To my boss.

Add to this that I was in the midst of a spiritual nightmare that was so macabre and so bizarre, I wouldn't even wish it on John Mulvaney, whom I was quickly beginning to abhor.

When I added it all up, I began to feel truly disoriented. Disoriented and afraid.

Afraid of what would happen to my career. Afraid of what would happen to my reputation. Afraid of the jewelry locked in my buffet. Afraid of flies. You name it, I was afraid of it.

So I did what most twenty-first century American Christians would do in such a circumstance. I sat there and worried about it. Sucking down a couple of gallons of tea, I sat there and fed the fear. Sheer, panicky, heart-fluttering, clammy-handed fear.

It wasn't until long after the sun came up that it dawned on me to pray. And even then, it was as a last resort.

Somehow, even as long as I've known the Lord, I remain convinced that secretly He wants me to make it without Him. Why I think this, I don't know. The entirety of Scripture defies this stupid little theory of mine. And I don't believe it in words, really. When I think about it, I know it doesn't make any sense. But I live it out every day.

I pray easily for others. Tony DeStefano had reminded me of that. And I randomly thank God for parking places and for unexpected M&Ms in the bottom of my purse. But for some reason, I resist praying for myself when I really need help. I seem to prefer trudging along without an umbrella, in driving rain, moving under my own power, when the Ferrari of the Holy Spirit is revved up and ready to go, right there beside me, if I would just bother to get in and fasten the seat belt.

But finally, I gave up. I fixed myself another cup of tea and bowed my head.

The words didn't come. They rarely do when I'm the subject of my own prayers. But I let myself sink into the fear and remembered Gavin's story about his dream. His prayer was so simple. He didn't want to be afraid anymore. Could God take away his fear? Would He?

It seemed like a good place to start. So that was what I asked for. Begged for, more like.

And I asked to be exonerated of the abuse charge. Immediately. I asked for clear and unambiguous information in that kid's file that would let me off the hook. Now.

Rarely do I get a direct answer to prayer, and rarely is the answer such a stunning, resounding no. But soon after I breathed my amen, the phone rang.

It was Helene.

"Bad news," she said.

"What?"

"Erik Zocci is a saint."

"You're kidding me."

"I wish I were. I pulled his case file and his academic file this morning." I heard her flipping pages. "Erik Michael Zocci. Hometown: Chicago. Religion: Catholic. Engineering major. SAT score 1480. Lived in Morrison dorm his freshman year. Takes a full load every semester. GPA 3.8." She flipped some more pages. "No psych testing in either file."

"You have my case notes there?" I asked.

"Right in front of me. You saw him three times over a period of two months. This was last summer, not this recent one. Looks like this was between his freshman and sophomore years. He'd be starting his junior year now."

"What was the presenting problem?"

"He was experiencing insomnia. Dropping weight. Having trouble with his summer courses. I'm getting this off the intake sheet."

"What's his diagnosis?"

"Diagnosis 309.28. Adjustment disorder with mixed features of anxiety and depression."

"Did I list a precipitating event? Anything set it off?"

She paused. "Not that I can see." I heard her turn the page. "Says he was waking up screaming. His roommate was the one who wanted him to see a counselor. Who could blame him?"

The light bulb went on in my head. "I remember him. Skinny kid. Tall. He was having nightmares, I think. Anything on the content of the nightmares?"

"Yep. Here it is. I'm going to quote directly. 'Patient describes recurring nightmare involving pale, sickly white man. In his dream, the man chases Erik. Typical dream response—Erik paralyzed, unable to run in the dream. Erik always wakes up before the man catches him.'"

I felt my skin get cold. "Anything else about the dreams?"

"No. You speculate that it may have something to do with his fears of failure. Maybe a parallel between the man in the dream and Erik's fears about himself. Running from his perceived weaknesses."

Weak psychobabble on my part.

"Any mention in the file of anything awkward between me and him?" I asked.

"Nothing. He didn't even terminate. He just stopped coming. You make a note that you called twice to follow up but didn't get a return phone call."

I thought for a moment. Nothing she'd read would help or hurt me. Half our students had adjustment disorders, which was just a fancy way of saying they were having a difficult but fairly normal experience in a time of their lives defined by change and adjustment. It didn't mean he was unstable and certainly not that he was mentally ill.

"What about the academic file? Is there a complaint listed in there or anything?"

I heard Helene turning pages again. "I don't see anything." I waited while she read. "But it does say he transferred. End of his sophomore year. To University of Dallas."

"Transferred? He's not even at SMU anymore?"

"Not according to this."

"Is there any way we can get his file from UD without having to explain why we need it?"

"What would be the point? He's been there a week. They won't have any information I don't have in front of me."

I paused, letting it all sink in. "What do you think, Helene?"

She paused. I knew she didn't want to say it. "I need to sit down with Erik Zocci and talk to him directly."

"So let's do it. Did you arrange to meet with him or anything?"

"No. I wanted to talk to you first. But I'll call him back and do a quick phone interview. And I'll set up a meeting with him early this week."

"Can I go with you?"

"Definitely not. Not until after I've spoken with him and figured out what we're dealing with."

"When are you going to call him?" I asked.

"What time is it?"

I looked at the clock on the wall. "Nine-thirty."

"I'll call him now. I'll call you back after I talk to him."

We hung up and I paced the kitchen for a few minutes until the phone rang.

I snatched it up. "What did he say?"

"What did who say?" It was my father.

"Oh. Hi, Dad. No one. I thought you were someone else."

"You should say hello when you pick up the phone."

"Hello."

"Much better. How are you, Dylan? I haven't heard from you in a while."

"Great. Doing just great. You?"

"Busy. Working a lot."

"Not slicing and dicing anyone this morning?"

"Not on a Saturday. I've got a tee time in twenty minutes, though. What do you need?"

I'd forgotten I'd called him. "Oh. I wanted to talk to you about mom's funeral."

"Her funeral?" he said, clearly taken aback. A rare chink in the armor for my dad. "Why would you want to talk about that?"

"Long story. I just needed to ask you a couple of questions."

"Okay. What?"

"Do you remember what she was wearing when we buried her?"

"A powder blue suit, I think. Why?"

"Anything else? Any jewelry?"

"Her wedding ring. You know that. That's all I remember. Probably some earrings or something."

"Do you remember seeing it on her hand? Her wedding ring, I mean. Or had we just talked about burying her in it?"

"What's this about, Dylan?" He sounded rattled.

"I'm just wondering. I thought I remembered seeing it on her finger, but I wasn't sure. I wanted to check with you."

"It was definitely on her finger. She never took it off."

"I know she never took it off. But do you specifically remember seeing it on her finger before they closed the lid?"

"Dylan, I don't remember." He sounded angry now. "I wasn't taking a detailed inventory of her burial attire at the time. My wife had just died."

"Ex-wife."

"Ex-wife. Fine. Why are you bringing this up now?"

"Do you remember if we saw them take the casket from the funeral home to the hearse? Or were we already in the car when they moved her?"

"I don't remember. How am I supposed to remember something like that? What's wrong with you?"

I heard my call-waiting click.

"I've got another call, Dad. I'll call you back. Have fun on the golf course." I hung up and clicked over.

"Hello?"

"Dylan, it's me," Helene said.

Something was wrong. I could tell from the sound of her voice.

"Well? What did you find out? Did you talk to him?"

"I called the number from this morning—the one he gave me. And it wasn't a working number. So I tried his parents in Chicago."

"And? Did you get them?"

"I talked to his mother."

"Well? What did she say?"

"Erik Zocci is dead, Dylan."

"Dead! Of what? What happened to him?"

"He committed suicide. He jumped off the balcony of the Vendome in Chicago. He fell twelve floors."

"This morning? After you talked to him?"

"Two weeks ago."

"That doesn't make any sense."

"I know it doesn't."

"Did he leave a note?" I asked.

"I didn't ask. She was upset, and I didn't explain why I was calling, for obvious reasons. I'll have to call back and get details."

I leaned back against the counter and tried to breathe. The air had completely come out of me. That nice kid. Dead. Just like that.

"What does this mean?" I asked. "For my situation, I mean."

"I don't know," Helene said. "I need to find out who called

me this morning. It's probably just a sick prank. Hopefully that's all it is and this will be the end of it."

"Helene?"

"What?"

"I'm scared."

"You should be," she said. And hung up the phone.

9
~

MY MEETING WITH LURCH BECKONED, whether my life was falling apart or not. I was determined to find out what had happened to my mother's wedding ring. So I showered and got ready for my visit to Sutter Funeral Home.

What does one wear to meet with a funeral director? A suit? Something somber and conservative? I stared at my closet, mentally trying on outfits. I flirted with the idea of waltzing in wearing a wild little Bohemian number, just to freak him out, but decided in the end that I should work out my hostilities on my own time, not his. I finally pulled a pair of black pants off the hanger, found a blouse that didn't need pressing, and threw it on.

Sutter Funeral Home is in the little town of Hillsboro, where my mom grew up. It's about an hour south of Dallas.

I tried to clear my head on the drive, to steady myself, to tamp down the panic that was bubbling up inside me. I started by mentally cataloging my questions. I decided to go in chronological order.

First, and perhaps most intriguing, who was Peter Terry? The man obviously got around. He'd had some at least fleeting contact with both Gavin and Erik Zocci. He'd turned up in the dreams of both boys.

Was he someone they'd both managed to cross paths with, in some glancing, inconsequential way? And had they taken subliminal note of him, thus paving the way to their subconscious? Or was he, as Tony and Bob seemed to suggest, a spiritual being?

He was just strange-looking enough that if you saw him at the grocery store or something you would notice him, but not so strange that you would find yourself staring at him. The brain would take in, process, and spit out obvious stimuli—a loud, angry man, for instance—but someone like Peter Terry could sneak in unnoticed…unless you saw the gash.

The other issue was that I'd somehow ended up involved in both boys' dreams. Zocci had told me about his dreams during therapy, and Gavin claimed I'd actually appeared in his. They both seemed credible to me. I believed them. It was too much of a stretch to be a coincidence.

Next question—the jewelry. I intended to make progress on that one by the end of the day. I was hoping Lurch would shed some light on the likelihood of my mother's ring being stolen the day of the funeral, as Silverstein had suggested. Perhaps whoever took it had simply returned it out of guilt.

That didn't explain the rest of the gifts that day at Barton Springs, however. All wrapped identically to the ring. Was the whole thing an elaborate ruse to distract from the ring's return? That didn't make any sense to me. The gifts had been carefully chosen and did, in fact, match the desires of their recipients. John Mulvaney had indeed expressed a desire for a new Day-timer, for instance. He'd reminded me of that the night he came to my house.

John Mulvaney. Another mess of unresolved questions. Who had written on his calendar, copying my handwriting precisely, suggesting we meet for supper? And how had he ended up with such a twisted version of that rather odd event?

The latter question was the only one so far I could answer. The man was an oddball. A misfit. Completely unable to process normal social cues. It would be natural for him to miss the boat entirely on what had transpired that night.

Moving on to the flies. What was that about? Odd as that battle had been, I was willing to chalk it up to bizarre coincidence. Maybe I had flies in my house. Maybe there was a little fly maternity ward somewhere that I didn't know about, turning out big fat flies one by one.

The boiled eggs? I'd never studied the presence of smells in dreams, but it had to be a fairly common phenomenon. That one would be easy to research.

Erik Zocci. This was the kicker. Why would anyone make such a dreadful accusation against me, using the name of a former patient? A former dead patient. A former dead patient who had committed suicide.

And what was the suicide about? Had this boy been so haunted by the Peter Terry-like figure that he'd thrown himself off a twelfth-floor balcony? Surely there was more to it than that.

I resolved to do some digging to find out what had been going on in Erik Zocci's life.

As I pondered this last item, I realized it was the one that was pressing the hardest on me.

As horrifying as suicide is, it is usually explainable, at least in hindsight. You could almost always retrace the steps of the person and find the path that led him to that terrible decision. It's harder to spot in present time, of course. But often perfectly clear after the fact.

That's one reason suicide is such a cruel choice. It leaves the survivors with nothing but the certainty and guilt of hindsight.

I'd never had a patient commit suicide on my watch. The

guilt I felt—though this young man had been in my care only briefly, a full year before he took his own life—was profound. Somehow, ludicrous as it looks in the light of day, I felt I should have prevented it. That I'd missed something toxic in this boy that had eaten him from the inside.

I felt like the physician who misses the tumor on the X-ray, only to find out a year later that the patient had succumbed to a treatable but virulent strain of cancer.

What had I missed? Why had this boy, haunted by Peter Terry, sought me out? Why had he abruptly ended therapy? Was he frustrated with me at the time because he felt I wasn't helping him? Had I failed to listen to him? Had I dismissed something important? Had I been careless? Frivolous with his pain?

As I pulled off I-35 onto the Hillsboro exit, I reached for my map, relieved to have something else to do with my mind. Erik Zocci, I knew, would haunt me as Peter Terry had haunted him. And my guilt would drive me until I either absolved myself of blame or made peace with my mistake. Neither would be possible until I found out what had happened to the boy.

Until then, I shoved my denial into place as I threw my truck into park and set a foot on the hot pavement of the Sutter Funeral Home parking lot.

Sutter Funeral Home was Proud to Be Family Owned and Operated. Since 1928, the sign said. Poor timing to start a business, surely. I wondered how the funeral home business had survived the '29 crash and the Depression of the '30s. But then death didn't respond to fluctuations in the economy. People were going to die either way.

Small town funeral homes are familiar territory for me. My mother's side of the family, prolific and gnarled farm folk, had died off one by one in the past couple of decades. Great Aunt so-and-so had "passed," my mother would say reverently, and we would all converge on some dinky Texas town.

A country funeral, usually in an unair-conditioned building, would be sparsely attended by surviving friends who would proclaim how very sad they were she was gone and how proud they were to have known her. Then we would spend the afternoon eating tuna casserole, three bean salad, and angel food cake, supplied by local Christian women.

My family would inevitably beat it out of there as soon as possible, hoping that great aunt so-and-so was too busy playing poker in heaven with Elvis to notice.

So when I stepped into the parlor of Sutter Funeral Home, I knew what to expect. Somber lighting. Musty carpet—in this case, a dirty nursing-home shade of green—and doors leading to viewing parlors named after pastoral scenes from Scripture. Thankfully, the faint spitting sound of window unit air conditioners accompanied the cheesy organ hymnal music playing softly over hidden speakers. At least it would not be wretchedly hot.

The smell of dust and mold took me back to the March afternoon my father and I had breathed this same air while planning the details of Mother's funeral. I felt a chill snake between my shoulder blades.

"Can I help you?"

I turned to see a handsome man of maybe twenty-eight, turned out in a nicely tailored black suit. Definitely not Lurch.

"I'm looking for…" Rats. I couldn't come up with anything other than Lurch. What was the man's real name? Not Sutter. It was something else. Tchaikovsky? Dostoevsky? All I could come up with were Slavic remnants of my liberal arts education.

"Mr. Shykovsky?" the young man asked pleasantly.

"That's it," I said, pointing at him. "Shykovsky. Mr. Shykovsky. Is he in? I have an appointment."

"I'm Mr. Shykovsky," he said.

"No you're not," I blurted.

"I could show you my driver's license," he offered, amused.

"No, no. I don't mean that. I mean, you're not the man I'm supposed to meet. He's older. Sort of…shorter. Black hair, sort of gray…sort of…" I cut myself off as I gestured with my arms. I didn't want to say fat. Hefty?

"Pear-shaped?"

"Yes! That's the guy. Is he here?"

"No, he's down the road a bit."

Down the road a bit. What was this, a *Hee-Haw* skit?

"When will he be back?"

"I'm afraid he's not coming back."

"Did he retire?"

"He died. We buried him three months ago."

"Oh." People kept dying on me. I thought I'd talked to the man yesterday. Was this another bizarre dead-people-talking-on-the-phone incident?

"Are you Dylan?" the man asked.

"Yes." Suddenly my brain cleared. "Are you the one I talked to?"

"The same." He shook my hand. "David Shykovsky. I'm sorry about the confusion. I didn't know you were asking for my father."

"I didn't know he'd died. I'm sorry."

He shrugged. "He lived to eighty and died of a heart attack in his sleep. Ate bacon and eggs every day of his life. Couldn't ask for a better ending."

"He was eighty? He looked so much younger."

"Yeah." He smiled, showing me a beautiful set of white teeth. "We liked to say he was well-preserved."

Hey. This was a likable guy. And he was cute. And looked

like he had a muscle or two under that nicely cut suit.

"Why don't you come on back?" he was saying. "I pulled the file for you already."

I followed him down a long carpeted hallway, past viewing parlors named "Green Pastures," "Still Waters," and "Restoration." Apparently no one had died in Hillsboro in the last day or two, because the rooms were empty.

We turned left at the end of the hall (avoiding the casket room, thankfully) and entered his office. He offered me a seat opposite his desk and leaned back into his leather chair. The man was a hunter. Stuffed trophy heads covered each wall, and a bobcat, teeth bared, poised in mid-leap behind his chair. It was unsettling. I kept wanting to tell him to duck.

"They're not mine," he said.

"What?"

"The dead animals. They belonged to my father."

"They're spooky," I said. "Why don't you get rid of them?"

He grinned. "It's hard to spook a mortician." He slid a manila file across the desk to me. My mother's name and death date were on the tab. March 15. The Ides of March.

I raised my eyes, questioning silently. He gestured that I should go ahead and open it.

I hadn't anticipated feeling so much emotion. But as I turned the cover, I swear I felt my mother's presence in that room. My eyes got wet.

David handed me a tissue from the box on his desk—a tool of the trade for us both, apparently—and left the room.

The information was clinical and dry. There was a copy of her birth certificate, a copy of her death certificate, a copy of her burial certificate. Lots of certificates were required to die, apparently.

There was a receipt for the casket, a detail of her funeral

expenses, an order form for the headstone, on which had been written "delivered and installed." A sheet of detailed funeral instructions were written in my handwriting. We had specified daisies instead of roses. My mom had always been more of a daisy chick.

I wiped my eyes and turned the pages until I found the description of her clothing and was surprised to see a Polaroid of her in her casket, paper-clipped to the description.

She was so pretty. My mother's hair was red. True red. And her skin, freckled and translucent in life, was lovely in this photograph. With her green eyes closed, she could have been asleep if she'd been in her jammies. Instead, she wore the blue suit my father remembered. A blue suit she never liked, by the way. Powder blue with a white blouse. The suit was the giveaway. It made the whole image seem artificial and waxy. I made a note to specify somewhere that I be buried in a really great set of flannel pajamas.

My eyes moved to her hands. I'd almost forgotten why I came. They were folded at her waist. There it was. 1.2-carat diamond and platinum band. It was so much part of her hand that it belonged there.

David returned with a glass of ice and popped the top on a Dr. Pepper. I listened to the pleasant sound of fizzy liquid trickling over ice as he poured it for me.

"You okay?" he asked.

I took a sip. "I guess everyone gets emotional in your office, huh?"

"Most everyone. Did you find what you need?"

"Sort of. Do you have some time for me to ask you a few questions?"

"Sure." He leaned back in his chair, the bobcat springing at him over his shoulder. He looked so…unsuspecting sitting there.

"My mother was buried in her wedding ring." I slid the picture across the desk and pointed at it. I read the description of her burial attire from the file, ending with "one ring, platinum with diamond (wedding) on left ring finger."

He nodded.

I reached in my purse and took out the little velvet pouch, emptying it into my hand. I handed the ring to him.

He looked at it and compared it to the picture, then looked up at me. "I don't understand."

"Neither do I. It was returned to me recently."

"Are you sure it's the same ring?"

"I spoke with the jeweler that made it. It's the same one."

"Was someone trying to sell it back to you?" he asked.

"No. It was boxed and wrapped. Someone clearly wanted me to have it back."

I waited for the news to settle.

"We had one incident," he said, rising from his chair and leaving the room. He came back with a file a few minutes later, saying "It must have been twenty years ago. A woman had been buried with a piece of jewelry, I think it was a pin or something, and someone later tried to sell it back to the family." He thumbed through the file until he found what he wanted and returned to the desk reading a newspaper clipping.

"Shirley Jean Lucas. It was a ruby and diamond brooch. Very valuable. It had been on the Titanic with her or something. Some big deal. There was a newspaper article about her and the pin before she died." He scanned the article. "They caught the guy. Juan Ramon Rodriguez. An illegal immigrant that had gotten a job digging graves at the cemetery. They determined he'd pried open the casket before closing the grave."

"So it is possible," I said. "Someone might have stolen it out of the casket at some point."

"It's possible. It's very rare, but it does happen."

"Who would have opportunity other than the grave digger?"

"The mortician," he said, "who in this case was my father. I think we can safely rule him out. Possibly the driver of the hearse. Usually there are two or three people from the funeral home staff on duty at a funeral, including the mortician. Probably in March of that year it would have been Everett Reed and Buddy Harriman." He reached for my mother's file and scanned the pages.

"Yep. They were both there." He looked up at me. "They were with my father for years. They both retired when he died."

"Do you think either of them would have done it?"

He shook his head. "Absolutely not. These were reliable men, longtime associates of my father's. There are firm ethics in this business, obviously. Believe me, even in a small town shop like ours, there's ample opportunity to steal. There's a fortune in jewelry planted in the ground out there south of town. You have to have people working with you that you can trust. And besides, if that were going on, something would have come out over the years."

"But who would know if anyone was stealing? Once they're buried, no one would know."

"True, but I've known these men all my life. Trust me, they're not the type. It's possible a grave digger or someone could have done it."

"And how could I find out who the grave digger was?"

"You could talk to Stan Harland over at the cemetery, but chances are you're on a wild goose chase. Nobody exactly chooses grave digging as a career, you know? Those folks are hourly wage workers who come and go. It takes half an hour to train them to operate the backhoe and they're hired. Know what I mean? Could have been anyone."

"So there's not an answer."

"No. There isn't. I'm really sorry."

There was an awkward moment of silence.

"You're not going to sue me are you?" he said, only half joking.

This time I was the one that laughed. "No. Definitely not. I'm not the litigious type. Besides, what would be the point? I have the ring."

"Would you like us to reinter?"

"You mean bury it again?"

He nodded. "I thought I'd offer."

"No. I think this ring wants to be with me. Maybe I'll fill you in on the rest of the story sometime."

"I've got time now. Want to go get a cherry soda?"

"You're kidding. A cherry soda?"

"At the drug store. They have a real pharmacy soda fountain there. Make a mean cherry soda. It's too early for beer or I'd take you dancing."

"How old are you?" I asked. We'd just looked at pictures of my dead mother together. Some sort of intimacy had been established. Directness seemed appropriate.

"Thirty. You?"

"Thirty-three."

"You look younger," he said.

"So do you."

"It's the embalming fluid."

So I went to the Hillsboro Main Street Drug Store with David Shykovsky, owner of Sutter Funeral Home, and had myself a genuine soda fountain cherry soda with a genuine small town guy.

At least it was a step up from John Mulvaney.

10

~

THE CHERRY SODA DATE turned out to be a pleasant surprise. I liked David Shykovsky. Though I kept picturing myself giving the "owns a funeral home in Hillsboro" answer at parties.

Interestingly, he'd seemed unfazed by the bizarre nature of my story. I didn't tell him everything. (I left out the teeny detail that I was being investigated for inappropriate sexual conduct with a client who had later committed suicide. That completely outdid "owns a funeral home in Hillsboro" as an automatic disqualifier for date consideration.)

He had my phone number. I suspected he would call me again.

David favored a spiritual explanation for this whole situation. He might have just said that to avoid liability on the part of the funeral home, but I didn't get the impression he was that sort of guy. He actually seemed to believe that an intrusive spiritual dimension was a plausible explanation for what I'd experienced. That made him a little more attractive in my mind. At least he didn't think I was a loony bird.

Driving home, I felt dissatisfied with the answers I'd gotten about the ring. It was too ambiguous. My gut feeling was that it hadn't been stolen. That it had been buried with my mother. I would have felt more at ease about this conclusion if there hadn't been some holes—one or two unlikely but possible opportunities for theft. I'd rather have had an airtight "no way." It seemed that certainty was not one of the things God was going to supply at this point. I was irritated about this to no end.

The drive seemed longer on the way back. Probably because my mind was still reeling and it was late afternoon now. Hot. Hotter than the eyes of hell, in fact. And all I'd ingested that day were about two gallons of tea, a Dr. Pepper, and a cherry soda with a side car of vanilla ice cream. Not exactly a strict observance of the FDA's food pyramid.

When I finally arrived home, I was beat. Just absolutely worn-out on every level. So I was even more annoyed than usual to find several messages on my answering machine, the red light blinking expectantly at me, a little scarlet strobe of obligation.

I hit the play button and fast-forwarded through two rambling and angry messages from my father. Apparently my abrupt conversation with him about mom's funeral had gotten under his skin. Which was fine with me. Let Kellee deal with him. She'd signed up for that, as far as I was concerned.

There was one message from Helene. She'd spoken with Erik Zocci's father this time and wanted me to call her back as soon as I had a minute to talk. And the last message was from my student, Gavin. Odd that he would call me at home. I wondered how he'd gotten my home number. Usually I make a point to be thoroughly unlisted. With the Damoclean sword of ethical allegations dangling over my head, I didn't need any suggestions of impropriety. I decided I'd just see him in class on Monday. I didn't return his call.

I did fix myself a large glass of ice water and sit down to call

Helene. She picked up on the first ring. Thank goodness for caller ID.

"Hi, Dylan," she said. "You ready for this?"

"Probably not. But go ahead. Is it bad news?"

"I can't tell yet." I heard her cover the phone and say something to someone else.

"Is someone there with you?" I asked.

"My son. He's just here to mow the lawn. He just stepped outside."

"Okay. What did you find out?"

"He mentioned you in the suicide note."

"What? Did he blame me for the suicide? What did he say? Why didn't his parents get in touch with me? Why haven't we heard from them?" Questions were whipping out of my mouth before I could stop them.

"Settle down. Do you want to hear this or not?"

"I'm listening."

"You don't sound like you're listening. You sound like you're arguing."

"I'm listening. Go ahead."

"I don't have it verbatim. But the note specifically said that you were right. That he wasn't the man he should be. Something to that effect."

"I never said that!"

"Shut up," Helene said. She'd never spoken to me so harshly before. "Just shut up and listen. I'm not going to debate this with you."

"Okay." I clamped my lips together and silently vowed to keep them there.

"According to the father, the kid had started having trouble at SMU his freshman year. Bad dreams. Insomnia. Same symptoms you saw. The father claims he went downhill while he was seeing you, and that your treatment was inadequate in some sort of catastrophically damaging way." She paused. "He also said Erik had told him about your improper behavior advances."

Silence.

"Well?" she said.

"You told me not to say anything."

"Now it's time to say something. What do you think?"

"I think I missed some paranoid psychosis in this kid."

"That's what I think."

"What else did he say?"

"He's contacted a lawyer, Dylan."

I closed my eyes. "They're suing me."

"And the university. The good news is that, in my opinion, your records completely dispute their claims. They haven't seen the files, obviously. But I can't see how they could possibly win that claim. Your professional credibility alone would stand against that sort of accusation. The bad news is you probably missed the diagnosis."

"That would come out at trial," I said, my heart sinking.

"If there is a trial. SMU's attorneys will defend this one aggressively. It will probably settle out of court with no admission of liability. That's how these things go."

"And what will happen to me?"

"Depends. You could lose your job."

"That's not fair."

"No, it isn't."

I listened to my kitchen wall clock tick seconds away.

"What's next?"

"I'm meeting with the attorney on Monday. He'll probably want you at the meeting. I'll let you know when we confirm the time. It'll probably be after your afternoon class."

"And until then?"

"If I were you?"

"Yes."

"Pray."

I took her advice and spent some time, literally, on my knees before I went to bed. Peace continued to elude me, though, and another sleepless night of deviled-egg smells had me wandering through the house at 3:00 a.m. looking for sources of the odor. I never could place it. I emptied every garbage pail in the house and garage, scrubbed out my garbage disposal, and ground up a fresh lemon in it. Still the smell remained. Every time I closed my eyes it would come again.

At least there were no flies.

The next day was Sunday, and I was relieved to step into the auditorium at my church. Something about the daylight, the familiar faces, the music—it all felt safe, familiar, insulated. Surely God would show up and comfort me. Maybe He would give me a hint or two about what to do.

I go to sort of a hippie church, so it's not terribly churchy looking. It looks more like an office building, with an atrium and an auditorium instead of a lobby or sanctuary. I greeted some friends and found myself a seat alone, hoping no lurking single male predators would home in on me that day. My church has a large single population, and any time I sit alone, I'm apt to have the seat next to me filled by some extremely awkward man desperate to make conversation for the sole purpose of scoring a date for the following weekend. No thanks.

So when someone took the seat directly next to me, though several around me were empty, I stiffened. I resolved not to turn and acknowledge his presence.

"Dr. Foster?"

Rats. It was someone who knew me.

I turned and saw Gavin sitting there.

"Good morning, Gavin," I said. I smiled, trying to be friendly. But in point of fact, I was feeling unfriendly, paranoid, and downright hostile that day. Great way to start out a Sunday, with a complete dearth of Christian charity.

"You didn't return my call." His tone wasn't accusatory. It was just a simple statement of fact.

"No, I didn't."

"Do you mind if I sit here?"

"Nope." Do lies in church count double? "I didn't know you went to church here."

"It's my first time. I don't really know what to expect."

His rookie status appealed to my helping instincts. I felt my attitude soften.

"Very few rituals here," I said. "I think you'll find it's an easy place to fit in."

The band started playing and we stood up with the rest of the crowd. I sang, feeling my attitude shift from horizontal hostility to vertical need and gratitude. I love that about worship. It applies appropriate perspective to my life. I felt some of my tension slip away.

Gavin didn't know any of the songs, of course. He just stood there with his mouth closed and his hands jammed in his pockets. But I wasn't going to allow my experience to be influenced by his. I have a terrible voice, but sang with abandon anyway, glad to get out of my head for a while and lift my mind and heart where they belonged. I felt much better by the time the sermon started.

Gavin took in the entire experience exactly the way he sat in my class. Attentive without being eager, critical without being cynical. He was a smart kid with a good mind. I liked him.

After the service was over, we walked out into the heat of the courtyard. I felt good for the first time in days.

"Do you want to know why I called?" he asked.

"I'd rather talk about it tomorrow at school."

"I think you'd rather know today."

Something in his tone stopped me.

"Okay. I'm listening."

"I found something yesterday."

I waited.

"A journal," he said.

"Whose journal?"

"Some kid named Erik Zocci."

I froze. "Where did you find it?"

"On the floor. Behind my desk."

"Your desk. In my classroom?"

"No. In my dorm room."

"Which dorm?"

"Morrison."

I was pretty sure it was the same dorm. "Room?"

"105."

I'd have to find out what Zocci's room number was.

"What did it say?"

"See for yourself."

He handed me a thin notebook, little wads of dust still clinging to the edges of the pages. I looked inside the cover and saw that Erik had written his name there.

"Who is Erik Zocci?" Gavin asked.

I could barely speak. My heart was in my throat.

"I can't say."

"Something's wrong, isn't it? Really wrong?"

"I can't talk about this with you, Gavin. You're a student of mine. The things that are happening don't involve you."

"The white guy showed up in my dream again last night." He met my gaze with steady brown eyes.

"And?"

"He told me to look behind my desk."

11

I SAID MY GOOD-BYES TO GAVIN, raced home, and cracked the pages of that journal.

There were dozens of entries, made between January and May of last year. His words were vague, as though he were hiding even from himself. His handwriting was erratic, an indication to me of his fluctuating state of mind.

Most of the entries were about his father, whom Erik had never mentioned to me in therapy, but who was obviously a central figure in this tortured boy's life. He talked of wanting to love him, but of hating him instead. And hating himself for hating his father. He anguished over his mother. Worrying for her, but asking himself time and again why she wouldn't do anything. He never mentioned exactly what he wanted her to do something about. He wondered if some day he'd have to do it himself. Whatever "it" was.

And over and over he mentioned the white man. The nameless white man who was gradually convincing him of his worthlessness. Of the futility and purposelessness of his life.

My newfound but fleeting, as it turned out, peace of mind evaporated. Anger took over. One kid had died. Another had caught the attention of the same freak that spooked the first one.

And now it seemed that said freak, weirdo Peter Terry, was directing the entire show.

One thing was abundantly clear. It was time to find Peter Terry.

I put the book down and logged onto the Internet. White pages search for Peter Terry. Hundreds of Peter Terrys across the nation. Narrowed my search to Texas. Down to seventy-six. Narrowed my search to Houston. No Peter Terrys in Houston. Which was where he'd said he was from.

I thought of the cancer center. There had to be some way to find out whether he was a patient there.

Time to make peace with my dad. I dialed his cell number.

"Dylan?" he said. No hello or anything. "Where have you been? Do you not answer phone calls from your father anymore? I hope you don't treat your patients this way."

"Sorry, Dad." I tried to sound sincere. "It's been an extremely busy few days. I've got a lot going on. Lots of emergency calls this week. You know how that is."

"Crazies getting to you? Flying off the bridges this week?"

I winced. The image of Erik Zocci flying off the balcony at the Vendome became instantly vivid in my mind.

"Actually, yes," I answered.

"Oh. Sorry. I was just making a joke."

"Don't worry about it. You know how it is to lose a patient."

"Lost one Tuesday. Forty-seven years old, congenital heart disease, smoked like a chimney, ate like a farm-raised hog. Guy had no shot. They'll sue me for it. Families like to blame everyone but the patient."

Who was this man and what had he done with my formerly likable father?

"I'm overwhelmed by your compassion, Dad." Before he could defend himself, I cleared my throat. "Hey, sorry about the confusion with Mom's ring."

"You upset me very much with that phone call, Dylan. You know I don't like to think about your mother's death."

"I know. Neither do I."

I debated whether to tell him about the ring. I decided to lie. That was twice today. Maybe this was why God was withholding peace and direction. Maybe my sorry spiritual state and pathological lying were blocking Him.

"I found a ring in an estate store that looked like hers. I got a little spooked. I thought maybe something had happened I didn't know about."

"Are you accusing me of taking her ring off her finger?" The other side of narcissism—paranoia.

"Did I say that? Calm down. I thought maybe someone else had stolen it before she was buried and sold it or something. I didn't know what had happened. I just wanted to check with you about it."

"Well, your mother was buried with that ring on her finger. I know that for a fact."

"Okay, okay. I believe you. Probably the other one just looked like hers."

"You know, we first saw that ring in Italy. I had it made for her. That's how much I loved your mother."

I was silently singing "It's All About Me" as he talked. I made a mental note to work on my attitude toward my dad.

"Hey," I said. "I need a favor."

This perked him up. He loved being asked for favors. Made him feel like Marlon Brando or something.

"I have a patient"—lie number three—"that's lost track of his brother. He thinks his brother may be a patient at the cancer center in Houston."

"M.D. Anderson?"

"I think so. I think the brother may be dying, and my

patient wants to mend their relationship before his brother dies. Do you know any way to track him down?"

"Confidentiality requirements are tight now, Dylan. Congress just passed a new law…"

"I know all about it. I'm subject to the same rules, remember? I'm asking for a favor, Dad. Surely you know someone who can help in a sort of unofficial way. My patient's really freaking out about this."

"I could make some calls."

"I'd appreciate it, Dad."

"What's the guy's name?"

"The brother's name is Peter Terry. Seems like he might be in stage four cancer. I don't know what type of cancer he has."

"Won't get any help on Sunday. I'll make some calls tomorrow." He hung up without saying good-bye.

My next phone call was to Tony DeStefano, my friend from the seminary. I looked up his number and dialed. His wife answered.

"Jenny," I said, "it's Dylan Foster. I hope I'm not catching you at a bad time."

"Dylan!" She sounded genuinely happy to hear my voice. "How are you? Tony said he'd seen you last week."

"I'm doing okay. I'm not sure if he told you my situation—"

"Of course not. The man never tells me anything. I think he believes his wedding ring is a mind-reading device that transmits his thoughts through the airwaves."

"Does your ring receive?"

"Absolutely not. I'm old-fashioned. I like to use words."

We both laughed. I could hear kids screaming in the background. Fifteen seconds with other people's children usually cured me of any impulse to have a family of my own.

"Is he around? I have a quick question for him."

"Sure. I'll rescue him from the kids. They've got him pinned to the living room floor. I blame you for all three kids, you know. If it hadn't been for you, I'd be a single career woman right now with no grape jelly stains on my clothes."

"Maybe you could name the next one after me," I said. "Just as a little reminder."

She came back to the phone a minute later. "We want to have you over for dinner soon," she said. "Here's Tony."

"Dylan. How's your demon situation?"

Tony was a get-to-the-point sort of guy. I wondered how his half of the conversation would sound to Jenny.

"Heating up, actually. Do you have a minute?"

"Yeah. What's up?" I heard a chair scrape the floor as he sat down.

I brought him up to speed. Told him everything. And felt like an idiot doing it, by the way. The whole thing sounded so ludicrous when I told it in sequence. I was actually suggesting to this man that I was being stalked by a demon who was trying to ruin my life.

Loony bird. I felt like a total loony bird.

"You got a problem on your hands," he said.

Something about talking to Tony was already settling me down. Maybe it was that New York accent again.

"You think? You went to graduate school for how long in order to come up with that assessment?"

"Eight years, I think," he answered. "I'm what they call an expert." He was laughing now.

I wasn't.

"Tony, I'm freaking out here. What am I dealing with?"

"I think you're dealing with some serious spiritual warfare. I told you that a week ago."

"You really think so? You don't think I'm crazy?"

"You might be crazy. You're the expert on that, not me. But you got some weird stuff going on. Only explanation that makes sense to me. What's your radar telling you?"

"Same thing. I just don't want to believe it."

"It's better than the alternative."

"What do you mean?"

"I mean," he said, "that if it's spiritual, you got Yahweh, Elohim, Adonai—all that Hebrew stuff—on your side. He's been in this fight for a while. On the winning side, if you get my point. Which is a distinct advantage in my book. Better than a hired attorney if this Terry guy is just a troublemaker."

I kept forgetting that I might actually be equipped for this fight. I vowed to myself to study Ephesians 6 before I went to bed tonight. I should muster some actual spiritual weaponry if this was what I was dealing with.

"What do you think of Peter Terry?" I asked. "What's he up to? And do demons regularly show up in bodily form to people? I mean, I had an actual conversation with the man…or demon…or whatever. It wasn't a dream like the other encounters."

"Hebrews mentions that angels show up in bodily form. Not much Scripture about this, though. Your guess is as good as mine."

"What does your experience tell you?"

"It happens. I seen it lots in Central America and Haiti."

"You've actually seen the demons? Or people told you about them?"

"I never saw them myself."

"So you don't know," I said.

"I heard lots of stories. Lemme ask you this. Anyone else see him? While you were talking to him?"

"I have no idea."

"Might be worth finding out. Answer to that question could be pretty useful. Nobody else saw him, you got a freaky situation on your hands. Demon-dudes don't like to make public appearances. At least what I hear."

"What about the slash on his back? Did anyone ever describe anything like that to you?" Picturing it still made me nauseous.

"I been thinking about that. I got a theory. Want to hear it?"

"No, Tony. I'm calling you because I have nothing else to do on a Sunday afternoon. That's how bad my social life is."

"You used to be nicer."

I hoped he was kidding. I didn't want to have to revamp my entire personality. I was sliding down the slope of bad attitude. I squared my shoulders and tried to behave myself.

"Sorry. Let's hear your theory."

"Wings," he said triumphantly.

"Pardon?"

"Wings. Think about it. What are demons? Fallen angels. Angels have wings. Maybe the demons, when they fell, they got their wings ripped off. Maybe they have to run around without them now." He sounded pretty pleased with himself. "What do you think? It does fit, doesn't it?"

"It does," I said. I tried to picture the confiscation ceremony. "I feel like I need to talk to this dude. I need to get some answers out of him. Am I playing with fire?"

"Yes. If you're thinking of some sort of séance or anything, put that idea right out of your head. People get sucked into the dark by sheer curiosity and it's hard to get out. Bad idea. Very bad idea."

"I didn't say séance. I never said séance. I just said I think he's the one with the answers."

"My thing is," Tony said, "this guy wants to talk to you worse than you want to talk to him. He's been pretty persistent up to this point. You ain't seen the last of him. You wait it out, you'll find out more than you ever wanted to know."

"That's a scary thought."

"Maybe. But here's something to remember. Demons, they're just created beings. They're not omniscient or omnipresent or any of the stuff God is. They're…finite, is a good way to put it. And they're obviously emotional and impulsive and make bad decisions or they would've kept the angel thing going in the first place."

"Are you serious?"

"Dead."

I'd heard that word too many times lately.

"I'll keep that in mind. Thanks for your time, Tony."

"You bet. And Dylan?"

"Yes?"

"We're praying for you."

"Good."

We hung up.

I called Helene immediately.

"Strange question for you," I said when she answered.

"Okay." She sounded wary.

"That day at Barton Springs. Did you see me talking to anyone at the rope swing?"

"I don't think so. Why?"

"You would probably remember this guy. Bone white and bald. Real sickly looking. Looked like he was about to keel over."

"I never saw anyone like that. Every time I looked up at you, you were alone. I kept wishing I was alone. Better company."

"So you don't remember seeing him anywhere?"

"No."

"Okay. Thanks."

"Is that all you wanted?"

"For now, yes."

12

~

FEW PLACES ARE LAZIER than a college campus on a Sunday. I don't know if it was the sleepy, hungover students or the serenity of empty sidewalks, but the whole SMU campus just had a slow, easy vibe to it that day.

My stress and anxiety level stood out in sharp contrast to the repose of that hot, still afternoon. I parked my car, very cleverly I thought, in commuter parking rather than faculty parking. And walked fast, head down, bag slung over my shoulder, keys wadded in my fist. Suspiciously purposeful. To anyone watching I'm sure I stood out like a powerboat on a stagnant pond.

I made it to the counseling center and walked around the building to the back door, stopping for a moment to catch my breath and quiet my heartbeat. Obviously, I was not cut out for espionage. All the more reason to hang on to my day job.

I stuck my key in the lock and felt a brief shock of panic at the sharp screaming sound that greeted me. It took me a minute to realize that the alarm was sounding.

That's why we have an alarm system, I scolded myself. To keep people like me from breaking into the clinic. I shut the door behind me and lunged for the alarm panel, somehow retrieving the code from the scrambled neurons in my brain.

The alarm stopped, leaving a sudden throbbing hum of silence. I listened, half expecting someone to storm around the corner and arrest me. But no one did, so I steadied myself against the wall for a second, walking myself through relaxation exercises. Breathe, I told myself. Breathe deeply, slowly. I tried to feel the air come into my lungs and fill my body all the way down into my toes. Just like I coached my clients.

It didn't work. I was lucky I didn't hyperventilate and faint right there. If nothing else, this horrible experience was opening my eyes to the lame inadequacy of my now chirpy-sounding interventions. I resolved firmly to get myself some new skills.

What did work, believe it or not, was praying. I closed my eyes and begged once again for help. And felt a surreal sense of calm settle into me as I finished the prayer. God, I felt, would not hang me out to dry. Even though I was breaking and entering. Well, not technically breaking and entering, since I have a key. But I'd been told in no uncertain terms to stay away from the clinic, and I was afraid I'd get in trouble with the brass for being here. Plus, I intended to pilfer any evidence that could and would be used against me. At least until I had time to take a look at it. So add stealing to my list of crimes. But somehow I felt there was an exception allowed for this circumstance.

With my newfound serenity, I walked, more slowly now—mindful of the necessity for quiet and trying not to crash into anything in the dim light—through the kitchen and into the hallway. I flipped on the light and checked my key ring, inserting the file room key into the lock. The door clicked open and I turned off the hallway light, stepping into the file room and shutting the door behind me.

Helene had the paper copy of the case file, of course, but there should be notes and demographic information in the computer system. I sat down in front of the screen and typed in my user name and password. The system thought for a second and then let me in.

I tapped keys for a while, poking around the file system, looking for Erik Zocci's information. I found him logged under "inactive patients" from the previous calendar year. So far so good.

I opened the intake page.

At first, scanning the little boxes of information yielded nothing. It was just a repeat of the details Helene had quoted me.

He was from Chicago. Age nineteen when he came into the clinic. Freshman going on sophomore. Engineering major. Catholic. I checked his campus address. Morrison dorm, room 105. The room Gavin was living in now.

He listed his parents' names: Joseph and Mariann. That was biblical. And this was interesting. I'd forgotten that he had seven siblings. He was number six. The oldest was only nine years older than he. Wow. Old Joseph and Mariann had been busy folks.

I wondered how the parents of eight children had managed to send one of their youngest to an expensive school like SMU. I paged down.

Erik had listed his father's occupation as "business." Mariann's occupation was listed as "charity work." What was that supposed to mean? I went back to the intake page. He had left the family income line blank.

We used that information to calculate fees, since the clinic has a sliding scale. I checked his fee. He had paid the full $110 an hour. I checked the line for scholarships—Erik had written "none."

My guess was, with an SAT score in the high 1400 range, he had turned down a number of scholarships. Perhaps, it seemed, because he didn't need one. Which meant the Zoccis had money. Probably serious money.

Despite what I'd read in his journal, Eric hadn't mentioned any family issues to me. Nor did I remember that his family was wealthy. Usually this sort of thing came out in therapy sessions. I'd have to check my notes when I got a look at the file.

I paged down to his Mental Status Exam, which was a standard observation-based intake procedure we did for every new client. Usually an intern did the intake, then reported the results to the therapist before the first session. I checked the box at the bottom of the page to see who had done the intake. It had been left blank. I'd have to check the hard copy to see if I could identify the handwriting. It was possible I'd done the MSE myself.

Paging back up, I scanned the form. Under almost every category, the standard answer "unremarkable" was listed. His appearance was normal, though he was very thin for his height. His clothing was age-appropriate and relatively neat, his affect tense. He was oriented as to time, place, and person. Which basically meant he knew what day it was, where he was, and who he was. His intelligence level was listed as "well above average." That sounded like my wording.

He was listed as having "anxious affect, but consistent with the content of the conversation." The interviewer had noted that Zocci bounced his leg and fiddled with a key chain throughout the interview. Common manifestations of anxiety.

I paged down to "delusions and hallucinations." Now it got a little more revealing. He had answered yes to several questions. Zocci reported that he'd recently experienced intense worry that something bad would happen to him. To the question "Have you ever felt someone was reading your mind or making you think things?" he had answered "sometimes, lately." When asked

"Have you ever had a dream that was so intense or real that you weren't sure whether you were asleep or awake?" he had answered yes. The interviewer had highlighted it for intensity.

When asked if he felt suicidal, he had answered "not really."

I checked the notes. The interviewer had written "when pressed, patient claims no suicidal ideation."

I felt a surge of guilt. I should have gotten to the bottom of that "not really." It sounded profoundly unconvincing in hindsight.

I scanned the rest of the file. Nothing else stood out to me. I printed it out, closed the program, and shut down the computer.

A few minutes later, I'd armed the alarm system and locked up the office, breathing a sigh of relief that I hadn't gotten caught. Jesus, it seemed, was cutting me a little break.

My next stop was the library. I seated myself at a research computer and started with a quick Internet search for Joseph Zocci of Chicago. Erik's father, it turned out, was indeed a businessman. He was the founder, president, and CEO of a sizable regional airline in the Midwest. Eagle Wing Air.

I went to the airline's website. Eagle Wing Air offered multiple daily flights to a number of Midwest locations. It was obviously a formidable regional airline. Not some rinky-dink start-up. I'd heard of it, but never taken an Eagle Wing flight. I was pretty sure it was mainly a commuter airline. I clicked on the company history page.

Eagle Wing Air had been founded in 1983 by Joseph Zocci, U.S. Navy, retired. He had started with a couple of small planes, ferrying local businessmen to their destinations. It sounded like it had started out as more of a charter airline than anything.

Utilizing small airports, Zocci had found a niche that was largely ignored by major carriers, and the airline, over the past twenty-odd years, had grown from a small two-plane operation into a large and enormously successful publicly-traded company. Eagle Wing now offered service to almost every major city in the U.S. And, I suspected, was the only airline in the country currently operating in the black.

Well. Bad news for me. Erik Zocci's dad was driven, ambitious, and had enormous amounts of money. He could easily obliterate little me in a lawsuit. This was one of those times when that whole omnipotence thing would really come in handy. I promptly began begging God to end this thing quickly and quietly. In my favor.

I clicked back to the search page and opened articles about Joseph Zocci. Most of them were business-related news stories. They didn't reveal much about him personally. I got the impression he was a man who guarded his private life.

I glanced through the articles quickly, building up to the one I didn't really want to read. Finally, I opened the most recent news item about Joseph Zocci. It was from the *Chicago Tribune*. "Airline Founder's Son Found Dead—Suicide Suspected."

I opened the article and was greeted with a grainy, black and white photo of the Zocci clan, staged to look like they were having a picnic. Erik stood behind his father's right shoulder. I recognized him immediately. I leaned in toward the screen, squinting.

He looked perfectly normal to me. Smiling, unaffected. Typical rich-kid-getting-his-photo-taken-with-the-family smile. He looked elegant, confident, and at ease, which was not at all how I remembered him. I checked the caption on the picture. It was taken the fall of his senior year in high school.

This was a kid who had been well loved. Not a kid haunted by self-doubt and delusional fears. Something had clearly changed for this young man between the time this photo was taken and the time he showed up in my office.

The article started out with the brutal details of the suicide. I read them with an anxious, morbid fascination.

Zocci had checked into the Vendome the night before he'd killed himself. The hotel staff was well acquainted with the family, various members of whom often checked in for an overnight stay. Apparently the family's primary residence was in the country. An estate on Lake Michigan.

Zocci had checked into a room on the twelfth floor. The following morning, witnesses reported seeing him on the treadmill in the hotel's fitness facility around 9:15. No one remembered seeing him leave the fitness center.

At 12:10 p.m. Zocci's body was found on the roof of the atrium facing Delaware Street. He had not left a suicide note.

Wait a minute. Helene had said the suicide note specifically mentioned me. I checked the date on the article. It was written the day after his death. Maybe the note had been found later. I'd have to ask Helene when it had been discovered.

The rest of the article was background on the Zocci family, particularly Joseph Zocci's success. Mariann Zocci was hardly mentioned.

I paged back up to the family photograph and studied her face. Mariann Zocci looked expensively groomed, but in an understated way. No big jewelry. No designer outfit. Her face was plain, drawn, and humorless. She was a tiny woman, dwarfed by her grown children. I wondered how such a fragile little person had given birth eight times.

I scanned the rest of the faces in the photo. The girls, a matched set of five, were lovely, graceful, taller versions of their mother. And the two boys were strapping. Erik particularly had the look of an athlete. I remembered him as thin and wiry. This photo showed a healthy muscular boy. He had his father's strong jaw line.

Something was bothering me about the photo. I studied it again, moving from face to face. They all looked so happy. So perfect.

But something was wrong. I couldn't put my finger on it. And then it dawned on me. There weren't enough kids. I counted. Five girls and two boys. Someone was missing.

I scanned the article again until I found the list of the children's names. There it was at the bottom of the final paragraph. Joseph Michael Zocci Jr., deceased.

Erik had specifically mentioned that he had seven siblings. Which meant he was including his dead brother in the count.

I had worked with families over the years who did that. When asked how many children she had, a mother might say, "We have four, including one child who died several years ago." I usually took that to mean that the family still had some mourning to do, or that they had an extremely strong sense of afterlife. Strong enough to refer to a deceased child in the present tense.

There was no mention in the article about what had happened to Joseph Zocci's namesake.

I printed it out and moved to the periodicals section of the library and found the microfiche of the *Tribune*'s archives.

I figured that, as the namesake son, Joseph Jr. had been the oldest boy. Erik's oldest living sibling was nine years older than he, which would put that child at about age thirty now. I started my search with obituaries from thirty-five years ago.

I found it after only a few moments of searching. Joseph Jr. had died in 1972 at the age of three. The obit said only that he'd died in a tragic accident. Survivors were listed as Lieutenant Joseph Michael Zocci, naval fighter pilot, serving in Vietnam, and Mariann Zocci, homemaker. No other children were listed.

I searched the rest of the paper from the previous week,

thinking maybe the accident had made the local news. I found it in the Tuesday Metro section.

Joseph Michael Zocci Jr. had fallen from the twelfth-floor balcony of the Vendome.

13

THE LIBRARY SUDDENLY seemed menacing to me. Bumps raised on my arms as I became aware, for the first time in the hour or so I'd been there, of the chill of the air-conditioning pouring out of the vent over my head. I felt bare, exposed, conspicuous. As though somehow the people around me were watching me. As if they were aware of my connection to these bizarre events.

I looked around and saw five or six people sitting at tables, mostly students bowed over thick reference books. No one even glanced back.

I wrote the sensation off as paranoia, but couldn't shake it. I could feel eyes on me.

I turned my attention back to the article. I wondered if Joseph had been in Vietnam when his son died. Or perhaps he'd been home on leave and the couple had celebrated by booking a weekend at the Vendome. I did the math. This would have been almost ten years before Joseph Sr. had started Eagle Wing Air. The airline had been founded in 1983, the same year Erik had been born. If Zocci was still in the Navy, I doubted they would have been able to afford such a luxury.

What a grim twist on an already unthinkable tragedy. I

didn't know what to make of it. Had Erik chosen the Vendome for his suicide in order to echo, in some sick way, his brother's death? It was not an unreasonable conclusion. He and his brother shared a middle name. Probably he felt some special kinship with the boy. And suicides sometimes choose methods reminiscent of some tragedy in the past. Something that reflects the legacy that had driven them to the edge in the first place.

I reached in my bag and retrieved the article about Erik's suicide, spreading it out on the desk in front of me. I studied the family photo again, focusing in on Mariann's face. I couldn't imagine her grief.

Curiously, I felt nothing for Erik's father. I peered at his picture again, wondering why I felt such a profound lack of empathy for the man. Something about his face put me off. He oozed power, authority. He didn't seem like a man given to softness of any kind. Or was this knee-jerk self-protectiveness on my part? Trying to steel myself against the enemy? He was, after all, the man who held my career in his very powerful hands.

The cold was starting to get to me. I made a quick copy of Joseph Jr.'s obituary and stuffed it in my bag with the rest of the articles, gathered my things, and got ready to leave.

I felt burgeoning paranoia as I stood up. I was certain someone was watching me. I'd read studies in graduate school in which subjects were blindfolded and then asked to guess whether or not they were being stared at. In a startling percentage of cases, the subjects had been accurate. Even blindfolded, they could sense when they were being watched.

I heeded the research and looked around again. Same students. Bent over the same books. No one seemed the least bit interested in me.

Finally I turned to leave, only to feel a surge of clammy fear as I caught a glimpse of Peter Terry out of the corner of my eye.

I saw his face distinctly, staring at me from between the stacks at the other end of the room.

By the time I whipped around toward the image, though, he was gone. I shuddered, but vowed to myself that I would not back away out of fear. I remembered Tony DeStefano's words, something about children of the King having protection.

I squared my shoulders, reminded myself that my Dad could beat up his dad, and stalked over toward the shelves.

I plowed the rows of books, one by one, passing a few students plucking tomes from the shelves. They looked up curiously at me as I whipped past them.

I realized for the second time that day that I was moving at a suspicious clip. To even a casual observer, my anxiety must have been obvious. I might as well have been setting off bottle rockets.

I slowed myself down and continued my search with ruthless, businesslike efficiency. Row after row. One by one.

About halfway through, I realized the futility of my effort. All he had to do was stay a few rows ahead or behind me, and I would never find him. The library had four floors, dozens of study carrels, and who knew how many closets, elevators, and bathrooms.

I went back to the reference section and stood in front of the microfiche desk, glancing again toward the shelves, hoping to convince myself I'd imagined the entire thing.

I walked slowly back to the spot where I'd seen his face and checked the label at the end of the aisle. Religions, Mythology, Rationalism.

I stepped into the aisle, studied the titles, and found myself in the comparative religion section. The selection was sparse. Most of SMU's religion and theology books would be across campus in the Bridwell Library at Perkins, SMU's theology school.

My seminary education included exactly zero courses in comparative religion. I didn't even recognize the authors' names. I pulled a few titles off the shelves, but stuck them back in their slots after looking them over. This wasn't going to get me anywhere.

I walked the aisles in the rest of the religion section until I reached the study area at the end. The large study table was unoccupied, except for one pile of books, a backpack, and a notepad with a pen sitting on it. The chair was empty.

I yanked a book off the shelf nearest me and sat down in the chair on the opposite side of the table, opening my book and pretending to read. Keeping my head as still as I could, I strained to see the titles in the pile of books.

On the bottom was an open concordance. The heading at the top of the page read "Flesh—Flock." On top of it sat *Studies in Isaiah* and *Isaiah: Yahweh's Salvation*. Apart from the pile, a Bible was open to the book of Isaiah.

The Bible looked brand new. The delicate silver on the edge of the pages was unblemished, and the pages still looked fresh and uncrinkled, as though the book had just come from the box.

A single sentence was underlined, in bloody red ink, on the otherwise pristine page. I strained to make out the words, reading them upside down and mouthing them slowly to myself as I deciphered them one by one:

> In that day the LORD will whistle for flies from the distant streams of Egypt.

The cold penetrated me then. And my flitty paranoia hardened into leaden terror, sinking into my heart so thoroughly and quickly that it pushed the air out of my lungs.

I sucked that same air right back in as a man's voice came from behind me.

"Are you following me?" he said.

I turned slowly, expecting to see Peter Terry. Instead I saw Gavin. Angry. Pale. Frightened.

"No," I said, my paranoia solid and icy now. "Are you following me?"

"Why would you ask that?" he said.

"Then what are you doing here?"

"Studying." He raised his chin defiantly. "What are you doing here?

"Studying," I said.

"Were you reading my notes?"

"Yes. How do you know about the flies?"

"How do *you* know about the flies?" he asked back.

"What flies?" I wanted him to say it.

"Exactly. What flies?" he said.

"Have you had problems with flies? Big, aggressive black flies?"

"Maybe. Have you?"

"Yes." I hesitated a minute. "Will you tell me about it?"

He shrugged, still mistrustful. "What's to tell? They're just flies."

"Then why are you looking them up in Isaiah? Why don't you just buy a flyswatter?"

"Is that what you did?" he asked. "Buy a flyswatter? Is that all there was to it?"

"There's something scary about these flies, isn't there?"

He nodded.

"Something evil," I said.

His unease began to shift from me back to the flies. "Do you have them in your house?"

"I had them one night. I haven't seen them since then. You?"

"Want me to show you?"

I was nervous about going to a student's room, especially with the charges pending against me. It was a terrible idea, really. But my curiosity won out. I nodded, and he wordlessly gathered his stuff, shoving it into his backpack. I followed him to the exit, stopping to gather my things at the reference desk.

We walked the length of the campus in the heat, neither of us saying a word.

We arrived at his dorm sweating and unsettled, both of us. I followed him into Morrison and onto One South, filing along behind him past rooms that smelled of dirty socks and stale food, until we reached 105. He stopped and unlocked the door.

"My roommate moved out," he said, as he swung the door into the room.

At first glance, it seemed I had stepped into a typical college dorm room. One mattress was bare, the other bed rumpled, unmade. A tiny refrigerator hummed in the corner. A computer sat on a fairly tidy desk.

And then I realized the refrigerator had been unplugged. The humming was coming from somewhere else.

I looked around more carefully now, spotting them at intervals around the room. Five of them on the wall over the bulletin board. Three on the post at the end of the bed. One walking slowly, zigzagging across his desk. Little black herds of them gathered in the corners next to the ceiling.

As we stood there, one broke loose from the corner and flew in our direction, buzzing between us and then circling around and returning to the corner.

I turned to Gavin. "When did they come?"

"They've been coming one by one for a week. I've swatted probably a hundred."

"Where are they coming from?" I asked. "Can you tell?"

"No."

"Is this why your roommate left?"

"That and the screaming. I keep having those dreams. With the white cancer dude."

He walked to the desk and picked up a paperback, flicking away a fly. He handed me the book. "I think he meant this to be funny. He's really not a bad guy—my roommate, I mean."

I looked at the book jacket. *Lord of the Flies*. I handed it back to him.

"I'm sorry," I said. There was nothing else to say. "Does the housing department know about the flies? I'm sure they'll exterminate."

"They're coming today." He looked around. "Somehow I don't think it will get rid of them."

I didn't either.

"Do you have anyplace else to go?" I asked.

"No, I don't really know anybody yet."

"You don't have family around?"

He looked up at me, utterly alone. "I'm from California. I don't really have much family anyway."

He had the haunted look about him that Erik Zocci had had. I resolved at that moment that I wasn't going to let this one slip away.

"Do you want a place to stay?" I asked.

"With you?"

"No," I said firmly. The implications of that terrible idea clanged in my head. "But I think I know a family that would let you stay with them."

"Do they have kids?"

"Three. Loud ones. That might be a drawback."

He smiled for the first time. "I like kids."

I called Tony and Jenny and explained the situation, giving them the details of Erik Zocci's suicide as well. They agreed immediately to take Gavin in, as I knew they would. We gathered his things quickly, shaking flies off each item before we stuffed it into his duffel. Then I dropped him at Fluff-N-Fold for a couple of hours to wash any remnants out of his clothes.

I took the time to go for a swim at the SMU pool, needing to feel the clean smooth water on my skin, needing to feel my muscles flex and my breathing regulate.

By the time I picked Gavin up, we both felt better. I dropped him off at the DeStefanos', finding a deep sense of peace leaving him in their hands. When I left, he was giving his first piggyback ride to one of Tony's kids.

14

~

I AM NOT A MORNING PERSON. I do not trust morning people. They are far too enthusiastic for me. But on occasion I find myself up with the dawn. I watch the sun come up over my cup of tea, heavy darkness dissipating slowly into watery blue and then the palest, most transparent yellow, and I feel the pull of the new day.

I am inevitably, in those moments, compelled by the universal force of morning. Watching the horizon show itself reminds me that somewhere, past the edge of it all, optimism awaits. That something else, maybe something better, is out there for the finding.

But I watched the sun rise that Monday, after another endless night, with no such hope. The dawn that morning brightened into the harsh, relentless light of scrutiny. Scrutiny I was certain I couldn't bear.

I had never in my life felt so vulnerable, so exposed. This spiritual attack was earthy, menacing. I had never felt the presence of evil so profoundly.

I couldn't shake the visual I had in my head of two Zocci sons, one an innocent little boy of three and the other a strong, seemingly healthy young man, flying over the railing at the

Vendome hotel. Screaming to their deaths. I had watched the scene over and over in my mind the night before.

I was beginning to have the same fear for Gavin. He was clearly being targeted by the same specter that had haunted Erik. I could see him beginning to slip. The traumatized young man I'd dropped off at the DeStefanos' was not the same boy that had approached me in class only a week before.

My fears for my own sake gripped me as well. I was freshly aware of my own fragility, of my tiny, inconsequential little place in the world. Of the true frailty of my grip on my own well-being.

Helene had taken my cases at the clinic. My professional credibility seemed already shredded beyond repair. I was certain I was going to lose my job, and was already casting about neurotically for a new way to make a living.

My meeting with the university's lawyers loomed over my afternoon. And with all this on my mind, I somehow had to manage to get through my day with some degree of aplomb and poise.

I'd taken my Bible on the porch with my tea, determined to summon some faith to see me through this day. I sabotaged my plan, of course, by looking instead for the Isaiah quote about the flies. I found it in chapter 7.

"In that day," it said, "the LORD will whistle for flies from the distant streams of Egypt and for bees from the land of Assyria."

Well. That could not be good. No matter what day we were talking about.

I looked around suspiciously for flies and bees—who needed a new insect to worry about, anyway?

Turning back to the pages, I scanned the surrounding chapters, looking for meaning, trying to come up with my own solution to the bug infestation problem. I finally realized that the answer was in the passage itself. If God could summon flies and bees, then it stood to reason He could call them off. The flies worked for Him, not for Peter Terry. ⚜

My first good news in days.

I bowed my head and had a long talk with the Lord about flies. And about Peter Terry. And about Gavin and the Zoccis and my job. And my professional reputation. All the rocks I was carrying around.

I had to fight with myself about my old niggling suspicion that God really is very busy and has no time for my dinky little requests.

I shot myself over to chapter 40 and pounded myself with more of Isaiah's words. "Why do you say, O Jacob, and complain, O Israel,"—I like to insert "O Dylan," though it doesn't have quite the same level of cosmic significance, I admit—"'My way is hidden from the LORD; my cause is disregarded by my God'? Do you not know? Have you not heard? The LORD is the everlasting God, the Creator of the ends of the earth."

I felt the peace come.

I paged over to Ephesians and refreshed my memory of chapter 6. The spiritual warfare chapter.

Sandals, belt, breastplate, shield, helmet, and sword. Head to toe, spiritual protection built to last. Not my usual attire, but perfect equipment for a fight.

All to be worn "when the day of evil comes."

My day of evil had certainly arrived. It was burning hot, bright, and ugly, in fact.

I vowed to wear my God-issued uniform faithfully. I resolved to myself that absolutely under no circumstances would I go down without a fight. I was determined to remember that I was on the winning side. After all, my General could summon flies.

I slapped my Bible shut and went into the house.

I'd gotten three phone calls while I was outside. I pushed the play button and listened to the messages.

Helene had called just a few minutes before, wanting me to meet her in her office for a working lunch today—she was bringing enough food for both of us. More good news. Helene's cooking always comforted me.

David Shykovsky had called just before Helene. He wanted to take me dancing Thursday night. He said he'd call back.

I had to hand it to the guy. Four days' notice. Didn't leave a number for me to call him back, because he intended to call me back. So far, I could bottle this guy and sell him. What a sugar pie.

And true to form, my dad had called at the crack of dawn, exhibiting his usual irritation that I hadn't answered my phone. He had information for me, he said, but I had to call him back to get it. He left his pager number.

I called his secretary instead.

"Hey, Janet. Dylan."

"Dylan! I was just thinking about you."

"You always say that."

"No. I really was. Your dad just asked me if you'd returned his call. Didn't you get his message?"

"I did," I said. "I'm calling him back. Is he around?"

"He just stepped out the door, but he said he was coming right back." I heard her flip the pages of her schedule book. "He's not due in surgery until nine. He probably just went down the hall for a minute."

"How are the wedding plans coming?" I asked. *Why do I do this to myself?*

"Oh, honey, what he sees in that woman, I will never know. Now she's got them riding in on matched white horses." Her tone shifted to imitate Kellee's nasal voice. "'The ceremony must start at precisely 6:07. We'll arrive on horseback at exactly the very minute the sun sets.' Do you know how hard it is to find two white horses in a town the size of Cabo San Lucas? Much less two that are exactly the same size. I'm thinking of having some spray painted."

I made another mental note to make my travel plans now. I intended to be anywhere but Cabo San Lucas come Thanksgiving.

"Oh," she was saying, "I'd prepare myself if I were you. Your name has come up a lot between him and Kellee lately. Every single time they talk about the wedding."

"Oh no. He's not going to ask me to be in the wedding, is he? Tell me he's not going to ask me to be in the wedding."

"I can't tell you any such thing, as a matter of fact. I'm just saying—Oh good, you're back, Dr. Foster. I have Dylan on line two." The line went numb as she abruptly put me on hold.

My dad's voice broke the silence. "Dylan, where were you when I called?"

"Why do you call me at 6:00 a.m., Dad? Who does that?"

"Did you get my message?"

"Of course I did. Hence the return phone call. What did you find out?"

"If you're going to ask me favors, you could at least pick up the phone when I call you."

"Are you going to answer my question?"

"No Peter Terry at M.D. Anderson."

"Are you sure?"

"Do I sound sure?"

"Who did you call?"

"Shollenbarger."

"Who's that?"

"Oncologist. Big guy. Seven handicap," he said testily.

"Oh." I remembered him now. Six five, two fifty. Very nice guy. "Did he check the whole cancer center? Or just his own patient list?"

His voice was getting louder by the word. "I called him this morning and asked him about Peter Terry. He called me back thirty minutes later and said there was no Peter Terry. That ought to be good enough for you."

"What time did you call him?" I was picturing my dad yanking this guy out of bed at five, and then Shollenbarger doing a cursory return phone call thirty minutes later to shut my dad up. Pretending he'd checked some magical database.

"What does that matter?" he said. "I do you a favor, you're complaining about how I did it. I called the man. There is no Peter Terry."

"Don't get so defensive," I said.

"I'm not defensive!"

With the temper he had, it was a wonder my dad hadn't ended up on his own operating table. He was about to blow.

"Who is this Peter Terry guy anyway?" he asked

"I told you. He's the uncle of a patient of mine."

"You said brother."

"Okay, brother. Whatever. Why?"

"Maybe I know him."

"What do you mean, 'maybe you know him'? Are you saying you know someone named Peter Terry?"

"I might have."

"Did you or didn't you?"

"I think so."

"Well, who was it? Someone you knew in school or something?"

"Not really."

"Know or knew?"

"Knew. But I didn't know him very well." His voice was faltering, the bombast wilting.

"I'm waiting," I said.

"He was a friend of your mother's."

Now we were getting somewhere.

"How long ago?" I said.

"While she was in the hospital."

"At M.D. Anderson?"

"Yes."

"Why didn't you mention that when I called?" My dad could be so exasperating.

"I'd forgotten about him."

"What did he look like?" I asked.

"I never met him."

"I thought you said you knew him."

"I didn't really know him. Your mother knew him. She spent a lot of time with him."

"But you never met him?"

"No."

"Then how do you know about him?"

"She talked about him a lot."

"What did she say about him?" I asked.

"Nothing, really. She felt sorry for him."

"Was he a cancer patient when she was?"

"She never said how they met, so I don't know." There was a long pause. "Mostly she said she thought he needed her. That he made her feel needed."

My dad, I knew, had never made my mother feel needed. In fact, he had never, at least since their first few optimistic years together, made her feel anything but neglected.

He was still talking. "I thought she'd made him up. No one

else ever saw him. Yet she claimed to be spending all this time with him." He gathered himself. "Was your mother having an affair with this man? I think I deserve to know."

"An affair? How did you conjure that up? Mom would never have done that. One of my patients knows him. That's all I know."

"But he's not your patient's uncle, is he?"

"Brother," I said.

"Whatever."

"No."

I heard Janet's voice in the background and looked at my watch. It was 8:15. She was probably telling him he needed to scrub.

"I have to go," he said, "But we are going to finish this conversation. I have something I want to ask you."

"Can you ask me later, Dad? I'm going to be late to work." No way was I walking behind those two white horses in Cabo.

"I expect you to answer my calls, Dylan."

"Sure, Dad. Call me later."

We hung up. I fixed myself one more cup of tea, then went into the bedroom and dressed for work, imagining my new war gear as I got ready to face my day.

15

I STOOD IN FRONT OF MY CLASS that Monday morning with a renewed love for my job, probably because I knew I was so close to having it yanked away from me. All my whining about the daily tedium of academic life seemed ridiculous now that I faced the possibility of doing without it. Simple, invisible elements of wealth—privacy, routine, security, respect—these I now realized I had taken for granted in the most frivolous, extravagant way.

My students, Gavin included, seemed dull and unresponsive. I didn't care. I taught gleefully, all the while silently begging Jesus to spare me from a fate flipping burgers for a living by the end of the week.

Gavin and I spoke briefly after class. He was getting settled in at the DeStefanos'. They had offered to let him stay with them as long as he needed to, and had assigned him some household chores. He referred to himself as "vice president in charge of babysitting and garbage removal," a title he seemed proud to have acquired.

His one night there had passed with neither nightmares nor flies. He was on his way to his dorm to pick up some more clothes and see if the room had been fumigated. He'd drop by my office later and give me the fly report.

I spent a few minutes returning phone calls in my office and then headed down the hall for my meeting with Helene. Her door was open when I arrived.

"Morning," I said, offering myself a seat.

She looked over her reading glasses at the wall clock. "Noon," she said.

"Picky." I popped the top on the soda she handed me.

"You don't look as bad as I thought you would," she said.

"You give the worst compliments."

"Well, I thought you'd look worse."

"What did you expect? Twitching? Drooling? I'm handling it."

She was unpacking lunch, stacking Tupperware on a cleared space on her desk. Helene had a thing about restaurants. She was convinced she could out-cook them all, so she rarely ate out. In the years I'd known her, I couldn't remember the two of us darkening the door of one single restaurant together. But we had shared countless Tupperware-stacked meals at her desk.

"I brought tuna," she was saying. "With cucumber. Do you want pita or regular bread?"

"Pita," I said, reaching for a plate.

She unfolded a piece of wheat pita bread, tucked a few fresh lettuce leaves into it, and loaded in a heaping spoonful of tuna salad. She layered some chopped cucumbers on top and poured on a little homemade dressing, moving deftly with practiced, gnarled hands.

She handed me the sandwich and then fixed one for herself. More open Tupperware lids revealed green grapes and freshly cut slices of ripe cantaloupe. Helene had a way of making food look so inviting.

The last lid she opened released a smell that turned my stomach.

"Deviled eggs?" she said, holding the little tub out to me.

I felt myself turn green and put my plate down. "No."

"I thought you liked deviled eggs."

"I've never liked deviled eggs."

"Well you don't have to get so testy. You could just say 'no, thank you.'"

"Excuse me a minute."

I bolted down the hall to the bathroom and leaned over the sink, fighting off nausea. It took me a few minutes to regain my composure. I splashed water on my face and stared at myself in the mirror. I was white. Shaken.

What sort of person is traumatized by a little plastic dish of deviled eggs? Helene looked up at me as I stepped back into her office.

"Now you look as bad as I thought you would," she said triumphantly.

"Thanks." I sat down and pushed my plate away.

Helene had put the lid back on the deviled eggs, forgoing them herself. I walked over and opened the window, then returned to my seat and took a sip of soda.

"You want me to put the rest of the food away?" she asked.

"No. It's fine. It was just the eggs, I think. That smell makes me nauseous."

"Suit yourself." She took a bite of her sandwich and chewed for a second. "How was your weekend?"

"Terrible."

"What time did you go up to the clinic yesterday?" she asked casually.

I looked at her. "What makes you think I went up to the clinic?"

"Don't make me audit the computer records. If you logged on, I'll know. Just tell me."

"About 2:30."

"Find anything out?"

"Nothing that will help me."

"Anything that will hurt you?" she asked.

My stomach was settling down. I reached for my plate and took a bite of cantaloupe.

"Not at the clinic. Afterward, at the library, though."

She raised her eyebrows at me.

"Zocci's parents have money," I said. "They can flatten me if they want."

"I wondered about that. When I called, it sounded like a maid or something answered. Both times." She paused. "How much money?"

"His dad founded Eagle Wing Air."

"Oh. That kind of money." She finished her sandwich. "I wouldn't worry about it. Leave that to the lawyers, honey."

"Easy for you to say."

"No, it really isn't." Her tone caught me off guard. "This is not just about you. I'm responsible for you. The university is responsible for you. We're all facing this thing together."

"Okay. Sorry."

"Besides, that's what lawyers are for. You'll feel better after we meet with them today."

"Is that what you wanted to talk to me about?" I tasted a grape.

"No. I wanted to talk to you about the faculty meeting."

"We're having a faculty meeting? I don't have it on my schedule."

"I just scheduled it this morning. It's about you."

I felt my stomach flip again. "I thought you said we'd fly

under the radar. I thought you said you were going to handle this quietly until we found out what's going on."

"I did say that. Zocci's father called the dean yesterday. At home. He asked that you be put on leave immediately."

"And she agreed?"

"I didn't know why until now. Money talks." She opened another Tupperware container. "Cake?" she asked.

I shook my head no. "You think it's because of the money?"

"Of course. That's the way these things work." She plunged her fork into a spongy slice of chocolate cake, swirling the icing onto the fork before taking her bite. "Anyway. I have to tell the faculty something."

"So I'm on leave? As of now? I can't teach this afternoon?"

"No, you can't," she said. "You're on leave as of now. Full pay."

"Oh."

"I'm sorry, Dylan. I really am."

"What are you going to tell them?"

"Your esteemed colleagues? As little as possible. I was thinking you need to have some sort of family emergency."

"Like what?" I couldn't think clearly.

"I don't know," she said impatiently. "Make something up. It doesn't matter. Just so you have something to tell people."

"Who will take my classes?"

"I will, for the time being." She looked across the desk at me. "I wouldn't do this for anyone else."

"Thank you." It was hard to come up with much to be grateful for, but at least my classes would be in good hands. "What time is the faculty meeting?"

"One o'clock," she said.

I looked at my watch. It wasn't quite 12:30. A lot had changed in half an hour.

"And the meeting with the lawyers?" I asked.

"4:15. In the dean's office."

"The dean will be there?" I longed for Mylanta.

"No," Helene said. "She just offered her office. For privacy."

"Oh. That was nice of her. What did you tell her? Does she know what's going on?"

"I talked to her this morning. I told her everything I know."

"Oh." One-syllable answers seemed to be all I could muster. "I guess I should go." I stood up. "What room?"

"Conference room."

I turned to leave.

"Dylan?"

"Yes?"

"I told the dean I believe you. I told her it wasn't true."

"Thank you."

"See you at 1:00."

I gave her a half-hearted thumbs-up and went back to my office. I closed the door behind me and sat at my desk, fighting off the urge to cry. The phone startled me out of my despair.

"Dylan Foster," I said.

"It's John," a voice said.

John. My mind went racing around. I know about forty men named John. I had at least three students named John and a couple of therapy clients. One of whom was in the middle of a psychotic depression. I'd given the clinic instructions to have him call me directly if he had an emergency. I wondered how I was going to tell him he was about to switch therapists.

"What is it, John? Did something happen?"

There was a hard pause. "What do you mean?"

"I mean, did your weekend go okay? Is there some emergency? Are you feeling suicidal or something?"

"Why would I be suicidal?" the caller said.

Suddenly I recognized the voice.

"John? Mulvaney? Is that you?"

"Of course," he said. "I'm returning your call."

"I didn't call you, John."

"You did and you know it." He sounded so childish. Like a seventh grader in a school yard spat.

"Check your caller ID, John. It wasn't me."

"I don't have caller ID, and it was you. And I want you to stop. Our relationship is over."

"We never had a relationship. Can we just agree on that?"

"We can agree you tricked me into coming to your house," he said.

"I didn't trick you into coming to my house."

"You have to stop calling me," he said firmly. "Why don't you say anything when I pick up the phone?"

"John, it's not me. Maybe someone else is calling you." I put my head in my hands. "I'm hanging up now."

"Don't act like there's nothing going on."

"I'm not acting," I said, and slammed down the phone.

I dialed Helene's extension.

"I can't come to the meeting," I said without saying hello.

"Which one?"

"The faculty meeting. John Mulvaney is delusional."

"That's what he says about you."

"Well, who do you believe?" I shouted.

"You're right. You can't come to the meeting. I don't want you cracking up in front of the staff."

"Thank you."

"What do you want me to tell them?"

"Tell them I had a family emergency."

We hung up.

I sat at my desk and looked blankly around me, flicking my

eyes across my bookshelves, my teapot, my photographs. Things that once seemed homey and familiar to me. They seemed foreign now. Quaint relics from a distant past.

I'd planned on prepping for my afternoon class after lunch, which of course wasn't necessary now. I hid in my office instead, watching the seconds tick by slowly. The phone rang twice. I let it ring both times. One caller didn't leave a message. The other message was from Gavin. The flies were dead.

At ten minutes after one, I gathered my class materials and my bag and tiptoed down the hall past the conference room, where I could hear the muffled sounds of the meeting through the door. I leaned in to listen, but couldn't make out any of the words.

Helene wasn't speaking anymore. Someone was asking a question, which meant the meeting would probably be over soon. How long could it take for her to tell them I was going on leave?

I scooted past the door, afraid to run into anyone, stopping by Helene's office on the way out. I left my class materials on her desk and then made a last stop at the reception area to check my box, grabbing my mail and stuffing it in my bag.

I made the short, hot walk to my truck feeling very alone.

I tossed my bag in through the open window and yanked on the door, which let out a groan. I decided to stop at the hardware store on the way home and buy that much-needed WD-40. Might as well make use of my newfound free time.

I walked around the store in a haze, aimlessly shuffling past pyramids of paint cans and walls laden with brooms and garden hoses. I couldn't remember why I'd come.

Finally, I spotted a small can of WD-40 and snatched it up, searching through my bag for my wallet.

At the checkout I paid the Helpful Hardware Man, whose

name was Alice and who was not a man at all, and then dropped my wallet back in my bag.

As I did, my eyes fell on my mail and I gasped.

On the top of the stack was an envelope from the Vendome hotel.

16

~

I RIPPED OPEN THE ENVELOPE as I hurried back to my
truck, opened my donkey-honk door, and tossed the unused
can of WD-40 on the seat beside me.

Inside the envelope was a receipt. For $664.48. From the
gift store at the Vendome.

I'd never been to the Vendome.

It wasn't itemized. I had no idea what the bill was for.

Maybe Erik Zocci had stolen my credit card number before
he checked in or something. I'm terrible about leaving my bag
unattended in my office. Anyone could walk in and take
anything they wanted.

Cursing my naiveté, I started my truck, threw it into reverse,
and raced home for the telephone.

I parked my car in the garage and shut the garage door. I
didn't want to advertise to anyone that I was home in the middle
of the day. I was half afraid that John Mulvaney would show up
again after today's faculty meeting.

I went into my study and sat at my computer and looked up
the Vendome online.

I felt instantly outclassed. It was a gorgeous hotel. Far more
elegant than anywhere I usually stayed. (My income level placed

me firmly at Holiday Inn status.) The photographs showed a tastefully decorated lobby with enormous sprays of fresh flowers. Beautiful rooms. Handsomely furnished suites. There was even a little orchestral number playing elegantly in the background on the homepage.

I poked through the website until I found the phone number.

"Good afternoon, the Vendome. How may I help you?" answered a polite voice.

"Could you connect me to the gift shop, please?" My voice was at least an octave higher than usual. I told myself firmly to calm down.

"Certainly."

A moment on hold with the same lovely string music playing in my ear, and then I was talking to Eloise in the gift shop.

Even the help sounded elegant.

"I have a little problem I'm hoping you can help me with," I said.

"Of course," she said. "How may I assist you?"

"I got a bill. In the mail. A receipt, I mean. From the gift shop there at the hotel." I sounded like a moron. A hick and a moron. I tried to smooth out my speech. "And I know this sounds silly, but I haven't the faintest memory of what I bought. Do you have any way of looking that up for me?"

"Certainly." If she thought I was an idiot, she sure wasn't showing it. Courtesy could be a grand and wonderful thing. "Do you have the receipt in front of you?"

"I'm looking right at it," I said.

"What's the date on the receipt?"

I gave her the date. The purchase had been made almost a month ago.

"Is there a transaction number? It should be in the upper right-hand corner."

I read her the number, which was printed in red ink right where she said it should be. I listened while she tapped on her computer keys.

"Here it is. $664.48?"

"That's it!" I said, a little too enthusiastically. "Is it itemized, by chance?"

"It was a phone order. I have eight items listed here, plus gift wrap and a delivery fee. Would you like me to read the entire list to you?"

"Please," I said.

"One Barrington fountain pen, black, $73.99; one leather Day-timer, brown, zip closure, $64.95; one set luxury bath salts, Origins, $47.99…"

As she read the list, my heart quickened. These were the gifts from the day at Barton Springs.

She was reading the last item. "One leather cord necklace, black stone drop, $62.50. Total items billed, eight; total amount billed, $503.65; gift wrap, $64.00; tax, $46.83; shipping and handling, $50.00; for a total of $664.48."

Shipping. "Is there an address listed?"

She read an address that I didn't recognize. I wrote it down and underlined the zip code. It wasn't a Dallas address.

"And what's the name on the charge?" I asked.

"Dylan Foster. Charged to a MasterCard. I'm sorry, but I can't give you the number over the phone."

"I understand." I dug my card out of my purse. "Can you just confirm the last four numbers for me? Is it 5466?"

"That's the one," she said. She was very genial. I liked Eloise. "I hope we've cleared up your confusion?"

"Yes, you've been very helpful."

"Is there anything else I may assist you with today?"

"No, thanks, Eloise. I appreciate the help."

I hung up the phone and stared into space. Someone had spent over six hundred dollars of my hard-earned cash to lead me straight to the Vendome. Six hundred dollars that, of course, I did not have.

I tried not to think about that. Six hundred bucks was the least of my problems.

That necklace was still locked in my sideboard. I unlocked the cabinet and took it out, along with the ring, and examined them both again.

Neither of them spooked me anymore. The ring was actually starting to feel comforting. I slipped it on the ring finger of my right hand and undid the clasp of the necklace, fastening it around my neck. If I'd spent $62.50 for the thing, I might as well wear it.

I got back online and went to the website for the U.S. Postal Service. I punched in the zip code of the address Eloise had given me.

It came up as a Houston zip code.

I did a search for realtors in Houston, calling the first big one on the list.

"I'm interested in buying a home in Houston," I said to a very grouchy woman named Belinda. "I have a particular address in mind and wonder if there's any way you can look it up for me?" I started my mental lie tally for the day.

Belinda wasn't nearly as helpful as Eloise. "Who's the listing agent?" she asked.

"I don't know the agent. Just the address. Is there some way you could verify the address for me?"

"What do you mean 'verify the address?'" she said. "What's there to verify?"

"I just want to make sure it's the right house."

"I don't understand. You just want the address?"

"No, I already have the address. I need to know who owns the house."

"I can't give out that information," she said. "All I can do is look it up on MLS for you and tell you who the agent is."

I didn't know what MLS was, but it sounded official. "That would be great. Would you do that, please?"

"What's the address?"

I gave her the address, and of course it wasn't listed. Dumb idea. I thanked her and was about to hang up when old Belinda redeemed herself.

"Have you checked the county?"

"The county? You mean have I found out what county it's in?"

"The tax records. You can check the county tax records."

"How do I do that?" I asked.

"The tax assessor's office has records of every county address. You might have to go down there. Their site is always down."

"Will it list the owner's name?"

"Owner's name, lot number, purchase price, date of purchase, assessed value," she recited.

"Thank you very much, Belinda."

I hung up and found the county's website online, which mercifully was up and running. I typed in the address. Belinda was right.

It was a commercial address, owned by a company named Garret Industries, Inc. I wrote down the information and did a web search for Garret Industries. Garret Industries did not have a website.

I looked it up in the phone book. Another dead end.

I looked it up in the Houston phone book's online business

pages. No listing. I was stumped. I couldn't figure out what to do next. I figured businesses must be registered somewhere. But I'm not a business person. I'm a shrink. And an academic. Thoroughly unfamiliar with the world of commerce.

So naturally, I decided to go back to the library. As an academic, I am firmly rooted in the belief that the answer to almost any question is at the library. It's part of the creed.

Maybe I'd get the added bonus of running into Peter Terry. Now that I was properly outfitted, I intended to corner him the next time I saw him and make him give me some answers.

I packed up the gift shop receipt and my notes and loaded myself once again into my truck, stopping first to spray the hinges of my door with WD-40. The door became satisfyingly silent as I swung it open and shut, working the oil in.

Two victories in one day. I was starting to feel downright celebratory.

I parked my truck behind the library, showed my faculty ID at the entry desk, and headed straight for the reference section.

The reference librarian on duty was named Cynthia. She'd helped me many times before.

"Hey, Cyn."

She looked up. "Dylan. How's the shrink business? Plenty of people getting work done on their brains?"

"I have a question for you," I said. "Do you know how to find out information about a corporation?"

"What sort of information?"

"I have the name and an address, but I don't know what the company does or who owns it. Is there any way to find out?"

"Is it a local company? You could try the phone book."

"Duh, Cynthia. Use your expensive library science degree. Help me out, will you?"

"Is it publicly traded?"

"No idea."

"Incorporated?"

I checked my notes. "Yes. Garret Industries, Inc."

"Then it would have to be registered with the state. Is it a Texas company?"

"Maybe. The address I have is in Houston."

"Let's start with the office of the secretary of state, then. All corporations have to be registered with the state through that office." She looked up their website and recited from the page, "'The secretary of state maintains a team of public information specialists to provide information from the agency's computer database. Business organization name availability or information about a specific entity may be obtained from the secretary of state via telephone, surface mail, or e-mail.'"

"Cyn, you're a genius."

"I know."

"What's the phone number?" I asked.

She checked her watch. "I'll write it down for you. But they're closed."

"Closed? On a Monday?"

"It's ten after five."

Sweet Moses. How could it be ten after five? I was supposed to meet with Helene and the lawyers an hour ago.

"Could you write all the contact information down for me?" I asked. "I'll get in touch with them tomorrow."

"Sure." She scribbled it all onto a sticky note. "If it's not a Texas corporation, you'll have to go state to state."

I took the sticky note and thanked her, waving behind me as I made a quick exit.

I arrived at the dean's office a few minutes later, sweating from the heat and from my rapidly heightening anxiety. The meeting was just ending.

"Dylan," Helene said crisply. "So glad you could join us."

I'd rarely seen her angry, and certainly never at me. I wilted. I can't stand for Helene to be mad at me.

"I'm so sorry," I said. "I got tied up."

I ignored her glare and held out my hand to the attorney closest to me, an icy blonde in a pale pink suit.

"Dylan Foster," I said.

"It would have helped to have you here," she said.

I smiled sweetly. "Want me to go to 'time out'?"

She didn't smile back. She stood up and handed Helene a business card. "Let us know when you can both be available."

She turned and walked past me, followed by the other attorney, a burly-looking man who clearly did not wear the pants on the team.

As soon as they were out the door, Helene turned her glare back on me.

"Inexcusable," she said.

"I'm sorry."

"Irresponsible."

"I know."

She reached for her briefcase. "I'm going home."

"You don't want to tell me about the meeting?"

She froze and looked over her glasses at me.

"Don't push me," she said. "You want to hear about the meeting, call that ice queen lawyer yourself. It's your rear end on the line." She handed me the woman's business card.

I pursed my lips and didn't say anything.

She brushed past me with her briefcase and her paper bag full of empty Tupperware.

"Thanks for lunch," I said.

"You're welcome." She started down the hall toward the elevator.

"I got something in the mail today," I said, following along behind her.

"I'm riveted," she said, without looking back.

"A receipt from the Vendome hotel."

She stopped and looked at me.

"I'm going to Chicago," I said.

She shook her head. "I hope you know what you're doing, Dylan. Because I sure don't."

She turned and walked away, leaving me alone in the hallway with the Ice Queen's business card in my shaking hand.

17

~

THE DAY HAD LEFT ME over six hundred dollars in the hole and reeling rapidly toward unemployment. A trip to Chicago was a stupid idea financially, no question about it. And probably a stupid idea period. I'd be walking into the lion's den.

But I felt compelled to go anyway, though I wouldn't have been able to swear why under oath. It just seemed to me that the road signs were pointing north to Chicago. Maybe it was the radar thing. I didn't know. And I didn't particularly care. I was going. I needed to go. I figured I'd know why after I got there.

I went home, fixed myself some supper, and spent the rest of my evening sitting at my computer putting my trip together.

I toyed briefly with the idea of booking my ticket on Eagle Wing Air, but gave up the notion instantly. I had visions of Joseph Zocci somehow getting wind of my presence on one of his planes and having me ejected in mid-flight or something.

I booked my flight on American, using every last one of my hard-won frequent flyer miles to save myself some cash. I'd been hoarding them for a trip to Italy, but that fantasy would have to wait. At times like this, desperation took priority over dreams.

I found a Best Mid-Western Motel in the lower-rent section of downtown, thus bumping myself even further down the ladder from my Holiday Inn status, and rented the cheapest, crummiest economy car I could find from some local Chicago company named They're Ugly But They Run. If I ate from vending machines, I could do the whole trip for less than three hundred dollars.

I was up with the dawn the next morning, once again hauling myself, my tea, and my Bible out onto my porch to summon my faith as the sun offered the first hint of the day's light. I actually felt well-armed and at peace as I loaded my bag into my truck and made the drive to the airport.

I slept on the flight, safe from encroaching flies and sulfurous egg smells for the first time in days, and arrived in the City of Big Shoulders refreshed and ready for battle.

Providence was with me that afternoon. My flight actually landed on time. And though Chicago's O'Hare is an enormous airport, it was surprisingly easy to navigate. A real, live, competent airline employee met the flight and directed me to the rental car area, which I found easily. I was batting a thousand.

I hit a glitch, albeit a small one, when I laid eyes on my rental car. The word *ugly* did not quite do that car justice. It was a ten-year-old purple Dodge Neon. The interior was gray vinyl, but in decent shape. The radio was A.M. only; no cassette, no CD player. The car's antenna had a little yellow smiley-face flag on it, and the bumper sticker proclaimed in bold, lime-green letters, "I'm Ugly But I Run," with the company's web address and phone number. A big blow to my dignity to save twenty bucks a day.

I thought briefly about spending that twenty bucks on pride going with another company, but I decided against it. So I loaded my stuff, got behind the wheel, and turned the key. The engine buzzed to life, sounding much more finely tuned than my cool but crummy pickup.

The company's name spoke truth. It was ugly, but that car ran like a top.

I followed the road signs out of the rental area and chugged along the simple route that the Ugly-But-It-Runs clerk had kindly highlighted for me on my Complimentary Local Map. I zoned out on the drive, lost in the mental mire of my life problems. Before I knew it, I found myself stuck in Chicago rush hour traffic. I crawled along listening to A.M. radio and getting crankier by the minute. At last I reached downtown, only to find myself stuck in a maze of one-ways and construction sites. I got lost twice. The second time, I rolled down my window (manually, of course) and asked a suited, briefcased businessman walking on Michigan Avenue for directions to the Vendome. The man knew the hotel and pointed me in the right direction, shouting "nice car," as I drove away.

I drove around the block a few times looking for a parking place, saying my usual parking space prayer. This time, for once, I felt I could make a legitimate case at the feet of the Almighty. Not only because of the urgency of my mission, but because there was no way on God's green earth I was valet parking this hideous car at the Vendome. I could take only so much humiliation in one day.

A spot opened for me just as I was about to give up, with the bonus blessing of a remaining forty-two minutes on the meter. I breathed a thank-you, fed the machine one more quarter for good measure, locked the car with the key (no handy alarm system here), and walked around the block to the Vendome.

I stood across the street from the hotel for a few minutes, taking in the sight.

The Vendome is a landmark. One of those old, historic downtown hotels with gargoyles on the parapets and flags flying over a columned portico. Uniformed bellmen paced the entryway, sweeping open the doors of arriving automobiles and offering white-gloved hands to the elegant patrons who stepped out of them.

Not one of whom arrived in a purple Dodge Neon.

I couldn't afford a class-based shame attack right now. I needed to focus on the business at hand.

I summoned my courage and crossed the street, holding my head high and smiling at the bellmen. One of them pushed the brass handle of the revolving door for me. I swished around the circle in the little glass-pie slice and stepped into the lobby.

The lobby was filled with the scent of stargazer lilies and roses from enormous arrangements set atop inlaid wood tables. Oriental rugs hushed the footsteps of hotel guests. The hotel staff, wearing tailored black uniforms with brass name tags, walked silently, crisply, purposefully.

It didn't dawn on me until exactly that moment, swept away as I was by all that elegance and that heady floral scent, that I had no plan. True to form, I had arrived on my mission completely unprepared. What was I going to do, walk up to the front desk and request the Zocci suite? Pretend to be a Zocci cousin? A reporter? I wasn't even sure what I was doing here. What exactly did I hope to accomplish? I kicked myself for sleeping on the plane instead of obsessing properly.

Though I was just standing inside the doorway, dumbly rooted in place, no one seemed to be paying any attention to me. I decided to seize the opportunity to blend and began a slow stroll around the lobby to study the situation and to think.

I made a circuit, limiting myself to one time around the room, lest I convince security that I was a call girl or something. For once, I had dressed conservatively, so at least I looked semi-credible. I tried to look as if I belonged there and perhaps was waiting for someone. I screwed a puzzled look on my face, looked at my watch, and dug in my bag for my cell phone.

I held the phone to my ear and nodded as though I was listening to a conversation, almost jumping out of my skin when the phone rang loudly in my ear.

"Hello?" I was grateful to engage in a real conversation. I was no good at faking it.

"Dylan, it's David."

Pleasant surprise. "Hey, there. How's the death business?" I asked. In our few conversations, I'd been relentless in teasing him about his occupation, and thus far he had proven to be a thorough sport about it.

"Smelly," he said, not missing a beat. "We had a real stinker in here today. Want details?"

"Pass," I said, laughing. I could feel myself settling into the easy sound of his voice.

"I left you a message yesterday," he said, "hoping you'll take me up on thick steaks, cold beer, and dancing on Thursday night. My intention is to sweep you directly off your feet."

What an offer. The man had some charm.

"How about Saturday instead?"

"Keeping me waiting? I like that. Never sound too eager."

I laughed. "It's just that I'm not sure I'll be back by Thursday. I had to leave town suddenly."

"Okay. Saturday it is. But I may have to warm up your beer a little, just to maintain a little edge here."

"I don't like beer," I said.

"Oh. Date's off. Sorry. Where'd you jet off to?"

"Chicago."

"You're not dumping me for some Yankee boy, are you?"

"How could I dump you? We haven't been on a date yet."

"You're not counting the pharmacy?" He faked incredulity.

"Definitely not," I said.

"Define 'date.'"

"You pick me up at my house, tell me I look beautiful and how could you possibly be so lucky, take me to a restaurant with cloth napkins, spend significant amounts of money on me, treat me like a lady, walk me to my door, kiss me on the cheek, and leave. Then you wait two days so you don't sound needy, then call me and beg me for another date."

"Wait a minute," he said. "I'm writing all this down. What comes after picking you up at your house?"

"The beautiful part."

"Do I have to do it all in order?"

"Order is optional," I said.

"This is complicated."

"It's part of the weeding-out process."

"So are we on? Saturday?"

"Absolutely."

"Pick you up at 7:00."

"Make it 7:30."

"Nice touch."

"See you then."

We hung up. I felt rejuvenated. Never hurts a girl's confidence to have a funny, good looking guy ask her out. Even if he does own a funeral home in Hillsboro.

I turned my eyes back to the lobby and watched the hotel staff for a minute, looking for an opening. I needed someone amiable to talk to. Someplace to start. My eyes settled on a porter clearing tables in the seating area by the bar.

I watched him for a minute. He was a wiry little man with coal-black skin and hair the color of graphite. He could have been fifty years old or a hundred. It was hard to tell. He bent over his task with the solitary burdened efficiency of someone who had emptied the same ashtrays and fluffed the same pillows for decades.

He was perfect.

I walked over to an empty grouping of wing chairs and had myself a seat, sinking into the feathery cushion with a surprising sense of relief. I hadn't realized until that moment just how tired I was.

I reached for a section of the newspaper that was scattered on the table in front of me.

"Let me get that out of your way," a voice said.

I looked up and saw the man's face over my shoulder, dark and lined as tree bark. I glanced at his name tag.

"Thank you very much, Earl. But I was just about to read it."

"That one's been read," he scolded. "I'll get you a new one."

"The words look the same to me. They don't evaporate when someone reads them the first time or anything, do they?"

He laughed. "You right about that. Don't know why everyone so worried about a newspaper's already been read. But I always like to offer a fresh one."

He stacked the newspaper and placed it neatly on the table in front of me.

"You enjoying your stay, ma'am?"

I decided I could not lie to this man. He was just way too dignified for that.

"I'm not staying here," I said. "I'm just stopping in."

"It's a good place to stop in, that's for sure."

"How long have you worked here?"

"Long time. I can't even say," he said, shaking his head. "Long, long time."

I leaned forward. "Can I ask you something? Earl?"

"Yes ma'am. I may not know an answer, but you can ask all you want."

"Were you here when that boy committed suicide a couple of weeks ago?"

"The Zocci boy? No, ma'am. I work the night shift."

"But you knew him."

"Everyone knows that family. They stay here all the time. Every one of them, and they's lots of them. Always ask for the same room. Up there on the twelfth floor. They like it up there on twelve." He straightened.

"Do you happen to know the room number?"

"You a reporter or something, miss?" He didn't seem at all concerned. Just mildly curious.

"No. Just a friend."

"Can't say the number. It's up there on the corner. Looking back on Delaware. You can see the water from the window." He picked up the ashtray. "I better get myself busy. They don't pay me to visit."

"One more question," I said. "Do you mind telling me where the gift shop is?"

He pointed. "Right over there, other side of those elevators. You have a nice evening, ma'am."

I watched him walk away. His stringy little body moved with surprising agility.

I sat there for a few minutes, contemplating my next move and wondering where I could find a McDonald's or something. I'd just realized I was starving.

The arm of a uniformed hotel employee startled me, reaching out of my peripheral vision and whisking the newspaper off the table in front of me, replacing it with a new one.

I looked up to see a young woman standing over my chair. She tucked the used paper under her arm. "May I offer you a drink from the bar?" she said.

"Club soda?" Surely that would be cheap.

"Certainly."

She returned in a few minutes with a club soda and lime on ice and a generous bowl of snack mix. What a jackpot.

I tried not to shovel down the snack mix, slowing myself down by perusing the paper. I started with the metro section, thinking there might be something about the Zocci family or about Erik's suicide. I didn't find anything, so I finished my drink, fished the last pretzel out of the bowl, and left a few dollars on the table.

The gift shop was closed. I checked my watch. 6:15. It had closed a quarter of an hour ago. The sign said it would reopen at nine the next morning.

I stepped back into the lobby, suddenly feeling the weight of the day. The weight of the week, perhaps. I was tired. And hungry. Snack mix wasn't going to cut it.

I decided I'd done enough sleuthing for one day. I'd figure out a way to see the twelfth-floor suite tomorrow.

I made it back to my parking space before the meter ran out. The purple car was still there, right where I'd left it, greeting me cheerily with its tacky happy-face flag. No one would be even remotely tempted to steal it. I had that going for me.

I checked my map and made a circuitous, inefficient, maze-like route to my motel, which it turned out was only six blocks from the Vendome, though it seemed like a universe away. I checked into my room and unpacked my sparse belongings.

The Downtown Chicago Best Mid-Western shared a parking lot with a Denny's. I walked next door, slid into a booth, and had a grilled cheese sandwich, a salad, and a slice of chocolate pie.

Then I went back to my room, took a shower, and got myself ready for bed, checking the lock on my door twice before turning my light out for the night.

18

~

I AWOKE TO THE SOUND OF SOMETHING clattering loudly to the floor in the bathroom. Afraid to move, I cracked an eyelid and looked at the clock, its numbers glowing red beside the bed. 3:30.

Keeping my head still, I rolled my eyes around and looked at the bathroom door. It was closed. I could see a thin strip of light under the door. I was certain I hadn't left it on. As I watched, the light clicked off.

I shot out of bed and made it to my bag in one leap, keeping my eyes on the bathroom door.

My purse (more of a backpack, really) has the weight and heft of a bowling ball. I don't know what leads me to believe I need everything I carry around in there—I couldn't possibly have a daily, urgent need for four different kinds of lip gloss, for instance—but for once I was glad to be so thoroughly disorganized and indecisive.

I hoisted the bag over my shoulder and froze, my eyes fixed on the bathroom door. I leaned in and listened, silently cursing the air conditioner for rattling so loudly over there by the window.

I heard nothing. Whoever was in there wasn't making a sound.

The room was pitch black, save for the faint red glow of the digital clock. I inched my foot sideways, sliding it across the floor toward the bed. After a few steps, the polyester bedspread scratched against my ankle, and I shifted my direction to ease my way around the bed.

When I reached the night table, I felt for the phone, my hand grasping the receiver just as I realized what a stupid idea this was. Did I really want to let the boogie man hear my voice so that he could come barreling out and kill me before I completed my first sentence? Besides, who was I going to call? 911? The front desk? "Excuse me. There's a monster in my bathroom. Could you send someone right away please?"

I didn't have to wait to find out. While I stood there indecisively, I heard the bathroom door click open.

I lunged for the front door, grabbing the doorknob and flipping the deadbolt simultaneously. I yanked on the door and heard a huge thwack as the door slammed, six inches open, against the inside latch.

I flipped on the light switch and whirled around, swinging my bag and screaming.

I faced an empty room.

The bathroom door was open.

My heartbeat almost choking me, I stepped forward slowly, bag at the ready, and moved toward the bathroom. I looked to the right as I passed by the bed. No one hiding behind it.

I stopped and listened again when I reached the bathroom door. I heard nothing. Not even breathing.

I leaped into the doorway, slamming the door against the wall with all my weight. No one was back there. I flipped on the light.

The shower curtain was crumpled on the floor, rod and all. I pushed the door flat against the wall.

The room was empty.

Lowering my bag, I stepped back out of the bathroom, went back to the bed, and threw the skirt of the bedspread up onto the mattress. Like most hotel beds, it was built to the ground. There was no space underneath at all.

I was alone in the room.

I sat on the bed and tried to breathe normally and bring my heart rate down to some level that might sustain life.

Had I imagined the entire thing? I didn't think so. It had seemed so vivid. So real. The shower curtain, surely what had woken me in the first place, was in a tangled heap on the floor. That, at least, was indisputable. As to the rest, I had lain there in bed and seen the closed door. I had watched that light go out. I had heard the door open.

I walked back to the bathroom and examined the crumpled shower curtain and rod. The screws that had held it in place were still in their brackets, drywall clinging to the threads. I dropped the end of the rod back to the floor, hearing the distinct hollow clatter that had woken me.

I reached up and examined the holes in the wall.

The beige vinyl wallpaper had six neat holes in it. Three on each end, in a triangle, at either end of the tub enclosure. The wallpaper was ripped slightly downward at each hole where the screws had scraped against it, coming out of the wall. Something had brought that rod down with force.

One thing I knew. Sleep was impossible. I needed to get out of that room.

I threw on some shorts and a T-shirt and grabbed my bag, my cell phone, my Bible, and the hotel's copy of the Greater Chicago Area telephone book, which weighed about twenty-five pounds. I unlocked the latch on the door and stepped outside into the warm night, the air conditioner chattering a farewell as I walked next door to Denny's.

168   MELANIE WELLS

Thank God for twenty-four-hour diners.

The restaurant was busy. Apparently lots of people eat at Denny's at 4:00 a.m.

I slid into an empty booth and ordered a cup of coffee.

I opened the telephone book first, hoping blindly that Joseph and Mariann Zocci were listed in the Chicago phone book. Of course, they weren't.

There were only fifteen Zoccis listed in the Chicago area. I pulled the *Tribune* article about Erik's death out of my bag and checked the names of the Zocci children. I found one match. Erik's older brother James Andrew. And there was one "V.A. Zocci." V.A. could stand for Virginia Anne, one of his older sisters.

I wrote down the addresses and phone numbers.

I hadn't brought the business pages with me, so I walked over to the phone booths by the front door and looked up Garret Industries. No listing.

The Chicago public library was listed, though. I wrote down the number and address of the main library, which I guessed would be downtown, near my hotel. I also wrote down the address and phone number of the University of Chicago's library. I flipped to the back of the phone book and ripped out the simple map of the city.

I returned to my booth and studied the map, sparse as it was. My Complimentary Local Map from They're Ugly But They Run was more detailed, of course, and would have been much more helpful. But the map was in the car and the car was parked right outside my room, and I wasn't going back there until the sun was shining.

A voice interrupted me.

"You needing directions, hon?"

I looked up. My waitress was back with the coffee pot.

"You don't happen to know where the University of Chicago is, do you?"

"Nope," she said. "You startin' school there?"

"No, I'm just looking for a good library."

"Can't help you with that. You want some breakfast?"

"How's the French toast?" I asked.

"Greasy."

"Hash browns?"

"Greasy."

"Sausage?"

"Greasy."

"I'll have oatmeal."

She smacked her gum. "Good girl."

I gave up on the map and stared into space, tumbling the week's details in my mind, hoping something would lock into place.

The oatmeal came, along with some brown sugar and a little pitcher of milk. It was warm and filling.

I finished my breakfast and opened my Bible, reading and sipping coffee until the sun came up and had hung in the sky a good long while.

I paid out and left my waitress a ten dollar tip. I'd taken up a table in her station for over three hours, and she'd filled my cup faithfully without the slightest trace of impatience.

I walked the parking lot back to the room and slipped my key into the slot, pushing the door open all the way with my foot before I stepped into the room.

The room was exactly as I'd left it.

The sheets were thrown back, the overhead light on. The bathroom door was open, the bathroom light on. Air conditioner rattling.

I checked the bathroom. The shower curtain was still on the floor.

That posed a particularly vexing problem. I pulled the shower curtain out of the room and filled the tub for a quick bath, my physician father's ominous warnings about hotel bathtubs ringing in my ears. He was convinced that viruses and germs lurked on every surface within reaching distance. My brother and I had spent our entire childhoods paranoid about touching stair railings or faucet handles. Probably the beginnings of my love affair with cleaning products.

I dressed quickly and loaded my things into my bag, grabbing my notes from this morning and my cell phone as I walked out the door. I stopped by the front desk and let the clerk know that my shower curtain had fallen in the middle of the night. She looked at me suspiciously and assured me it would be fixed by this evening.

I studied my map in the car. From what I could tell, the University of Chicago was pretty far away from where I was. I'd probably be better off with the public library, given my rotten navigational luck so far. But I couldn't find that address on my map.

My cell phone service, I remembered suddenly, had dial-up information. It was one of those tricky, useful little things that I'd never quite learned how to use. Supposedly the operators would look up anything for you. Movies. Restaurants. And, perhaps by extension, libraries. I dialed.

"How may I help you?" the operator asked.

"I'm in downtown Chicago," I said. "Near the Vendome hotel. Can you tell me where the nearest library is? University or public. Either one."

"Hold one moment, please."

I heard him tap keys.

"Loyola University Library."

Like magic. I wrote down the address and thanked him, congratulating myself on my spontaneous stroke of genius.

I found it easily on my map. It was six blocks from the Vendome.

I decided to go to the Vendome first.

My parking luck ran out this time. No gifts from the heavens today, so I had a hike to the hotel. I was sweating a little by the time I'd reached the lobby and made it to the gift shop.

The gift shop was open and empty of patrons. It was surprisingly large for a hotel gift shop. A lone clerk polished silver picture frames with a blue cloth. I recognized the frames. I had apparently purchased one here recently, for the bargain price of thirty-eight dollars.

"Good morning," said the man. "May I help you find anything?"

"I'd just like to look," I said. "Thanks."

I poked around for a minute, not sure why I'd come.

"Lovely necklace," he said, a knowing smile on his face.

I touched the stone at my throat. I'd forgotten I was wearing it. "Thank you. I like it a lot. It's unusual."

"That designer is very good. We sell quite a few of her pieces."

"Do you have any more?"

"Right over here."

I followed him to a lighted jewelry case. He stepped behind it, unlocked the door, and took out a velvet tray of necklaces.

They were lovely. Each one had a heavy, chunky feel to it. They were all done in sterling silver with some sort of stone on a leather cord.

"The designer's name is Rosa Guevera. She does wonderful work. Each piece is one-of-a-kind," he said.

"Do you remember this necklace particularly?" I asked. "It was purchased here."

He frowned. "Not that piece per se. Her pieces don't stick around very long."

"Do you happen to remember taking an order for a necklace of hers recently? This one was ordered by phone."

"I don't remember it myself, but there are only three of us working here. You might talk to Eloise, our store manager. Was there some problem with the order?"

"No, no, nothing like that. I was just wondering. It was sort of a gift. An anonymous gift."

"A secret admirer," he said, smiling.

"Something like that."

"Lucky girl."

"Something like that."

"Eloise comes in at noon on Wednesdays," he said. "You might stop back by. Or if you like, I can have her phone your room when she arrives."

"No, thank you. I'll just give her a call in the morning. Thanks for your help."

"Certainly," he said.

I picked up a business card as I walked out, sticking it in my back pocket.

From the Vendome it was about the same distance to my car as to Loyola. It was a nice day, so I decided to take the long route and walk along Lake Michigan. Loyola fronted the lake.

The walkway along Lake Shore Drive was buzzing. I passed by runners, bikers, skaters, walkers, loiterers, tourists, dogs, and one monkey riding on its owner's handlebars. Frisbee and volleyball were being played on the sand beach. And a bagpiper stood on a rock jetty and played his mournful tune into the wind. I was enchanted.

I wondered if Loyola or the University of Chicago needed any psychology professors. Maybe I could outrun my soiled reputation by moving to the Midwest.

Too soon, I arrived at Loyola and stepped off the walkway onto the manicured lawns of the campus.

Feeling suddenly at home in the anthill atmosphere of the university, I asked someone where the library was and was pointed toward Cudahy Library, in one of the large buildings on the main square.

The faint ring of my cell phone reached my ears from the depths of my bowling ball bag just as I walked up the library steps.

It was Tony DeStefano.

"Ready for this?" he said.

"No. What?"

"Your boy cracked up last night."

"Gavin?"

"Jenny's at the hospital with him now. We checked him into Green Oaks."

"The psych hospital? What happened?"

"He tried to hang himself from the shower curtain."

19

~

I SAT DOWN ON THE LIBRARY STEPS, the heat of the sun suddenly blinding, stifling, unrelenting.

"What time was this?" I asked Tony.

"I don't know. Between 3:00 and 4:00 a.m., I think. Jenny heard it. She thought it was the dog."

"Who found him?"

"Annie did."

I winced. Annie was their three-year-old.

"At around 6:00 this morning," he was saying. "Kid was unconscious. Passed out, drunk out of his mind. Annie thought he was asleep. Came and got us because she didn't want to use the bathroom with him in there. She was afraid she'd wake him up.

"I found an empty Jack Daniel's bottle in his room. He'd probably been drinking all night. Annie goes in there and he's all sprawled out, got a belt around his neck, passed out on the bathroom floor, all tangled up in this pink plastic Cinderella shower curtain. He picked the girls' bathroom for some reason. Probably would've killed himself if the rod hadn't fallen. Thank God for cheap construction. I always knew there was a good reason I'm poor."

"How is he now?"

"Hung over, probably."

"He wasn't hurt?"

"Nope."

"I'm sorry, Tony. I had no idea he was in that kind of shape."

"It's not your fault. That kid's in the grip."

"Of what?"

"God only knows. We'd been up the night before, him and me, talking about demons. He told me his stories, the ones he's telling you, about old Slash Back."

"Peter Terry."

"That's his name?"

"Yep."

"I always thought demon names would be more exotic. Something sort of Aramaic. Or medieval."

"I'm sure it's just an alias."

"Well, whatever his name is, the dude's got this kid scared. Scared him right out of his mind, I think."

"So you think this is in direct response to the demon thing?"

"Gotta be."

"Is this how demons usually work?"

"Think about all the people in the Gospels. Tortured, basically. They get inside your body and make you sick. Get inside your head and mess with it. Mess with your thinking."

"You think he's possessed?" Tony and I hadn't yet uttered the word. It scared me just to think about it.

"I don't think so. I seen that before, and it's got a whole different feel to it. This guy—he's just scared. Scared from the inside."

"Like Erik Zocci."

"Like Erik Zocci. Exactly," Tony said. "What I can't figure out is, why them?"

"I'm working on that. I'm in Chicago right now."

I gave Tony a quick update on my situation, ending with my own version of the shower curtain story.

He whistled. "You got a target painted on your face. Someone's got you all singled out."

"Terrific," I said. "I wish I knew what to do about it."

"Stand firm," Tony said, quoting Ephesians once again. "And wear your gear. I mean, God went to a lot of trouble to provide it for you. And never, ever forget whose side you're on."

"How's Annie?"

"Oh, she's fine. She doesn't know what's going on."

"And everyone else?"

"They're doing fine. You gotta remember, Dylan. Jenny and me, we spent our whole marriage in Haiti and Nicaragua. My kids don't spook easy."

Thank God for that. I dug in my bag for a pen. "Do you have the Green Oaks number on you?"

He looked it up and gave it to me. "Jenny's probably on her way back. I got class. Her turn to wrangle these kids."

We hung up and I dialed Green Oaks. They wouldn't let me talk to Gavin, of course. Without a signed consent, they couldn't even confirm that he was a patient there. But they did allow me to leave a message and assured me that if he was a patient there, he would receive the message. I left Gavin my cell phone number and asked him to call me, saving the Green Oaks number in my phone so I would recognize the incoming call when it came.

Before heading into the library, I spent a few minutes alone on the steps, praying. For Gavin. For myself. For the DeStefanos. For the Zoccis. For myself again.

Sitting there, watching the sun flick off the waves of Lake

Michigan, students swarming around me, priests and nuns walking briskly on the tidy concrete walkways of this lovely Catholic campus, all I could think was that God had obviously made some serious error in judgment. I was completely in over my head. I was drowning. Drowning in fear, in confusion, in self-doubt. What was He thinking leaving me, of all people, in the target zone?

I, who felt no capacity whatsoever to withstand this assault. I, a lay person with a stale seminary degree, weak faith, crummy flailing self-discipline, and vast blank spaces in my head where all those Scriptures I hadn't memorized should be. I, with my limited ability to rebound and my endless capacity for panic. I, who regularly failed to pray, and who fell asleep most nights without cracking a Bible. I, for some reason, had been allowed to wander into the shooting gallery, toddling dumbly along behind the little tin ducks.

I didn't want to keep fighting this fight. I didn't want to go inside the building. I wanted to sit there, on the steps of the library in the hot sun, and disappear. I wanted my old, easy, comfortable life to materialize, and for this all to have been some horrid bad dream.

But it wasn't a dream. Erik Zocci was dead. Gavin was working on it. And my formerly ordered life was coming apart around me, pieces of it flying off in every direction. There was nowhere to go but forward.

I gathered my stuff as I gathered myself and trudged up the steps into the library.

I showed my SMU faculty ID in order to get a visitor's pass.

"Welcome to Loyola, Dr. Foster," said the guard.

Right. If he only knew. I fought the urge to warn him off. Keep a wide berth, I urged mentally, else you might get caught in the cross fire.

I tucked my ID back into my bag and headed straight for

Reference, where I seated myself at a computer and retrieved a detailed map of Chicago.

Typing in the two addresses I had for the Zocci children, I could see that they lived in different parts of the city. Virginia Anne lived in an apartment downtown. Probably in one of those beautiful high-rise buildings overlooking the lake. James Andrew seemed to live in the suburbs. Something called Highland Park. I pictured kids, a dog, a barbecue. Maybe one of those plastic wading pools.

I used the trick the surly Realtor had taught me and went to the county appraisal district's website, punching in each address, increasing the scope of my search to include the surrounding counties.

James Andrew's home, purchased four years earlier in the name of James Andrew and Elizabeth Zocci, was listed on Lake County tax records for $2.2 million.

So much for my kid, dog, barbecue scenario.

I adjusted my imagination to accommodate the new image, feelings of fear creeping up the back of my neck as I envisioned ivy-laced stone walls, a circular brick driveway, a vast green lawn. I was reminded again of the magnitude of the forces lining up against me. This family had serious cash. Scary cash.

Virginia Anne's address yielded more useful information. Her apartment, valued at $673,000, had not been purchased in her name. It had been purchased five years earlier by Garret Industries, Inc.

In my rush to get to Chicago, I'd forgotten to contact the Texas agency that would lead me to corporate information about Garret Industries. Now I couldn't remember which agency I was supposed to call. I looked around. No reference librarians in sight. I stepped into the foyer with my cell phone and called the reference desk at SMU's library.

"Cynthia. Dylan Foster."

We exchanged pleasantries.

"I'm still trying to find out information about that business I asked you about," I said.

"Garret Industries?"

"I can't believe you remember the name."

"I'm smart. And I'm a librarian. Besides, I ran the search for you myself."

"And?"

"No Garret Industries, Inc., registered with the secretary of state in Texas."

"Rats. It was worth a try."

"But…"

"But?"

"But…since I'm smart, and since I'm a librarian, and since I'm devoted to my job even though I'm severely underpaid, I did a little more digging for you."

"And?"

"And Garret Industries, Inc. is registered to do business in the state of Texas. Just with a different office."

"Which one?"

"The Railroad Commission."

"It's a railroad?"

"No. Garret Industries is an oil and gas company, licensed to drill land wells in the panhandle and to do offshore drilling in the Gulf of Mexico. Oil and gas permits are regulated by the Railroad Commission of Texas. Don't ask me why."

"Cynthia, you're a genius."

"I know."

"How did you come up with the Railroad Commission?"

"A hunch. I'd run every state agency I could think of. The company name sounded so generic. It's industrial, obviously, and in Houston, that probably means oil and gas. According to the RCT, Garret Industries has offices in Brownsville, Houston, and Galveston. The U.S. Department of Energy shows offices in all the other Gulf states. Louisiana, Mississippi, Alabama, Florida. Bing bing bing bing. Right down the line."

"Who owns the company?"

"It's a partnership. Guy named Sheldon Garret and something called MAZco." She spelled it out for me as I wrote it down. "I pulled some history on Garret, which is incorporated in New York State, and a few things on MAZco, but that's as far as I got."

"Do you have all this in a file or something?"

"Of course."

"Can you send it to me?"

"Hard copy or electronic?"

"Send it to my e-mail address."

"Your university address?"

I thought better of it. "No. Let me call you back in a few minutes with a fax number."

We hung up.

Since I was already making calls, I dialed my office voice mail and my home machine to check my messages.

I had one call from David, one from Helene, one from the pink Ice Queen lawyer, and fourteen calls from my father. He must have lost my cell phone number again. Each message was increasingly agitated. By now, he'd probably blown an artery or something.

I dialed his office number and got Janet.

She flew into her fussy-mother voice. "Honey, your father has been out of his mind with worry. We were just about to give you up for dead."

"I'm fine. I just left town for a few days. Is he around?"

"Of course not. I'm going to page him, though, and tell him you're all right. He'll want to talk to you right away."

"What does he want?"

"That same favor. It's something to do with the wedding, that's all I know. Kellee's dogging him. You know how she is. He's been hell on wheels all week."

"Janet," I said. "I cannot be in that wedding."

"Well, you're going to have to tell him yourself. You can't dodge him forever."

"Help me out here. Tell him I'm out of town and I forgot to bring my cell phone and that you didn't ask me where I was staying."

"Now, he'll know that's a lie," she said. "He knows me better than that."

"Then don't tell him anything. Don't even tell him I called. Just buy me a couple of days, Janet. I can't deal with him right now."

"Honey, are you okay?"

"I'm working on it."

"You haven't gotten yourself in any sort of trouble, have you?"

"No, of course not. I'll be back by Saturday. I'll call him when I get home."

"He won't make it that long. Heck, I won't make it that long. He'll have me calling the FBI by then."

"Then tell him I called and left you a voice mail and didn't leave a phone number. That ought to settle him down."

"Okay," she said reluctantly. "But you call him the second you get back. You promise me?"

"I promise."

Back in the library, I found a staffer who supplied me with

a fax number, then called Cynthia and stood by the fax machine as the pages rolled in.

I glanced through her research as it came out of the machine, realizing that there was too much information to digest quickly. I set it aside for now and went back to the computer.

It dawned on me that the appraisal district's records might work backwards. Each time before, I had started with the address. I widened my search to include other local counties and tried again, this time typing in the name of each Zocci family member. None of the other children lived in the area, apparently. I finished with Joseph and Mariann Zocci.

I got a hit. Joseph Michael Zocci, Sr. owned a home in Lake County, purchased in 1987, worth $10.7 million. On thirty acres. Mariann was not listed as a co-owner.

Back to my map. Since it was a country home, the best I could do was locate the county, which was north of Chicago, fronting Lake Michigan.

I printed out my research, slipped it all into a folder with Cynthia's information on Garret Industries, and then shoved it all in my bag.

I looked at my watch. It was almost two in the afternoon. I had eaten before sunup. I'd find myself a burger and then head back to the Vendome.

20

~

BY THE TIME I MADE it to the Vendome, I'd gotten myself completely freaked out thinking about Gavin. I was worried about him. But beyond that, it occurred to me that two suicides on my watch would be more than any professional's reputation could withstand.

I decided the best thing to do was call Helene and confess now. It wouldn't do for her to hear this from anyone but me. I called her office and left her a message that I needed to talk to her right away.

Walking into the lobby of the Vendome felt less daunting this time. But still, I had no real plan. I was here because I'd been led here. By whom or what, I didn't know. And what I was supposed to do remained a mystery. I decided to follow my own curiosity—look into the things that were puzzling me—and hope it led me to a next step.

I said a brief prayer for guidance and started with the gift shop.

Eloise, it turned out, was exactly as I'd pictured her. Silvery gray hair, conservatively coiffed. Pearl stud earrings, a silvery gray sweater twin set that matched her hair almost exactly, black pants. She was prim and elegant. Cordial without being friendly.

"Good afternoon," she said as I walked in the door. "Please let me know if I may be of help to you."

I went with the direct approach and walked right up to her, dispensing with the charade of browsing.

"I'm hoping you can help me. We spoke on the telephone the other day. I called about an order that had been charged to my credit card? I couldn't remember what I'd purchased. Do you remember me?"

"Why yes," she said. "I do remember. Ms...was it Foster?"

"Exactly. Dylan Foster. Good memory."

"And what may I do for you today?" she asked.

"I'm not sure, to be honest. The truth is, I never placed that order. I think someone used my card and ordered the items in my name."

"My goodness! I do apologize. Have you spoken with your credit card company?"

"Not yet," I said. "And I'm not terribly worried about that. I'm not shaking any trees to get my money back or anything. I'm just trying to clear up my own confusion. Do you happen to know who took the order?"

"I can look." She asked me a few questions, reminding herself of the date of the transaction and the amount involved, and then stepped into an office at the rear of the shop. She'd retrieved the records within a couple of minutes.

"I took the order myself," she said, coming back into the room. She handed me the ticket with the list of items and prices, pointing at her initials at the bottom of the ticket.

"Do you remember anything about it?" I asked. "Any details of the conversation at all?"

She shook her head. "I'm sorry, but this was several weeks ago. I'm certain I couldn't—"

"Look, I know this is going to sound strange, and I do

apologize for imposing. I don't want to put you on the spot. But it's really important that I find out who placed this order. Do you mind trying something for me? I think I might be able to help you resurrect something about that phone call."

She raised her eyebrows skeptically.

"Please," I said. "It'll only take a minute.

"You're not a hypnotist or anything?"

I smiled. "A psychologist. I promise I'm not going to wave a pocket watch at you and tell you you're getting sleepy."

She looked around the empty shop for a moment, then relented. "All right."

"Great." I tried not to sound overly eager, which I was, of course. "Where do you usually stand when you're taking a phone order?"

Eloise nodded at the other end of the room. "At that counter."

"Could we walk over there, please?"

She obliged.

It was a bizarre moment, her compliance to move at my request. It felt almost as if I were committing a holdup or something, like I was herding the shopkeeper into the back of the store so I could make off with the cash. The only thing missing was a gun.

She stopped beside the counter.

"Do you usually stand in front of it or behind it?" I asked.

"Behind," she said. I could tell she was starting to get intrigued.

"Do you mind?" I asked.

She walked obediently around the corner of the counter and stood there looking at me.

"Do you mind moving over by the telephone?" More holdup vibe. "Try standing exactly as you would when you receive a call."

She stepped sideways a bit until she was to the left of the phone.

"Are you right- or left-handed?" I asked.

"Right."

"So you usually hold the phone with your left hand and hold the pen in your right?"

"Yes, I guess I do."

"Would you mind trying that? If you have a pen and an order pad, that would be great."

She pulled out a pen and an order pad from behind the counter and set them on the table.

"Just hold the phone up to your ear, as if you're receiving a call."

She picked up the phone with her left hand and held it to her left ear.

"Okay," I said. "Now believe it or not, we haven't gotten to the weird part yet."

She raised her eyebrows at me, but didn't say anything. I had to hand it to old Eloise. She was a sport.

"Try looking up and a little to the left," I said.

She cocked her head up and moved her eyes to the left.

"Now just try to clear your head for a second while I ask you some questions."

"Okay."

"You said it was a Wednesday. This was three weeks ago now." I read the date off the receipt. "Do you remember anything about that day at all? Were you having an ordinary week? Are you normally in on Wednesdays?"

"I was planning a trip for the weekend, I believe. So I had a short workweek. I left Thursday morning."

"Great. Do you remember what you wore that day, by chance?"

She thought for a minute. "Now that you mention it, I do. A black skirt and a lavender silk blouse. I remember because I wore something I knew I wouldn't need to pack."

"And what time did you come to work?"

"Noon."

"Was it a busy day?"

"Not terribly. Much like today. Mornings can be busy, but the afternoon was slow, I think."

"What time did the call come in?"

"Shortly after I arrived." She lowered her head and looked at me, startled. "I guess I do remember something, don't I?"

"You're doing great," I said. "Look up and to the left again while I read you the list of items." I read them off one by one, leaving the prices off.

She dropped her chin and looked at me. "It was a man's voice. I remember that now. What was the name on the order again?"

"Dylan Foster," I said.

"I guess I didn't catch the fraudulent use of the card because Dylan could be either a man's or a woman's name."

"Did he list the items specifically? Or did he have you shop for him?"

"He had me choose the items," she said. "He told me he was buying gifts for his girlfriend's family."

"Which gift was for the girlfriend?"

"The necklace." She met my eyes. "The one you're wearing."

I felt my skin crawl.

"How did you choose the items? Did he tell you anything about the recipients of the gifts?"

"He described each person in detail."

"What did he say about the girlfriend?"

She'd been looking at me while she answered my questions.

Now she went into a natural posture for a right-handed person trying to summon a memory, her head cocked up and to the left.

"Creative, free-spirited, smart. Auburn hair, green eyes." She looked at me. "He described you. Where did you get the necklace?"

"It was an anonymous gift," I said. "I don't have a boyfriend."

"Maybe you do now."

"If I do, he's guilty of credit card fraud. Doesn't sound like boyfriend material to me."

"So you received the gift and then the bill?"

I nodded. "Weird, huh?"

"I remember something else," she said. "He mentioned a room number." She reached for the ticket, which I handed her. "There." She pointed to a handwritten number on the bottom corner of the ticket. 1220.

"Is that a room here at the hotel?"

"I assume so," she said.

"Twelfth floor?" I could feel my heart quickening. "Do you recognize the room number? Have you heard anything about that room recently?"

Her eyes widened the tiniest bit. "I believe there might have been an accident in that room."

"A suicide. Not an accident."

She didn't respond.

"It was a suicide, wasn't it?"

"I believe so."

"Is there any way we could find out if it's the same room?"

"Did you know him?" she asked.

"Yes."

She picked up the phone and dialed an extension. "Mr. Molina, if you have a moment. I'm trying to clear up some bookkeeping. I've got a charge in front of me." She read the date and the room number. "Can you tell me who was registered in that room on that date?" She waited a minute. "A little after noon," she said. "I see. And isn't that the room…? I thought so. But no one checked into that room until evening. Thank you very much, Mr. Molina. Must be my mistake." She hung up the phone.

"1220 was empty until nine o'clock p.m. on the date this charge was called in. But it is the same room the Zocci boy stayed in." A hint of suspicion crept across her face. "How did you know him? He was too young to have been—"

"No, he wasn't my boyfriend." I took a breath and violated Erik Zocci's confidentiality. "He was a patient."

"Oh, I'm sorry."

"I'm telling you this because I'm trying to figure out what happened to him, Eloise. I think these gifts must be related somehow to his death. It can't be a coincidence. I've never been to the Vendome before in my life."

"His family stays here often," she said. "They're always very courteous. Very generous with the staff."

"Is there any way I could see the room?"

She looked at me. Deciding whether or not to go out on a limb for me, probably. She picked up the phone again. "Mr. Molina, could you step into the gift shop for a moment, please?"

We waited together for a few minutes, neither of us saying anything. A man stepped into the store, wearing a well-cut black suit and a brass name tag.

"Sam Molina," Eloise said. "I'd like you to meet Dylan Foster."

I offered my hand. He looked as if he had just been offered a salamander.

"Mr. Molina is the manager of the hotel," she said to me. I tried to look impressed.

"She'd like to see the Zocci boy's room," she said to him. "She was his psychologist."

Sam Molina didn't say anything. I could read nothing from his face. The man could make a fortune at poker.

"I treated him briefly, a year ago," I said. "I didn't know him well. I came to Chicago at my own expense. I'm trying to piece together what happened to him. For my own information."

"I don't see any harm in showing you the room," he said at last. "No photographs, of course. And you must agree not to publicize anything you discover. The Zoccis are longtime customers of the hotel. We're very protective of the privacy of our guests."

"Understood," I said. "I'm here for my own information only."

"Call the bell stand," he said to Eloise. "Have Carlos show her upstairs."

He turned and walked away without saying anything to me.

I turned to Eloise. "Thank you."

She dialed the bellman's stand and called for Carlos, who arrived a moment later with a master key.

"I do appreciate your help, Eloise. You have a good memory."

"Good luck," she said. "I hope you find what you're looking for."

The twelfth floor was tomb-like. A long vast hallway greeted me as I stepped out of the elevator. More sprays of flowers punctuated the tunnel of carpeted space, walls muted with tasteful wallpaper and gilt-framed mirrors.

Carlos led me to 1220 and clicked the lock open with his key. He swung the door open for me and I stepped inside.

The room was enormous. Bigger than any hotel room I'd ever been in. It actually had a hallway. I stepped around the corner and into the suite's living room. The sitting area had two chairs, a fireplace in the corner, an inlaid wood desk, and a round table with upholstered chairs encircling it. The doors to the balcony were curtained and closed. I sat down on the edge of a couch for a few minutes, taking in the details of the room. Trying to imagine Erik Zocci's last hours on this earth.

He'd probably sat on this couch to tie his shoes before he went down to the fitness center the morning he died.

The bedroom was to the left. I got up and walked through the doorway to find a king-size bed flanked by inlaid wood bedside tables and brass lamps. There was an armchair and reading lamp, and a second fireplace.

I walked over to the bathroom and flipped on the light. The bathroom was almost the size of my entire hotel room at the Downtown Chicago Best Mid-Western, bathroom and all. My shoes echoed loudly, intrusively, on the tile as I walked over to peek in the huge whirlpool tub and separate, walk-in shower. I turned around. Twin vanities. Marble everything.

Stepping back out of the bathroom, I walked past the bed to the balcony doors, pulling back the drape and unlocking the latch.

The sounds of the city below rose up to meet me as I pushed open the doors. Traffic noise, car horns. A siren in the distance. The air up here on twelve was different from the air on the street. It was warm and soft. With enough of a breeze to take the edge off the heat. I stepped forward to the rail and felt the wind on my face, my eyes taking in the view of Lake Michigan to my right. No wonder the Zoccis always requested this room.

Looking down, I could see the atrium roof directly under the room. It was a long, long way down. Erik must have landed on the narrow concrete ledge between the stones of the building wall and the glass roof. I tried to picture his body sprawled on that ledge below me. As the image crystallized in my head, I caught a glimpse of little Joseph Michael Jr. in my mind's eye. I could see his body there as well, crumpled next to his brother's.

I felt myself getting dizzy. Standing in this spot made both boys' deaths so graphic to me. I hadn't anticipated being thrust so vividly into the scene. My hands were shaking, clammy.

I raised my eyes to the blue sky, dotted as it was with white puffy clouds, and took some deep breaths until I felt myself calm down. I closed my eyes and offered yet another silent prayer for the Zocci family.

I don't know what I'd hoped to find in that room. Somehow it had just seemed important to see it. But I'd been there long enough. I was ready to go.

I pulled myself together and stepped back into the room, locking the door behind me and drawing the drapes against the light, leaving myself in muted afternoon shadows.

I stopped in the bathroom and yanked a tissue out of the box, wiping away a tear and blowing my nose.

Carlos was waiting stiffly by the door, an odd, uncomfortable look on his face.

I drew my eyebrows together. Something was wrong.

As I approached the door, Carlos stepped aside to let Sam Molina in through the doorway. A hotel security guard followed him. The two men met me in the center of the living room.

"Dr. Foster," Molina said, "I'll have to ask you to come downstairs."

"Why, is there something wrong? I was just leaving."

"Please come with me."

"Not until you tell me what's going on."

"I'd like to have a word with you. It will only take a minute."

I thought about it. I hadn't broken any laws. Could hotel security guards arrest people? Surely they couldn't throw me in the pokey or anything. Maybe the man had something he wanted to tell me about the Zocci suicide.

I agreed, and the three of us walked out of the room and into the elevator, which Carlos was holding for us.

A long silent ride to the first floor, and then a long walk down yet another elegant Vendome hallway, down an elevator, and through double doors that read "Hotel Staff Only."

I trailed obediently behind Molina, following him down a maze of industrial-looking back halls. At last he stopped in front of a suite of offices, slid a security card through a slot, and led me past a mug-shot gallery of somber-looking men, one of them Sam Molina. We stopped at an office in the back corner of the suite. The guard turned and left.

As I followed Molina into the room, I saw that someone was there waiting for us.

The man stood up. I recognized him immediately.

"Dr. Foster," Molina said, "I'd like you to meet Joseph Zocci."

21

~

I WISH I COULD SAY that I succumbed to Christian
charity and concern at that moment. That I was swept away by
compassion for Joseph Zocci, who had lost two sons on the
twelfth floor of this building. But I wasn't. I loathed him
instantly and thoroughly.

I had been ambushed, obviously. Which surely accounted
for at least a portion of my hostility. But it was more than that.
Something about this man was just off.

We stood there, the two of us, staring at each other
wordlessly, sizing each other up.

He was a handsome man, dressed expensively in a gray suit,
blinding white starched shirt, and silk tie. Salt and pepper hair,
olive skin. Slim, athletic build. He seemed coiled and taut, his
body and mind tuned for combat. He'd been a naval fighter pilot
in Vietnam, I knew. He still had that look about him. The alert,
forward look of a predator.

He put his hands in his pockets and stood there wordlessly.
Not at all uncomfortable with the silence.

Molina was the one that spoke up. "Sit down, Dr. Foster.
May I offer you a refreshment? Something to drink, perhaps?"

I downshifted into defiance mode. One advantage to having such a blustery, threatening father is that I am not easily intimidated. Clearly both men had expected more fear out of me than I intended to give them. I continued standing, continued staring into the eyes of Joseph Zocci.

"No, thank you," I answered, without looking at Molina.

Another moment of silence passed as Zocci waited for me to sit. This was a man accustomed to compliance. I sensed his unease and knew I'd found a small edge.

I finally looked at Sam Molina, who stood stiffly a few feet away, watching the tense scene. "What can I do for you, Sam?" I said.

He shifted uncomfortably. I could tell it bothered him that I called him by his first name. Like Zocci, he too seemed accustomed to deference, perhaps even servitude from the people around him.

"Mr. Zocci has some questions for you," Molina said.

"He does? I would have appreciated your letting me know that before you herded me downstairs." I reached into my wallet for the Ice Queen's card and handed it to Sam. "If Mr. Zocci has some questions for me, I suggest he give—" I glanced down at the card—"Ms. Montgomery a call." I turned to leave.

Zocci spoke at last. "Dr. Foster."

I stopped and turned. "Yes?"

"I apologize if Mr. Molina offended you. I asked him to invite you downstairs. Clearly, I should have specified that he mention the purpose for our meeting."

"Why don't you mention it, then? Somebody ought to, don't you think?"

"I'd like to speak to you about my son," he said coldly. "I think I have the right."

"You're suing me, Mr. Zocci. I can't talk to you about your

son. Why don't you give my attorney a jingle? I'm sure she'd be happy to talk to you about your son."

"I don't appreciate your disrespect, Dr. Foster."

"Nor I yours, Mr. Zocci."

We stared at each other.

"I do not appreciate your intrusion into matters personal to my family," he said.

"What matters would those be?"

"The death of my son, Dr. Foster."

"Which son, Mr. Zocci? Erik or Michael?"

Zocci flinched, almost imperceptibly. I'd scored a hit. A below-the-belt, dirty, nasty, unfair hit, for which I felt instantly ashamed. I would deal with myself later. For now, I sensed I was in a fight that needed to be won. No matter what the cost.

I glanced aside at Molina, catching a brief glimpse of surprise on his face. I suspected he knew nothing about little Joseph Michael's death.

"My attorneys have issued a subpoena for your records," Zocci was saying. "You are not to spend time alone, professionally or personally, with any student between now and the time this matter is resolved. You are not to breach the premises of the Vendome under any circumstances. And you are not to approach any member of my family, in proximity or via any avenue of communication."

"This is America, Mr. Zocci. I don't recall electing you to run my life."

"I strongly recommend you do not test me."

"Thank you for the advice. I appreciate your concern for my well-being. Truly I do."

I shot my eyes over at Sam Molina, who looked as if all the blood had drained out of his head. "Sam, you've been a big help. See you soon."

I turned and walked out of the room, closing the door behind me.

I stood still for a moment, gathering myself and looking around the empty suite of offices. My legs were shaking. So much for not being easily intimidated.

The adjoining office door was open an inch or two, so I slipped inside and closed the door, leaving it cracked slightly. I seated myself on the floor behind the desk, hugging my knees, my back to the shared wall between the two offices, and strained to hear their conversation.

It was muffled, but from what I could make out, Zocci was chewing Molina out for letting me into the twelfth-floor suite. I caught a few phrases. "Unconscionable," "breach of privacy," "unprofessional." Molina was obsequious. Apologizing. Practicing the fine art of kissing up.

I heard the door open and the two men stepped out of the office. Zocci was still talking "—in a timely manner," he was saying. "Alert hotel security. I leave for New York in an hour. I'll leave the number with my secretary."

The two men closed the suite door behind them as they left. I winced, hoping I wouldn't hear the door lock. Just my luck to get locked down here in the dungeon. I'd probably get myself arrested. Trespassing. Breaking and entering. My mind reeled with dreadful possibilities.

No click, though. I waited until I could no longer hear their footsteps in the hallway and then lunged for the door.

My plan for a quick exit was thwarted by the fact that I'd paid absolutely no attention while Sam Molina had led me into the catacombs of the Vendome. I could not find my way out. I trotted down several different hallways, dead-ending myself each time. I finally stepped into the women's bathroom, locked myself in a stall, and tried to settle down.

My cell phone rang loudly, echoing around the tile in the small room.

I clutched my bag to my stomach, muffling the sound while I groped for the phone to silence it. I found the right button and brought the phone out of the bag to check the caller ID. It was my father.

The perfect ending to a perfect day.

I ignored the call and waited another few minutes before poking my head out the bathroom door. The hallway was still empty. I slipped out of the bathroom and hurried to the elevator at the end of the hall. The twenty yards or so between me and the elevator seemed like a mile. As I covered the distance, I saw the lighted numbers above the brass doors begin to descend from the second floor. In a few seconds, the elevator doors would open and someone would step into my path. My day's luck would ensure it was Sam Molina.

I ducked behind a silk ficus plant as the bell dinged and the doors whispered open. Two black-outfitted hotel employees stepped off and walked past without noticing me. I waited till they were several feet down the hall, then slipped into the elevator just as the doors were about to close and pushed the button for the lobby.

As the doors opened on the first level, I found myself at the south end of the lobby. The concierge desk buzzed with activity as hotel guests made their evening plans. The bar had filled up as well, with businessmen occupying most of the wingbacks.

I shouldered my bag and kept my eyes focused on the revolving door, the brass gateway to my escape. As I passed the bar, I brushed past a waitress, barely sparing her tray of martinis. A quick glance around the lobby revealed a couple of security men engaged in an animated conversation with a suited man, the three of them laughing. Talking about football perhaps. That sort of conversation. Neither of the uniformed men glanced my direction.

I breathed a prayer as I covered the last few feet, then turned to survey the room before I crossed the threshold to the street.

The only face I recognized belonged to Earl, the porter I'd met yesterday. He stood erect behind a wingback, watching me.

Our eyes met. He shook his head slowly, no.

I stopped, my head cocked in silent curiosity.

He shook his head again.

I looked through the glass just as Joseph Zocci ducked into the backseat of a black Mercedes, the driver shutting the door behind him, closing him in behind a dark curtain of glass. The car pulled out quickly. I watched it exit the circular drive and slide into the traffic on the street.

After I'd lost view of the taillights, I turned to meet Earl's eyes again. He was gone, folded back into the late afternoon swirl of activity in the lobby.

Clearly the staff, or parts of it at least, had been briefed. I slipped out the door quickly. Why Earl had helped me, I had no idea.

My car was several blocks away, and I walked the distance uneasily, once again troubled by the feeling I was being watched. Paranoia in this situation was starting to make sense, though, so I tried not to make too much of it. Someone, I suspected Sam Molina, had ratted me out. And I'd come face to face with the enemy.

Though the possibility of being followed on the crowded streets of Chicago seemed absurd, I whipped around a few times just to make sure, making a thorough fool of myself and annoying the pedestrians marching along at my heels. But I saw nothing suspicious. Certainly no glance of Molina or Zocci. Or Peter Terry, for that matter.

My purple Neon looked downright gorgeous to me, I was so happy to see it. I slipped into the driver's seat, locked the door, and then sat there for a good five minutes and cried, allowing myself a brief meltdown after a stressful afternoon. Then I blew my nose, wiped my tears, and picked up my cell phone.

Back in the saddle.

My first call was to Helene. She answered this time, and I explained as briefly and clearly as I could the situation with Gavin. She held her tongue, though I'm certain she was as appalled as I was about this recent development. Appalled on Gavin's behalf, of course. But probably more so on mine. My mentor was being forced into a front row seat to view the demise of my career. Her anger and pain were palpable to me.

Our conversation was quick and to the point. She asked me how things were going in Chicago. I told her fine, but left out the details. Somehow we shared a tacit understanding that there were things better left unsaid for now. Hopefully, I could get to the bottom of all this and clear my name. And our mutual nightmare would be over.

I called my father next. Some sort of masochistic impulse on my part, I guess. And since he'd tracked down my cell phone number, he'd be calling me a dozen times a day until he got what he wanted anyway, so I might as well take the bullet now.

He picked up on the first ring, cuss words flying out of his mouth.

I started listening when he finally got to my name.

"…Dylan. I just cannot believe you. Just the height of irresponsibility."

"You want to calm down? I'm thirty-three years old, Dad. I don't need to check in from the movies anymore, okay?"

He let a few more fly, but his anger eventually ran out of steam. "So you're okay, then."

"Of course I'm okay."

"Good. You worry me, Dylan."

"You worry me, Dad. What do you need?"

"I had to call your brother to get your number."

"Guthrie had my number?"

"Cleo did. Your sister-in-law knows how to get in touch with you. Your own dad has to call—"

"Dad, can we move on? What do you need?"

"I need you to do me a favor."

"I don't think I can do it, Dad."

"I haven't even asked you yet."

"I do not want to be a bridesmaid."

"Are you insane? I can't have you in the wedding, Dylan. Kellee specified no family. No family at all. I'm sorry. I just can't do it."

"Oh."

Why was I hurt? I had spent days avoiding the man so he and his bubble-head fiancée wouldn't ask me to be in their tacky, expensive, over-the-top wedding. And he'd just kicked me off the roster and now I was hurt.

I needed therapy. Badly.

"Your mother needs a trustee," he was saying.

"What?" Nonsense. The man was speaking complete nonsense.

"A trustee. Your mother's estate. A trustee."

"Dad, I don't understand what you're asking me. Use verbs."

"The trustee," he recited, "makes fiduciary decisions and handles all administrative responsibilities for the various entities of the estate."

"You want me to manage Mom's estate?"

"She needs a trustee. Someone to manage her estate. Yes. That's it. That's the favor."

"Who's doing it now?"

"I am."

"So what's wrong with you? Why can't you do it anymore?"
I knew what the answer would be.

"I think it would be better for Kellee if you did it."

"Better for Kellee. You want me to do it because it would be better for Kellee."

"Better for me, Dylan. It would be better for me."

I couldn't remember the last time my father had asked me to do anything for him. "Why me? Why not Guthrie?"

"He's moving, his life's up in the air. He and Cleo—those two could split up any minute. I just think…you're the stable one."

Except for the part about the pending malpractice charges, the lawsuit, and the looming unemployment. None of which he knew about, of course.

"Your mom would—"

"I'll do it, Dad. I'd be happy to. No problem."

"I'll have Janet box up the files and ship them to you."

"Ship them? How many are there?"

"Your mother left a sizable estate, Dylan."

"I didn't know that."

"Maybe four, five boxes."

"What am I getting myself into?"

"It's fine. Don't worry about it."

We agreed to speak when I returned so he could go over it all with me. I hung up with the distinct feeling that I'd just stepped into a quagmire of paperwork and responsibility.

The meter had run out on my parking place. I sat there for a minute, trying to decide what to do next. I finally decided I was on a roll. Why not slay one more dragon before day's end?

I started the car, shoved it into gear, and reached for my

map. I'd overheard Joseph Zocci say he was flying to New York tonight. If the traffic was good, I could make it to Lake County before dark.

22

~

ONCE AGAIN, I HAD NO PLAN. As I barreled north, breaking multiple laws of the state of Illinois—speeding, rolling through stop signs, talking on my cell phone while driving—I became fully aware that once again, I was acting on instinct. Impulsively throwing myself into a situation I was completely unprepared for.

I went anyway, fighting the urge to turn tail and run back to my crummy, haunted hotel room, pack my stuff, and haul my unemployed self to Mexico to start an outlaw life.

I busied myself in the car by checking my messages and returning phone calls. The Ice Queen had called me, insisting in her cold, shaming voice that I call her immediately, and did I fully understand the gravity of my situation? I left her a message, feigning contrition and explaining that I'd had to make an emergency trip out of town. I suggested a Monday morning meeting.

Several of my students had called as well, wanting to know when I would be back in the classroom. Apparently, Helene's dictatorial teaching style wasn't engaging them in the manner they'd hoped to become accustomed to. I didn't call them back. They were in college. Let them take responsibility for their own learning, whether they were entertained or not. Welcome to grown-up life.

My final message was from Gavin. He'd called from the acute care unit at Green Oaks. He sounded terrible. He was on suicide watch, he said, which I knew from my experience working on locked units meant he was under close surveillance, denied even the simple dignity of shoelaces or pencils. He'd left my name on his call list, though, meaning that if I called the unit, they would put me through to him.

The Green Oaks number was still in my phone, so I called him back immediately, hoping I'd catch him between supper and the evening process group. It took me a while to get through the maze of security checks, an annoying gateway of fairly hostile, suspicious questions that, though off-putting, are necessary to protect patient confidentiality.

I finally made it to the unit, where the psych tech took my name, checked Gavin's list, and agreed, after some cajoling, to pull him out of group so I could talk to him.

"Hlo?"

"Gavin, is that you? It's me. Dylan Foster."

"Hlo."

"You doing okay?"

"Mmm."

"Is that yes? Or no? How are you, Gavin?"

"Mmm. Did he find you?" he asked.

"Who? Did who find me?"

"Peter Terry."

I had never uttered the name Peter Terry in Gavin's presence, had never told him about my encounter at Barton Springs.

"Is this the same man that's been in your dreams, Gavin?"

"You know him. The white guy. He's looking for you."

"He's visiting your dreams again, Gavin?"

His speech was slow, slurry. "No, no. No. Not in my dreams. He's here."

"He's where?"

"My roommate."

"Peter Terry is your roommate in the hospital?"

"Peter. Yeah. He's looking for you."

"Does he know me?"

"Of course."

"What did he say, Gavin?"

"He thinks you're pretty."

Strangely flattering.

"He's worried," he was saying.

"About what?"

"Ask him yourself."

I heard him put the phone down.

"Gavin? Gavin?" He must have walked away from the telephone. I was talking to dead air.

"May I help you?"

It was Diane, the charge nurse. She and I had crossed paths before and knew each other professionally.

"Hi, Diane. It's Dylan Foster. I was just talking to Gavin."

"He's very agitated. I don't think this is a good time," she scolded.

"I understand. Could you just tell me—"

"I really can't answer your questions, Dr. Foster. You must know that."

"Sure, sure. I know. I was just wondering, could you tell me if Gavin has a roommate?"

"No. Of course not. He's on suicide watch."

"Is he stable? Does he exhibit any psychotic symptoms?"

She paused. She really was not supposed to talk to me at all.

"I do believe he is, yes," she said.

"Is what? Stable or exhibiting psychotic symptoms?"

"The second one."

"Listen Diane, could you call me if he worsens? I'm really his only local contact."

"He'll have to sign a release for that."

"If you wouldn't mind asking him, I'd appreciate it."

"I'll check, Dr. Foster."

I thanked her and hung up.

The drive was congested but beautiful, the sun setting to my left and Lake Michigan calming itself for the evening on my right. My nerves were beginning to fray, the once heroic-sounding idea of hunting down Mariann Zocci now sounding foolish and dangerous. My Neon was buzzing along I-94, cutting in and out of traffic. I calmed myself listening to the tinny buzz of the car engine and the crackly A.M. radio. I made the exit onto U.S. 41 and headed toward the little city of Highland Park, Illinois, population 31,365.

I had an address but no map. The Zocci estate was on Lakeside Drive, the geography of which seemed fairly obvious to me. I headed east toward the lake, found Lakeside, which indeed ran along the lake shore, and made a left, heading north, craning my neck for address numbers.

The houses were mostly large, stately colonials. One well-behaved Republican house after another. Golf-green lawns. Clipped bushes. Orderly trees. Color-coordinated flower beds. American flags posted by doorways. I felt like I was on a movie set. I half expected little herds of paper-doll children to spill onto lawns and play touch football with their golden retrievers.

The street addresses told me I was about ten blocks off. As I went north, the traffic disappeared completely. The lawns became larger, the houses set further back, until at last, a few blocks before the Zocci address, the houses on the Lake Michigan side were not visible at all from the road. I found myself slowing almost to a crawl, peering through hedges designed to keep people like me from peering through them.

From the road, I could see no posted address for the home I suspected was the Zoccis'. I drove the surrounding blocks again, just to make sure I had homed in on the right house, then parked my car down the road, locked it up, and walked along the hedge-covered wrought iron fence toward the gate.

I was alone on the road. I suspected the neighborhood employed private security services, which would no doubt spot my Ugly But It Runs smiley-face flag in no time. I'd be outed as an imposter and promptly sent packing. That is if Joseph Zocci had not briefed his local security about me. If he had, I was liable to get myself arrested.

A brisk walk from the car took me to the black metal gate in the hedge. It was wide enough for only one car, meant to go unnoticed, I think. Maybe it was a back entrance or something. From the gate, I could see a long curved drive lined with trees, and could catch only a glimpse of the house, which was set a few hundred yards back from the road and obscured by foliage. There was no indication as to who lived in the house, but the numbers on the mailbox matched the ones on my list. I crumpled the paper and stuffed it in my pocket, trying to figure out what to do next.

I could probably climb the fence, but doing so would give anybody that caught me a legitimate reason to arrest me for trespassing. I didn't want to take the chance. Finally, for lack of a better idea, I pressed the intercom button on the keypad by the mailbox and waited for an answer.

A female voice answered. "Yes?"

What had I intended to say? I couldn't think of anything. Naturally, I panicked.

"UPS."

"Pardon?"

"UPS. Delivery."

I looked around nonchalantly, wondering for the first time if security cameras were installed around the gate. I couldn't see any.

"What is the name on the package, please?" the voice said.

"Mariann Zocci," I said.

"Return address?"

I recited the address of the SMU campus.

"One moment, please."

I waited in silence, fighting the urge to run. What was I doing? Faking a delivery from Mariann Zocci's dead son. Claiming to be a UPS delivery person when I was driving a purple Neon and wearing a black dress and sandals. What was I going to do if they let me in? Claim someone had heisted my truck and uniform?

The voice was back. "Please proceed to the delivery entrance."

"I'm sorry, I'm new. I don't know where that is."

"To the north of the gate. You'll see it on your right."

There were no sidewalks on this end of Lakeside, only a strip of lush green grass running between the hedge and the asphalt. I walked the yardage quickly, the heels of my shoes sinking into the damp sod. As I neared the gate, I slowed and folded myself into the shadow of the hedge.

I peeked around. There was a guardhouse at the gate. With a real live guard in it. And security cameras.

I chickened out.

I walked back to my little purple car, started it up, and

drove off, circling back the way I'd come to avoid passing the guardhouse. Scolding myself mercilessly.

A few miles down the road, I turned off Lakeside into a little shopping center and found myself a Starbucks. I needed a cup of tea.

Times like this made me wish I smoked. It just looked so calming, sitting at a little round table, drinking a cup of coffee and smoking a cigarette. I ordered a piece of carrot cake instead, creamed and sugared my tea, and seated myself at a table outside.

My situation begged for a Plan B. I had no Plan B. I'd had no Plan A. I was driving around Highland Park, Illinois, impersonating a UPS driver, and I had no plan.

Once again, I found myself out of ideas, without resources, and in over my head. And once again, I followed my instinct to worry instead of pray. I sat there through two giant cups of tea before I thought of God, of asking for help. Discussing my little problem with the Creator of the universe occurred to me only after I'd exhausted every other possible option.

I didn't seem to be learning my lesson.

So at last I prayed.

I drank my tea and prayed. I scraped the last of the cream-cheese frosting off the plate, licked it off my finger, and prayed. I pulled my crumpled notes out of my bag and prayed. I pored over all my thoughts and research and prayed.

I thought about Peter Terry and prayed.

I thought about Mariann Zocci and prayed.

I finally settled on the thought that this woman was an important piece of the puzzle. I needed to speak with Mariann Zocci. I was certain of it.

I didn't think there was any way I could make it past the fortress at the Zocci mansion to see her. My eyes fell on the other

Zocci addresses on my list. Maybe one of the other family members would be more accessible. Virginia Anne lived in the city. I could try to track her down once I got back to Chicago. James Andrew lived in Highland Park. I checked my map. His home was less than a mile from where I was sitting. Might as well check it out. I prayed for guidance and got in the car.

I found the house easily and was relieved to discover that James Andrew's house wasn't nearly as intimidating as his parents'. He lived in one of the big Republican colonials. Circular drive. Huge trees. Bursting flower beds. And a rope swing. A rope swing hanging from one of the huge oaks in the front yard.

I saw that rope swing as a sign from Jesus.

I parked my car and marched myself up to the front door, stepping over a plastic Fisher-Price dump truck, and rang the bell.

I could hear children running, a dog barking, and a woman shouting for someone to answer the door. As I stood there, the red-painted door swung open.

My eyes dropped to meet the gaze of a skinny little dark-haired girl dressed in footie pajamas. She couldn't have been more than four years old.

"Hi," I said.

"Hello."

"Is your daddy here?"

"Mommy!" she shouted. She stuck her thumb in her mouth and waited calmly for the next question.

A woman's voice came from inside the house. "Who is it, Punkin?"

"A lady."

The owner of the voice appeared, toddler on her hip. She wore a pink sweat suit, no makeup, had pulled her brown hair back into a pony tail, and carried a copy of *Green Eggs and Ham* in her free hand. A little blond-haired boy clung to her thigh.

"Can I help you?" she said.

"I'm looking for James Andrew Zocci," I said. "I'm sorry to bother you. You've obviously got your hands full."

She laughed. "It's the witching hour. They go nuts right before bedtime."

"Is he here?" I said. "I just need to talk to him for a minute."

"Daddy went on the plane," Punkin said.

"Andy won't be back this evening," the woman said. "Was he expecting you?"

I decided to tell the truth for a change. She seemed like a good egg. It was worth a try. "No, he wasn't. I knew his brother, Erik. I wanted to talk to James...Andy about him. Could I leave him a note or something?"

She put the toddler down. "Punkin, take your brothers for a minute, will you honey? Put in a movie if you want."

The little girl stared at me. "You know my Uncle Erik?"

"I used to."

She turned to her mother. "I told you she'd come." Then back to me. "Does he miss me?"

"Yes, sweetie, he does," I said. "I think he misses you very much."

"Will he bring me a present?"

I looked at her mother.

She leaned down. "I don't think he can, honey. But Daddy's bringing you a present when he comes home tomorrow, okay? Now take your brothers for me. I need to talk to Erik's friend."

She shooed the kids off and came back to the front door.

"I'm sorry I left you standing out here. Would you like to come in?"

"No, thanks. I'm really sorry to intrude."

"How did you say you knew Erik?"

"I was his psychologist."

I watched the recognition settle onto her face. "The one from SMU." She looked at me for a moment without saying anything. "Joe's got his sights on you."

"He does."

"I think you'd better come in," she said. "Knowing Joe, he's got somebody watching the house." She looked out onto the street. "Is that your car?"

"Sadly, yes. My rental."

"It's ugly."

"But it runs," I said.

"Hey, I've heard of them. I guess that's truth in advertising. I'm Liz Zocci," she said, extending her hand.

"Dylan Foster."

"Why don't you park your car in the garage and come inside? I think you and I should talk."

23

~

I MOVED MY CAR TO THE GARAGE, then followed Liz through the back door into the kitchen. She cleared Spaghetti-O-crusted plates from the table and stacked them in the sink, moving easily among the pleasant kid clutter and opening the Sub-Zero for a bottle of wine.

"Join me?" she said.

"Sure."

"I swear. Three kids under age five would turn any sane woman to drink. I'm thinking of bagging the whole thing and becoming an alcoholic."

"You'd need to find yourself a good codependent first," I said. "Someone to over-function for you so you can become passive and irresponsible."

"I'll work on that," she said laughing. "Andy's pretty responsible. Maybe if we found a really good nanny…"

She poured us both a glass of white and raised her glass.

"To Erik," she said.

"To Erik."

We both took a sip. "He was a great kid," she said. "A really great kid."

"I know he was," I said.

"Why do you think he did it?"

"I was hoping you could tell me. I didn't know him very well. I only saw him three times. A year ago."

Liz leveled her eyes at me. "I thought you'd been seeing him regularly since he got to school. That's what Joe's telling everyone." She took a sip of wine, holding the taste on her tongue and closing her eyes. "So you don't know why he did it."

"No. I didn't even remember him at first," I admitted. "I had to look up his records."

"The way Joe talks about it, you're the one that drove him off the balcony. You might as well have shoved him off yourself. He'd love to blame the whole thing on you."

"Do you think that's true? I mean, do you believe him?"

"Erik had plenty of reasons to commit suicide," she said. "I doubt seriously that you're one of them."

I waited silently. I didn't want to push.

"It was a tough family to grow up in," she said at last. "Andy's completely estranged from his father."

"Joe seems like a hard man to be close to."

"Delicately put. You've met him?"

"Once. Today. At the Vendome hotel."

She raised her eyebrows. "You went to the Vendome?"

"I wanted to see the room."

"I hate that room," she said. "I won't stay there anymore. Christine won't go past the doorway."

"Mommy." It was Punkin.

"Yes, Punkin."

"Jamie took the movie out and he's pulling all the tape out of it and Mikey's eating my purple. My favorite."

Liz looked at me. "We go through hundreds of purple crayons. I'll be right back."

I waited in the kitchen while she got the kids under control.

She came back a minute later with all three in tow. "I'm going to try to get them down. Mind waiting for a minute?"

"Can I help?"

Liz turned to her daughter. "You want Miss Dylan to tuck you in?"

Punkin came over and grabbed my hand. "Will you say my prayers with me?"

I looked over at Liz for permission. She nodded at me.

"Sure, honey," I said.

I got up and tagged upstairs with her, following her into her pink and yellow bedroom while Liz carried both the boys down the hall. I wondered why Liz Zocci trusted me to be alone with her kid. Not that I wasn't trustworthy, but how could she know that?

Letter-shaped pillows on Punkin's bed spelled Christine. She yanked the covers back, pushed all the pillows into a heap on the floor, grabbed a worn teddy bear missing its nose and one eye, and stuck her thumb in her mouth.

"I knew you'd come," she said.

She'd said that earlier.

"How did you know, sweetie?"

"The angel told me."

"What angel?"

"My angel," she insisted, as though that were plenty of information for anyone. "He told me you would come to see me. He said you knew my uncle Erik."

"When did you see the angel?"

"I always see him."

"Do you see him now?"

She took her thumb out of her mouth and rolled her eyes. "No, silly-bean. He's not here now."

Surely Peter Terry hadn't gotten to sweet little Punkin. If he was coming around this kid, I'd hunt him down and skin him myself.

"What does the angel look like? Is he all white?"

"He looks like Mr. Martin."

"Is he all white and sick looking?"

"No." She shook her head emphatically. "He looks like Mr. Martin."

That was as far as we were going to get with that.

She stuck her thumb back in her mouth and said, "Pray."

"I'm supposed to pray? Don't you pray when you say your prayers?"

"No, you," she said.

"Who do you want to pray for?"

"Mommy and Daddy and Mikey and Jamie and Erik. And Gramma."

I dutifully prayed for Mommy, Daddy, Mikey, Jamie, and Erik. And Gramma. "Anyone else?" I said.

"You. Pray for you."

The kid had good instincts. I needed praying for. I prayed for myself.

I opened my eyes again. "Anyone else?"

"The babies in Africa."

I prayed for the babies in Africa. "Anyone else?"

She stuck her bear in my face. "Kiss No-Nose."

I kissed No-Nose.

"Amen," she said.

"Amen," I said.

She stuck her thumb back in her mouth. I was clearly being dismissed. I told her good night and turned off the bedside light.

"Door open or closed?" I said.

"Open."

I left the door open and went back downstairs to wait for Liz.

In the kitchen, I busied myself cleaning up the supper dishes. I wondered if Liz had a maid or anything. The house was sort of a wreck. Not dirty, just cluttered with kid gear. I got the feeling she was on her own. For a family with Zocci-level money, Liz and Andy seemed very down to earth.

"Oh, thanks," Liz said as she came into the room. She started the dishwasher. "Leave the rest. Housework can always wait." She handed me my glass and we sat again at the table.

"Has Christine mentioned an angel to you?" I asked.

She nodded. "She talks about him all the time. That's how she knew you were coming. Her angel told her."

"Who is Mr. Martin?"

"He's her school principal."

"Is he bald and white, sort of sickly looking, by chance?"

"As a matter of fact, he's black. Full head of hair. Why?"

"Christine said the angel looks like Mr. Martin."

"News to me."

"Do you believe her?" I asked.

"What, that he looks like Mr. Martin?"

"No. That there's an angel. That he's real."

She shrugged. "Don't know. Christine has always had a good radar. She sees things no one else sees. That's why I let you tuck her in. If you'd been dangerous, she would have known it."

"I wondered."

"She won't go into that twelfth-floor room unless her angel is there."

"At the Vendome?"

"Yep."

"Andy took the kids there last week. I was at my mother's.

Christine wouldn't go in. Said the bad man was there."

"Who's the bad man?"

"I have no idea." She took a sip of wine. "Have you eaten?"

"No."

"Neither have I."

She got up and dug in the Sub-Zero for a minute, producing a plate of lunchmeat, cheese, and fruit and set it between us on the table. She tossed a napkin across the table for me and sat herself down.

"How did you know Joe was gunning for me?" I asked. "Did he tell you?"

She shook her head. "I never see the man. At the funeral, of course. And later at the house. Mariann told me."

"Are the two of you close?" I asked.

"Mariann is sort of a broken woman. She's not close to anyone. But we talk a few times a week. More since Erik died. She spends a lot of time with the kids. Christine loves her."

"What broke her, do you think? Erik's suicide?"

"Erik is just the last stick on the pile," she said. "Joey, her first son, died when he was three. And she's had almost forty years living with Joe Zocci."

"What's he like?"

She reached for a piece of cheese. "Joe? Cruel would be accurate, I think."

"Abusive?"

"Very."

"Physically, emotionally, verbally? What?" I asked.

"Pick one. Erik didn't tell you?"

"Erik never said a word about his father."

"I'm not surprised. Lots of silence in this family. Everyone's afraid of him."

"You don't seem to be afraid of him. Otherwise you wouldn't be talking to me."

She looked at me. "I'm through being afraid of things."

"Why did you want to talk to me? Why did you invite me in?"

She thought a minute. "I think because Christine had said you'd be coming. I'm learning to listen to her. And because Erik was a good kid. I'd like to know what really happened to him." She drained her wine glass and reached for the bottle. "Top you off?" she asked.

"No, thanks."

She filled her glass, corked the bottle, and returned it to the fridge.

"How long have you and Andy been married?"

"Seven years," she said. "Andy's a good man. Nothing like his father."

"How long have he and his dad been estranged?"

"Seven years."

"Since you married."

"Easy math," she said. "Joe's not too crazy about me. He didn't want Andy to marry me."

"Why not?"

"I think it's because I stood up to him."

"To who? Andy or Joe?"

"Both, I guess. But Andy doesn't need much standing up to."

"How'd you stand up to Joe?"

"I convinced Andy not to help him run the airline."

"And Joe wasn't too happy."

"That's putting it mildly."

"How did he react?"

"He cut Andy off."

"Financially?"

"Every dime."

"But…" I looked around. They were obviously doing very well.

"Andy's done this on his own," she said.

"What does he do?"

"He owns an oil and gas drilling company."

"Garret Industries?"

She looked at me. "How do you know about Garret Industries?"

"Long story," I said.

"Andy's company is called A&E Oil. Garret Industries is Joe's attempt to put Andy out of business."

"Joe started a rival company?"

"Just a subsidiary. Garret has been around for a long time. But it didn't go into the oil and gas business until Andy did."

"Wow."

She took another drink of wine. "Yeah. Wow."

"I'd like to talk to Mariann," I said. "I stopped by the house earlier. I pretended to be a UPS delivery person. Hoping to get my face in front of hers so I could talk to her."

"You'd never get past security."

"I figured that out."

"I'll call her for you."

"Would you? I'd really appreciate it."

"When do you want to see her?"

"What time is it?"

"Almost nine," she said. "You want to see her tonight?"

"I'd like to. Joe's out of town. I don't know when he's coming back."

She picked up the phone and exchanged a few words with

Mariann Zocci, then hung up the phone and looked at me. "She's waiting for you."

"Should I—"

"Just ring the bell at the family gate. The first one you tried."

I looked at her.

"She saw you the first time you were there. She would have let you in."

"Did she know it was me?"

"She'd already looked up your picture on the SMU website. She recognized you."

I needed to check out that picture. Everyone had seen it but me.

"Thanks, Liz. I can't tell you how much I appreciate your help."

We exchanged phone numbers.

"Good luck," she said. "You have no idea what you're up against."

24

~

THE TRIP TO THE ZOCCI ESTATE seemed shorter this time. Probably because I was so nervous. I didn't really want to get there, I don't think.

My planless state persisted along with the inevitable accompanying panic. I wasn't sure what I was going to say to Mariann Zocci.

Hi, I'm the psychologist your husband is blaming for your son's suicide.

So sorry for your loss, but could you put your grief aside and help me, because my career is going down the tubes?

Have you seen a scary white man with a big slash on his back?

I pulled my Neon up to the family gate and cranked down my window to press the button. The gate opened before I even got my hand out of the window. So much for my theory that there were no video cameras at this entrance. I looked around for the cameras, but never spotted them. Which made me even more nervous. I was tired of the continuing unease of being watched. And how did I know Joe Zocci wasn't lying in wait for me, watching my little smiley-face flag as I curved along the driveway to his home?

The house was enormous and sang of old money, which intimidated me immediately, of course. Grey stone walls were laced with ivy. The slate roof was speckled with the unmistakable signs of permanence—blue-green lichen, small patches of bright green moss, and coppery water stains. Gargantuan marble planters guarded the doorway, each spiked with a spiral, groomed topiary and spilling over with more ivy.

Mine was the only car in the drive. I shoved the door open with my shoulder, grabbed my bag and what remained of my courage, and stepped onto the flagstone walk. The front door opened before I made it up the steps.

I'd counted on a little time in the foyer to gather my thoughts. I had pictured being greeted by a balding man named Chauncy, I think. As it was, I found myself face-to-face with the tiny woman from the newspaper photograph, her face aged exponentially since the photo was taken.

She looked like a child in the cavernous doorway, not more than five feet and change to her slight frame, her careful hair and makeup somehow making her seem smaller and more vulnerable. She wore a red velour Chanel sweat suit. I didn't even know Chanel made sweat suits.

She held out a delicate hand.

"So pleased to meet you, Dr. Foster. Won't you come in?"

"Thank you."

I followed her into the foyer, my shoes clomping loudly on the marble, echoing through the stony silence of the house.

"We'll talk in the library," she said. "May I offer you a drink?"

"No, thank you," I said, trailing along beside her.

The library. I'd never been in a house that had a library.

"I appreciate your seeing me," I said.

"Not at all. I was hoping we would get a chance to talk."

The library door stood open, and we walked into perhaps

the coziest room I'd ever seen in my life. Worn leather couches flanked a fireplace, in which a storybook fire burned brightly. An oriental rug covered most of the hardwood floor, its fringes framing the seating area. Tall French doors were open to the cool, breezy evening, leading out to a stone patio and framing a spectacular view of Lake Michigan.

Floor-to-ceiling bookshelves held what was obviously someone's treasured collection of rare books. The bindings on many were old but in remarkable shape. I glanced at the shelf nearest where I stood. The entire shelf was full of Bibles.

"I collect rare Bibles," she said, following my eyes.

"They're beautiful." I walked over to the shelf.

She reached for one and handed it to me. "This is an Aitken Bible. The first Bible printed in English in the United States. 1782. Fewer than a dozen remain in existence in the world."

Suddenly I felt grimy. I had the urge to bolt for the powder room to wash my hands before I touched it. But I took the book gingerly and opened it, studying the irregular print on the frontispiece.

The scholar in me was moved by this woman's love of books, and of Bibles, of all things. She was a woman I would have wanted to know under different circumstances.

I handed the book back to her. "It's beautiful. How do you go about finding them?"

"Rare book dealers. Auctions."

"How long have you been collecting?"

"Twenty years or so."

Around the time Erik was born. Around the time Joe had started Eagle Wing Air. Around the time she came into money.

She gestured toward the couches and seated herself near the fire, indicating that I should sit across from her. The marble coffee table between us seemed like a football field.

"I'm not sure how to begin," I said. "I'm terribly sorry for your loss. I can't imagine what you're going through."

She nodded at me. I could tell she still had trouble talking about it. The sparkle of a tear edged into the corner of her eye.

"Why do you think…" she began. "I mean, in your opinion as a professional. Why…? He was such a wonderful young man. Always so happy."

"Many students have a great deal of trouble adjusting to college life," I said. "Was he? Happy before he left home, I mean?"

"Always. Our family has always been very happy."

"I had understood—" how was I going to put this?—"that there was some ongoing tension in the family."

She met my eyes squarely. "That's a lie. If Erik told you that, he was lying."

"I'm sorry. I didn't mean to offend—"

"I don't know where you would have gotten such an idea," she said. "We have always been so fortunate. My husband is a wonderful, kind man."

I hadn't mentioned Joe. Yet she had jumped in to defend him anyway.

"My understanding is that Joe has a temper. That sometimes—"

"That's a lie," she said again. "My husband is a wonderful, kind man. He wouldn't hurt a fly."

Interesting choice of insects.

"Do you want to know what I really think, Mrs. Zocci?"

"Please."

"Are you a woman of faith?"

"I always have been." She gazed into the fire, talking more to herself than to me. "Faith. Evidence of things not seen?" She shook her head. "The evidence of things seen is…more compelling at times."

The smell of burning pine crackled into the still air, a tangible comfort in the face of the heavy sadness and tension in the room.

"I believe Erik was caught in some sort of a spiritual battle. Something that was larger and more powerful than he was," I said.

"And how did you determine that, Dr. Foster?"

"I saw him as a patient only a few times. Over a year ago. But my notes indicate that he was having nightmares. Spiritual nightmares, if you will. Involving some sort of evil presence. I know it sounds strange—"

"The white man."

"He told you about him."

She nodded.

"What did he say?"

"We were talking about how fearful he had become. He had always been such a confident boy. He had this natural...exuberance."

"Did he say what the fear was about?"

"About himself, actually. He said that this man, this white man, haunted him. He had begun to believe him. That he was," she struggled to keep her composure, "worthless, I believe he said. My precious son. Worthless."

Her voice broke at last and the tears came.

"Would you excuse me for a moment, Dr. Foster?"

"Sure."

She left the room. I sat there alone for a few minutes—longer than I'd expected her to be gone. Then got up and perused the bookshelves again, my old habit of sizing people up via their bookshelves proving too tempting.

I wandered the room, cocking my ear for her returning footsteps.

An enormous wall of shelving held Bibles and other rare books. Theology books were arranged in careful order. She liked some of the same theologians I did: C. S. Lewis, Henry Nouwen, though her collection was sprinkled with tomes by the early church fathers—Augustine, Justin—and numerous Catholic scholars.

Mariann's charity work was cataloged on this wall as well. I counted a dozen or so framed photographs of Mariann standing among little gaggles of socialites, holding cartoonish, oversize checks or cutting red ribbons with enormous scissors. She'd worked with a number of different charities, it seemed, though the one cited most often was something called Angel Wing Air. Its similarity to Eagle Wing Air made me wonder if this was a Zocci-founded nonprofit. I made a mental note to check into it.

Another entire wall was clearly Joseph Zocci's territory. Books on business. Biographies of military leaders. Sprinkled among the shelves were various military citations awarded to Lieutenant Zocci during the Vietnam War. A Navy Cross. Two Purple Hearts.

There were framed newspaper articles regarding his service, mostly from the *Chicago Tribune*. I squinted to scan the yellowed pages. Zocci had been shot down twice. Once in 1969. And later, in 1971, at which point he'd been taken prisoner. He'd spent two years in a Vietnamese prison camp.

No wonder the man was so angry.

Mariann Zocci's voice startled me.

"Joe was a war hero," she said proudly. "He could have requested stateside the first time he was shot down."

"Was he wounded?"

"Not badly. He ejected. His nose was broken and he dislocated his shoulder, I believe. He almost refused his Purple Heart. He didn't feel his wounds merited it."

"How long was he in Vietnam?" I asked.

"Two full tours, plus two years in captivity. Six years in all before he was released."

"That must have been hard for both of you. Did he ever get leave?"

"After he was shot down the first time. In '69. He spent a month at home. We'd only been married two years at that point. Still newlyweds really. Most of the time he'd been away."

That leave must have been when Joseph Jr. was conceived.

My eyes moved to the framed family photographs on the table next to me. I leaned down, spotting Andy and Erik right away. All the pictures portrayed what seemed to be a picture-perfect happy family. If what Liz had said was true, the Zoccis were masters at hiding their dysfunction.

I spotted a picture of a very young, beaming Mariann Zocci holding a toddler. "Is that Joseph Jr.?" I asked.

She looked at me, startled. "Why yes. It is."

"It must be hard, having lost two children. Two children in the same way."

"I can't talk about that." She straightened and walked away from the table. "Some things, Dr. Foster, are just too painful…"

"I'm sorry. It's just that it's so unusual. Do you think that's why Erik chose—"

"Erik never knew how his brother died," she said stiffly. "We don't talk about it. It was a terrible accident. A terrible time for me. He was my firstborn."

"What do you make of the fact that Erik jumped off the same balcony? Surely you must realize—"

"Dr. Foster, it's late. I'm afraid I'm going to have to escort you to your car. Thank you so much for visiting with me."

And that was it. Conversation over. She didn't say another word until we'd arrived at the front door.

"Thank you so much for stopping by, Dr. Foster."

"Thank you for seeing me, Mrs. Zocci. May I contact you again?"

"I don't think that would be a good idea. My husband—"

"Is suing me," I said.

"I think it's best he doesn't know we've spoken."

"I'll leave my number anyway. In case you think of anything you'd like to discuss with me." I wrote my cell number on the back of my business card. "I'm staying at the Best Mid-Western downtown. In the city. I'll be leaving in the morning."

She held out her tiny little hand and took my card. "Good night, Dr. Foster."

"Good night."

I got in my car and circled around the driveway, watching her swing the enormous door shut, closing herself into that cavernous cathedral of a house.

As I wound down the dark, half-mile ribbon snaking through the trees, I saw a pair of headlights stop on the road, the gate swinging open to let the car through.

The car eased through the gate and made its way straight toward me. I couldn't see anything but the headlights. The road was too dark to make out the outline of the car. I slowed down and briefly considered scooting off the side of the road into the trees and turning off my headlights. As though I could make myself invisible. It was a ludicrous thought.

The road was too narrow to turn around, and my headlights had surely been as visible to the occupant of that car as the other's had been to me. There was no place to go but forward.

As the car neared mine, I felt my heart miss a beat. It was the long black Mercedes from the Vendome. The car that Joe Zocci had driven off in.

The windows were tinted black, obscuring the interior of

the car. But I knew that whoever was in that car would have a big, fat headlighted view of me. Me in my purple Neon. In all my glory.

The car pulled beside me, slowed, and then continued past me without stopping. I downshifted and floored it.

Once on the road, the gate swinging slowly shut behind me, I barreled down Lakeside toward the lights of Highland Park, somehow finding comfort in the idea of witnesses. Surely Joseph Zocci wouldn't come after me if I was surrounded by his neighbors.

As I neared the lights of town, a police cruiser passed me slowly. I hoped that Zocci hadn't already gotten to the local police. I felt conspicuous. I envisioned the car flipping on red and blue lights, blocking my exit, an officer hopping out, gun drawn.

None of that happened. The cruiser passed me without pause.

I took the opportunity to beat it out of Highland Park. I wanted to get out of Chicago, in fact. Whatever I'd hoped to accomplish, I was convinced I'd failed thoroughly. And I was just as thoroughly out of ideas. I'd danced in the face of danger long enough.

I stopped to fill up the car with gas, got myself a cup of decaf tea, and then headed back into the city, back to my crummy, haunted hotel room. I'd try to steal myself some sleep, ferreting out some rest for my addled, stressed-out mind.

And then I intended to get on the plane and get myself back to Texas where I belonged.

25

~

MY ROOM AT THE BEST MID-WESTERN was just
as I'd left it, untouched by the healing hands of housekeeping.
Sheets were still rumpled. Pillows awry. The shower curtain had
finally been removed but not yet replaced. Someone had left a
pile of folded towels, a set of hotel toiletries, and a fresh roll of
toilet paper just inside my door.

My heart sank. This day had shed the last of its appeal. My
give-a-hooter was officially broken. All I wanted was out.

I carried in my pile of fresh towels and slung them onto the
foot of the unmade bed, then gathered the used towels as I
walked around the room and hurled them in a pile by the front
door.

I picked up the phone and called American Airlines.
Tomorrow's flights were full, but I could fly standby in the
morning for a fifty dollar fee. I gave the rep my credit card
number and prayed that a seat would open.

The hotel's bath gel, a noxious vanilla-scented concoction,
sounded better to me than anything I'd experienced all day, my
standards were so low. So I filled the tub, emptied the tiny bottle
into the warm running water, and sank myself into the suds.

My temples throbbed. My body ached. My mind reeled. I practiced deep breathing and prayed to all three members of the Trinity, covering my bases by hitting the Father, Son, and Holy Ghost in quick succession. I needed relief. Surely the Lord could see that. Maybe I could get it by knocking hard on all three doors.

My headache was just about gone when I was jolted out of my near-coma by a thunderous knock on the door.

Cursing does not come naturally to me. I'm not good at it, and the words take on a strange, tinny timbre as they pass my lips. But on this occasion, I made a good faith effort. I cussed a streak as I wrapped a tiny, thin hotel towel around my slippery body and stomped to the door. I hooked the inside safety latch, opened the door, and peered through the crack.

I expected hotel staff. Someone bearing a replacement shower curtain. Someone who would see the distress on my face and feel appropriately guilty for failing to properly service my room.

What I got instead was the Chicago Police Department.

"Officer Pruitt. CPD," the man said. "Looking for a Mr. Dylan Foster."

"Mister?"

"Dylan Foster."

"Dylan Foster is a woman. Ms. Dylan Foster. Or Doctor. That works too. Either one."

"Okay, Missus. Have you seen her?"

"How much more do you want to see? I'm standing here in a towel."

Officer Pruitt clearly wasn't burning up the Bell curve on his IQ test. "You're Dylan Foster?"

"Yes," I said slowly. "I'm Dylan Foster."

"You are under arrest."

More cussing. Mentally this time. I coached myself to keep my composure. Hysterics would only make the situation worse.

"On what charge?" I asked.

"Trespassing."

Rats.

"Breaking and entering."

Cuss, cuss, cuss.

"Assault and battery."

Whoa. I tried to remain calm.

"Who did I allegedly," I dragged the word out, "assault and batter?"

"Mariann Zocci." Officer Pruitt pulled his cuffs off his belt, suddenly all business. "You'll have to come with me."

"Mariann Zocci was assaulted?"

"Mrs. Foster, I need you to cooperate. Would you like me to call for a female officer?"

"Is she okay?"

"Mrs. Foster, how much time do you need to prepare for your departure?"

I stammered. "What do I…? Do I leave my stuff? Should I pack?"

"I'll need you to dress for departure, Mrs. Foster. Would you like me to call for a female officer?"

"No. I just need a few minutes." I started to close the door.

Officer Pruitt shoved his foot into the doorway. "I'm afraid I can't leave you unattended, Mrs. Foster."

"You mean you need to watch me dress?"

"Afraid so, ma'am."

"I'd like you to call for a female officer."

"Will do."

He reached for his belt and pulled out what looked like a walkie-talkie. The kind my brother and I played with when we were kids. Only this one was big and black and official-looking. He asked dispatch for a female officer, specifying the hotel name, address, and room number, adding that, "the suspect is cooperative but is unclothed."

Great. Let's advertise and see if we can draw a crowd.

He disconnected the call and stared at me. Officer Pruitt clearly had no intention of letting me out of his sight.

"What happened to Mariann Zocci?"

"You have the right to remain silent."

"Was she badly injured?"

"If you choose to forego that right, anything you say can and will be used against you."

"Is she okay?"

"You have the right to an attorney."

"You're not going to tell me anything, are you?"

"If you cannot afford an attorney, one will be appointed for you."

"Is she in the hospital?"

He stared at me.

I tightened my towel and stared back.

We stood like that, staring at each other until the female officer arrived.

She had a peppermint-red hairdo, pink shimmery lipstick (certainly non-regulation), and a big black handgun strapped to her belt. I was afraid of her.

"Officer," she said to Officer Pruitt.

"Officer," he said back. "Mrs. Foster would like a female officer to chaperone her preparation for departure."

"Mrs. Foster," she said to me.

"Ms.," I said.

"Ms.," she said. "Please unlatch the door so I can step inside."

She followed me inside and shut the door behind us.

"Do you have a name?" I asked. It seemed a fair request for such an intimate experience.

"Officer Simon," she said. "I know this is awkward."

No kidding.

"But if you'll just dress quickly, we can get you down to the station and get this over with."

I turned my back to her and reached for my suitcase, fishing around for some clean clothes.

She turned aside discreetly as I dressed.

"I don't understand," I said. "What's going to happen? Where are you taking me?"

"County lockup," she said. "You'll be processed there, arraigned in the morning, and then assigned to a cell."

"I'm going to jail?" I shoved my legs into a pair of jeans. How did one dress for jail? Comfort seemed a priority, so I reached for a sweatshirt. "But I didn't do anything. I'm innocent."

"Everyone's innocent, honey."

"Can you tell me what happened to Mariann Zocci?"

"Who is Mariann Zocci?"

"The woman I didn't assault and batter."

"I have no information, Ms. Foster. I'm just here to assist in your arrest."

Assist in my arrest. Like she was doing me a favor.

"What should I do with my stuff? I'm supposed to check out in the morning."

"I suggest you leave it and have someone pick it up."

"I don't know anyone in Chicago," I said.

"I'm very sorry, ma'am."

The Chicago Police Department wasn't interested in my problems, apparently. And I was going to jail. Alone. For something I didn't do. In a city where I knew no one.

And Mariann Zocci had been assaulted and battered.

"Can I make a phone call?" I asked.

"Not until you're processed."

"Look. You seem like a nice enough person. I'm asking for a break here. I'm not a criminal. I've never done anything wrong in my entire life. Can I just please make a call? One?"

She looked at me, considering my plight. Surely she'd heard this a thousand times. For some reason, still unknown to me, she relented.

"Hurry it up," she said.

I raced for my phone and dialed Liz Zocci. It was after midnight. She answered on the second ring. Maybe it was true that mothers never sleep.

"Hello?"

"Liz. Dylan Foster."

She didn't seem at all fazed. As though we were old friends and I always called her at 12:15 in the morning.

"Dylan. How are you?"

"Have you heard from Mariann?"

"No. How did it go?"

"Fine. But I think she's been beaten. I'm being arrested for assault."

"You assaulted her?"

"Of course not. I'm just being arrested for it."

"Did Joe come home while you were there?"

"I think so. As I was leaving," I said. "Can you find out what happened to her? Someone needs to check on her."

"Where are they taking you?"

I covered the phone and spoke to Officer Simon. "Where are you taking me?"

"Cook County lockup. Downtown." She recited the address, which I repeated to Liz.

"Is this your one phone call?" Liz asked me.

"I don't think so. I think I get an official one later."

"Don't make your phone call until morning. You may need to save it for an attorney. I'll try to find out what happened and let you know. Maybe they'll put me through to you."

"Thanks, Liz."

"And Dylan?"

"Yes?"

"Christine woke me up to pray for you tonight."

"Good. I need it."

"Obviously."

We hung up. I was ready. As ready as I was going to get, anyway. I hoped silently that no press had gotten wind that Mariann Zocci, the matriarch of a prominent Chicago family, had been beaten. I didn't need any pictures of myself splashed on the front page of the *Tribune*. Not without mascara or a lawyer.

Officer Simon escorted me to the police cruiser. Officer Pruitt cuffed me, which ranked right up there as one of the most humiliating experiences of my life. As I was loaded into the backseat, he put his hand on the top of my head, helping me duck into the car. Just like on TV.

The ride to county lockup was depressingly short, my sense of dread accelerating the entire process to warp speed.

Within a span of a half hour, I'd been booked, photographed, fingerprinted, and escorted into a holding cell that housed twenty other women.

Jail, it turns out, is an efficient leveler. The luxury of self-righteousness became immediately unavailable to me.

Most of my cellmates were clothed, shall we say, less modestly than I. And were surely due some grace from the Almighty, experienced sinners that they were. For once in my life, any sense of safe superiority I'd cultivated with good behavior and higher education fled my heart entirely. I was one of them.

We were all in the pokey. Together. Twenty pathetic examples of miserable, needy humanity.

I found myself a spot on the floor—a space relatively clean of urine and sputum—and curled myself into a ball, hugging my shins, my chin on my knees.

If I were even a moderately decent Christian, I would have sung praises to the Lord, like a real disciple. Or witnessed to my jailers like Paul. Or forgiven my accusers like Jesus Himself.

What I did instead was cry. And wallow in fear and self-pity. I had never felt so alone in my entire life.

I watched the clock on the hallway wall tick off a second at a time, until 2:16 a.m., when one of my jailers approached my communal cage.

"Foster?" he said loudly.

I looked up. "I'm Foster."

"Phone call."

The few women in the holding cell who were still awake taunted me, mainly out of jealousy, I guess. A 2:00 a.m. phone call could only be good news.

I trotted down the hall after the female officer, who was businesslike and efficient. She never once looked at me, and I'm sure if asked to describe me, would not have been able to. I was a nonperson to her. One of the inmates. Someone to be herded and kept under control.

She stepped aside as a door opened electronically. A bank of black dial phones was attached to a wall in the otherwise empty room.

"Five minutes," she said.

I picked up one of the phones. "Dylan Foster."

"It's Liz."

"Thank God. I'm so glad to hear your voice. How's Mariann?"

"Not too good," she said. "She's at Chicago Memorial."

"She's in the hospital?"

"Broken arm, fractured eye socket. Multiple contusions."

The breath came out of me.

"Dylan? Are you still there?"

"Yeah. I'm just…stunned."

"Don't be. It's not the first time."

"Did you talk to her?" I asked.

"Joe did it."

"She told you that?"

"Not in so many words."

"Was he standing right there?"

"I couldn't tell. I think so."

I didn't know what to say.

"Can you make it through the night?" she asked.

"Of course."

"I can get you out in the morning."

"I can't ask you to do that," I said, though I desperately wanted to ask her to do that.

"You didn't ask. I offered."

"Thank you."

"I'll see you in the morning," she said.

I hung up the phone and knocked on the steel door. My jailer pressed a button, motioned for me to step into the hall, and escorted me back to the cell.

~

26

No ANGEL FLUNG OPEN the doors of Cook County lockup that night. Maybe that's because I wasn't doing the singing and praising required to precipitate such a miracle. As it was, though, I spent the next miserable hours curled on the floor of that holding cell, wondering where God had run off to. Where had He been when Joe Zocci was knocking his wife around? And why was He letting them blame me for it? Just what was He thinking abandoning me like this?

I must have dozed, because I spent the rest of the night in the company of Peter Terry. My first encounter with him since the library. He hunted me through a rapid, violent series of dreams.

In one, Mariann Zocci stood beside me, tapping me awake, urgent with something to say. Peter Terry arrived and grabbed her by the ankles, swinging her around by her feet, smashing her head into a telephone pole.

Then Gavin was standing in a creek, watching the sun rise. Peter Terry eviscerated him. Literally. Stem to stern. And hung his mangled body by the neck from a shower curtain rod.

In another, Peter Terry sat beside my mother's hospital bed, holding her hand and gradually squeezing the life out of her, her face purpling as she gasped for breath.

And finally, Peter Terry, his white skin glistening, whispered into a blindfolded Erik Zocci's ear, leading him slowly, a step at a time, to the brink, shoving him over the edge of a cliff and laughing hysterically as the boy hurtled toward oblivion.

I awoke with my hands clammy, my heart pounding. Wishing for the simple nuisance of flies instead of this new plague of bizarre, terrifying images.

Weak morning light at last squeezed through the dirty wire mesh windows, rousing my cellmates one by one. As the cell slowly shook awake, communal toilets were utilized and sometimes flushed. Faucets were turned on at the trough along the wall. Women stood in front of the sinks and brushed their teeth with fingers. I stayed in my corner, huddling alone, shivering.

Occasionally a guard would rattle the cell door and call out a name, and the corresponding inmate would shuffle out behind her. These inmates did not return. Maybe they'd been assigned to cells. Maybe they'd been released. I didn't know.

At five of nine, a burly wrestler of a guard shouted "Foster!" I jumped to my feet and hustled out of there, following her down a series of desolate hallways.

My destination, it turned out, was the county courthouse. For my arraignment.

I had no attorney. I'd never made my one phone call. Never been offered the opportunity, as a matter of fact. So I stood in front of the judge alone, the court room buzzing around me, a hive of disinterested parties, going about their business. Oblivious to my desperate plight.

The judge looked at me over her glasses. "You have no representation?"

"No ma'am."

"Can you afford an attorney?"

I didn't quite know how to answer that. "It depends on what you mean by afford."

"Don't be smart with me, Ms. Foster." She scanned the courtroom and chose an attorney, pointing for the man to come to the bench. A skinny black man in a badly fitting suit trotted up to the defense table with his briefcase.

"You'll be representing Ms. Foster for the purposes of this arraignment," the judge said to him. "How does your client plead?"

I stood there mutely, convinced for once of the wisdom of keeping my mouth shut.

"Absolutely not guilty, your honor," the man said.

"Calm down. Bail?" said the judge.

"The state requests that bail be denied," came a voice from the other side of the aisle. I peeked around my lawyer to see yet another badly suited man standing behind the prosecutor's table.

"On what grounds?" asked the judge.

"The defendant brutally assaulted one of Chicago's most prominent citizens, a frail, defenseless elderly woman. Ms. Foster is not from the area and has no family here. She's clearly a flight risk. And an imminent danger to society."

"Counsel?" the judge said to my attorney, whose name I had never heard.

"Uh," he said, "we deny all that. Yes. We do." He leaned over to me. "You going to show up for trial?"

"Yes," I whispered back.

He looked at the judge. "We request the defendant be released. Right away."

"You want O.R.?" said the judge.

"Yes. O.R., that's what we want," he said.

"You want the defendant released on her own recognizance?" she said.

"Yes," my attorney said confidently.

I wasn't feeling too confident about my attorney.

"The people object to that," the prosecutor said.

"Bail is set at two hundred thousand dollars." The judge rapped her gavel, dismissing us all without another glance. "Next case."

My attorney turned to me, his face seeming familiar suddenly, in some distant sort of way. "I'll come see you later today," he said. "Don't talk to anyone."

"Okay," I said.

He picked up his briefcase and rushed off. And I was alone again. The entire procedure had taken less than five minutes.

As the guard turned me toward the door to escort me back to jail, I caught a glimpse of Joseph Zocci sitting alone in the back of the courtroom. Just looking at me. No expression. No movement. Like a reptile. Waiting.

The guard led me out of the courtroom and through another maze of hallways, doors slamming open and closed as we walked through them. Clanging in my ears. My head pounded. I felt weak. I was hungry and exhausted.

A final door shoved itself open and I walked into a cell. Six feet by ten—I know because I paced that route back and forth like a cat—with two bunks, a sink, and a toilet. The other bunk was empty, which meant I had my own room. My first break in twelve hours.

I alternated between pacing my cell and sitting on my cot trying to figure out what to do.

Lunch arrived, a single slice of fatty ham on white bread, a smeared dot of yellow mustard staining the bread and reminding me of the smiley-face flag on my rental car. A plastic cup of mushy fruit cocktail sat next to the sandwich, along with a bite-size 3 Musketeers bar and a carton of skim milk. I picked at it and paced some more.

Still I had made no phone call. I had not heard from Liz Zocci. Or my nameless attorney.

With all that time on my hands, I contemplated my situation, trying to fit the pieces together. It was like a puzzle with no solution. As though someone had thrown together the oddly shaped pieces of a dozen different jigsawed images.

If I'd had pen and paper, I would've tried to draw it all out, inking connections onto the page as well as into my thoughts. But since I had neither, I had to make do with my brain alone, which was filled with static and fogged by fatigue.

The last two days had been packed with characters and events. As I catalogued it all—suicides and shower curtains, my adventures at the Vendome, the disparate members of the Zocci clan—it occurred to me that I hadn't yet finished my conversation with Mariann Zocci. I hadn't asked her about Erik's suicide note. Also, she'd refused to talk to me about Joe Zocci's cruelty, which seemed to me central to the entire mystery. And she'd refused to talk about her first son's death. Little Joseph Jr. The lost boy.

I must have fallen asleep with my head spinning like that, for I dreamed again. This time Peter Terry, instead of delighting in his cruel mischief, was wary. Restrained. In the shadows behind him, a sinewy dark figure watched him. Peter Terry seemed to fear this figure, darting away from it, looking over his shoulder as he ran away.

The jangle of metal jolted me awake. I opened my eyes to see the guard who had escorted me to court.

"You made bail," she said without animation. "Congratulations."

I stood up and followed her. I was getting used to following people down hallways.

She stayed with me as my captors processed my release. There were several pages of documents for my signature, verifying my address in Dallas, promising that I'd show up for trial. The last piece of paper said I'd been treated well and that my rights had been respected. I signed.

The guard led me through a swinging door and then walked away wordlessly.

A child's voice shouted my name.

"Miss Dylan!"

I scanned the room. It was Punkin, standing there all dressed in pink, holding her mother's hand.

She ran over to me and hugged my legs. I thought my heart was going to explode. Nothing ever felt so good to me as that nutty little kid squeezing my knees.

Liz walked over behind her.

"Okay, Punkin," she said. "You don't need to tackle her."

"I prayed for you," Punkin said to me, releasing my legs and gazing up at me.

"I know, sweetie. I could tell."

"Did my angel come?"

"I don't think so."

Her face fell. "He said he would."

"I'm sure he meant to," I said. "Maybe you're my angel."

"No, silly-bean! He looks like Mr. Martin."

I knew better than to argue that point.

Liz grabbed her hand and looked at me. "You ready to go?"

"You have no idea," I answered. "Thank you so much for coming for me. I'm so grateful. I feel like I should mow your lawn for the rest of my life or something."

We made our way out of the courthouse and began the walk

to the car, the late afternoon sun slanting warm against my face.

"Did you have to post bail?" I asked, guilt already sinking in on me.

"It was kind of an adventure," Liz said, her eyes wide. "Practice for my boys some day, I'm sure, the little hoodlums. This one," she looked down at Christine, "I'm not too worried about."

If my sketchy knowledge of legal procedures was accurate, I now owed Liz Zocci twenty thousand dollars. Ten percent of my bail money, which had been posted as a bond. And about a million percent of my meager self-worth.

I couldn't even let myself think about that.

"How's Mariann?" I asked.

"She's out. They released her this morning."

"Did she go home?"

"She checked into the Four Seasons."

"Not the Vendome."

"I don't think she'll ever go back to the Vendome," she said.

"Does Joe know where she is?"

"I don't think she told him. I drove her there myself."

We loaded into her Suburban, Liz buckling Christine into her car seat while I flicked Cheerios off the passenger seat and settled myself in. I had never been so happy in my life. A jailbird. Out on bail. Intoxicated by the luxury of riding in a car without handcuffs on.

"Where to?" Liz asked.

"My hotel." I gave her the cross streets. I had no idea where we were. "If I don't take a shower and brush my teeth, I'm going to come out of my skin."

"You didn't take a toothbrush with you?" She was incredulous.

"I lost my ability to plan ahead when the cops showed up at my door. I panicked."

She nodded. "I could see that. Still…no toothbrush."

"No kidding." I waited a minute. "Do you think Mariann would talk to me again?"

"She's in pretty bad shape."

"I know."

I waited. We both knew I was desperate.

"I'll call her while you're in the shower," she said.

We finished the drive in silence, Christine singing gaily to herself in the backseat.

At the Best Mid-Western, while Liz and Christine waited next door at Denny's, I took a hot shower behind a newly installed plastic shower curtain, putting myself back together slowly, luxuriating in every detail of the experience. Clean towels. A mirror. A blow dryer. Mascara. Astonishing wealth to me now.

Once I was showered and dressed, I flew around the room, shoving my things into a suitcase. Whatever the rest of this day brought, there was no way I was spending another night at the Downtown Chicago Best Mid-Western. Not only did the place have bad mojo for me, but Joseph Zocci, the Chicago Police Department, and Peter Terry had all managed to find me. It was time to move.

I locked my stuff in the Neon, checked out of my room, walked next door, and slid into the booth with Liz and Christine. They were sharing French fries and a chocolate shake. Christine was dipping the fries in the shake and drinking her ketchup with a straw.

I ordered a club sandwich and a Dr. Pepper, both of which I inhaled. Christine chattered to herself and colored on the back of a place mat while Liz and I talked.

"I talked to Mariann," Liz said. "She said she'll see you. She didn't sound too good. She's in a lot of pain."

"Thank you for asking her," I said.

I waited a minute and then asked the question that was tugging at me. "Why are you helping me?"

Liz jerked her head over to her daughter. "My kid has good instincts. It was her idea."

"Thank you for posting bail. I don't know when I'll be able to pay you back."

"Don't worry about it," she said. "They return the bond money if you come back for trial. So I'm in good shape. Unless you move to Mexico or something."

Little did she know. Mexico was sounding pretty good to me right about now.

"What's Mexico?" Christine asked.

"It's a place with blue sky and a beach," Liz said. "Like Lake Michigan but warmer."

Christine started drawing yellow sand and a blue sky.

"Did Mariann tell you anything?" I asked.

"She told me everything."

"Was it who we thought?" I didn't want to be too specific in front of Christine.

"Of course."

"Will she leave?"

"I doubt it."

We sat silently for a minute, listening to Christine hum. She ran out of paper, so her mother handed her another kids' menu.

"Has he done this before?" I asked Liz.

"Many times. But I've never seen it this bad."

"Grandpa's mean," Christine said, without looking up.

So much for shielding her from the brutal truth.

Liz smiled at me. "I told you. Good instincts."

I watched Christine choose a brown crayon. She drew an awkward, thin stick figure, festooning it with golden wings and a silver halo.

"Mommy, how do you spell my angel's name? I can't remember."

Liz said the letters slowly as Christine drew them.

I watched her scrawl the name awkwardly in purple: E–A–R–L

27

~

L IZ GAVE ME MARIANN'S room number and hugged me good-bye, Christine reminding me once again that her angel looked like Mr. Martin and would I come see her tomorrow. I promised her I'd try.

I couldn't decide where to go first, the Four Seasons to talk to Mariann Zocci or to the Vendome to hunt down Earl, the porter who might really be an angel, or perhaps a defense attorney. I eventually opted for the Four Seasons, reasoning that even though Earl had said he worked nights, angels surely followed no regular schedule. He, after all, needed no sleep, at least as far as I knew about angels.

I kept a wary eye out as I drove to the hotel, half expecting Joseph Zocci's black Mercedes to shadow me.

In the lobby of the Four Seasons, I passed two members of the Dallas Mavericks basketball team drinking martinis in the hotel bar, a man wearing silk pajamas and slippers asking the concierge for pipe tobacco, and a woman carrying a terrier that was wearing a little red doggie sweater. But no Joseph Zocci. The coast seemed clear.

Another brass elevator. Another silent ride to another

tasteful hotel hallway. And then I was standing in front of Mariann Zocci's door.

I hesitated before I knocked, gathering my thoughts as well as my resolve. I wanted to make sure this time that I asked everything that needed asking.

My knuckles barely made a sound as I rapped on the heavy door. I wasn't sure if the knock would even be audible from inside the room. But the door swung open in a minute, and I was looking at a shattered version of the woman I'd met the day before.

The entire right side of her face was the color of Christine's favorite crayon, puffy and shiny as an eggplant. Her right eye was swollen shut. Her left hand was a matching aubergine, the arm splinted and supported in a black canvas sling. She wore another Chanel sweat suit. Black this time. As though she had finally gone into mourning.

"Good evening, Dr. Foster," she said, as though nothing at all were unusual about her appearance.

"Hello, Mrs. Zocci," I replied. "Thank you for seeing me again."

"Please come in."

She moved slowly, painfully, as I followed her into her suite. I stifled the urge to help her. As she passed each piece of furniture, she steadied herself with her good hand, reacquiring a modicum of balance so she could move again.

We arrived at last at a formal seating area. She eased herself into a wing chair, raised her chin, and met my eyes.

"What did you want to speak to me about, Dr. Foster?"

"I meant to ask you a few things. About Erik." I hesitated, unable to speak past the obvious legacy of violence on her face. "Are you sure you're up to this?" I asked awkwardly.

She smiled weakly and nodded, a tear leaking out of the corner of her good eye.

"I'm so sorry, Mrs. Zocci. That he's done this to you."

She shook her head and cried silently.

I leapt out of my chair and brought tissues back from the bathroom. It's a therapist reflex. Always hand your crying client a tissue. It conveys sympathy without being invasive.

She accepted my offering silently, dabbing at her eye as I took my seat again.

"I won't press charges. Against you, I mean." She blew her nose daintily. "Joe told them it was you."

"I figured."

"I'm very sorry," she said. "Liz tells me you spent the night in jail."

"It wasn't so bad." This broken woman wasn't getting a finger wag out of me. Not tonight, anyway, sitting there looking like that.

"I really am very sorry," she said. "I'll speak to the detective tomorrow morning."

"Are you going to tell them?" I asked gently. "About Joe?"

Her shoulders shook with noiseless sobs. "I don't think I can."

I'd worked with enough battered women to know that trying to coerce her wouldn't do a bit of good. After all, she'd been letting him beat her for almost forty years.

"Do your children know about this?" I asked.

"They know. They've always known."

I waited for her to continue.

"He came back from Vietnam a very angry man. So angry."

"He wasn't like that before he went?"

"I don't know, really," she said. "The truth is, I didn't know him very well when I married him. He was just so dynamic. So charming and handsome. And powerful. I was young. Naïve. I let myself be swept away by him. I didn't know."

"You got more than you bargained for, didn't you?" I asked.

"That's putting it mildly."

"How old were you?"

"Nineteen. And such a child. I had been very sheltered. My family—my father, especially—was very protective."

"When did he hit you the first time?" I asked. I knew I was pressing. I longed for a cup of tea and a spoon as my therapist posture took over.

"The night Joey was conceived," she said, staring at her hands, watching herself twist and untwist her tissue. "We'd had a fight. He was very angry, and I always felt so guilty when he got angry. He hit me on the back of the head. With his belt. I'll never forget the sound the belt buckle made, like being inside a bell tower." She reached for another tissue. "And then he— That was the night Joey was conceived."

"Why didn't you leave him? That first night?"

She looked up at me, surprise on her face. "We're Catholic, Dr. Foster."

"What about grace, Mrs. Zocci? Don't Catholics believe in grace? In forgiveness?"

"Yes," she said. "And I forgive him. I always forgive him."

I decided not to fight that one.

"How did Erik feel about his father?"

"Conflicted. Like the rest of us." She shrugged. "He's a very hard man to…"

"Love?"

"I was going to say hate," she said.

Not for me. I was great at hating him. Getting better at it by the minute, in fact.

"Did Erik mention his father in his suicide note?"

"I wish he'd left one," she said wistfully. "Some words for me. So I could have had some idea of what he was going through."

"He didn't leave a note?" I asked. "I'd been told that he'd specifically implicated me. That his note was the basis for the lawsuit against me."

"If there was a note, Dr. Foster, I have no knowledge of it. I never saw it."

I felt my heart quicken. "Was there an autopsy?"

"I believe there was. I never asked about it." She shuddered, her eyes glazing, as though she'd suddenly gone somewhere else. Someplace terrible. "I can't bear to think of it. To think of them cutting my boy like that."

"You said Erik didn't know how his brother died. Joe Jr."

"No one knows," she said. "No one has ever known." She looked at me again, suddenly coming back into the room. "I'd like to know how you found out."

"I read it in the archives of the *Tribune*."

"It was so long ago."

"It was just a small article. Printed the day after he fell, I think."

"What did it say?"

"Nothing, really. Just that he fell from the twelfth floor of the Vendome."

"Did the article mention Joe?"

"I'm not sure," I said. "Why?"

"I just wondered."

Her manner was such a strange, almost mystical combination of forthrightness and mystery. I couldn't quite seem to wend my way to the heart of the truth with her.

"Why do you think Erik chose to kill himself that way? By jumping from the same floor of the same hotel? How could he not have known?"

"I wouldn't know, Dr. Foster."

"Was it the same room?"

"I couldn't say."

I looked at her for a moment, neither of us saying anything.

"Is there something you're not telling me?" I asked at last.

She squared her chin, a small gesture of defiance. "There's much I'm not telling you, Dr. Foster."

"Are you lying to me?"

She considered my question. "More to myself, probably. You have to lie to yourself a lot when you're in a situation like mine."

I accepted her words, silently wondering which situation, exactly, she meant.

"You said Erik mentioned the white man to you."

"He believed he was a demon," she said.

"Okay. Demon. Did you believe him?"

"Of course."

"You believe in demons, then?"

"Of course," she said. "Don't you, Dr. Foster? Aren't you, as you said, a woman of faith?"

"I am." So far, anyway. "Have you ever seen him?"

"Erik's demon?"

"Yes."

"Demons needn't bother with me, Dr. Foster. I defeated myself long ago."

I could feel seeds of anger sprouting in me, like weeds among the compassion she clearly needed. Anger and pity. All at once. She *had* defeated herself. The mottled battle-plan was traced in bruises across her face. It was infuriating to watch. And yet I had no experience with the kind of brutal intimidation she faced every day. I couldn't possibly understand the battles being waged in the deepest part of her soul.

"Was there anything else you wanted to say to me, Dr. Foster?"

"Probably. But nothing I can think of now."

"Then would you mind excusing me?" she said. "I'm very tired. I'd like to get some rest."

She pushed herself up out of her chair with her good hand, barely maintaining her balance.

I stood and reached to help her, out of reflex, really. She submitted to the assistance wordlessly, a strange, newfound intimacy passing unspoken between us.

"Can I do anything for you before I leave?" I asked.

"If you could get my pain medication from the bathroom. And bring me a glass of water."

She made her way slowly to the bedroom while I followed behind her, watching her carefully to steady her if she fell. We parted at the door to the bedroom.

I flipped on the light in the bathroom and spotted the pill bottle on the marble countertop. I checked the label. The prescription was a refill. For thirty forty-milligram tablets of OxyContin, one of the more potent narcotic pain relievers.

I was surprised to see such a high dosage prescribed for such a tiny woman. And I was surprised to see it written as a refill. OxyContin was so addictive that prescribing physicians recommended patients flush the unused pills down the toilet when the medication was no longer needed. I knew, because we dealt with this addiction commonly at the clinic. It was the cachet drug of choice among prescription drug junkies.

When I emerged from the bathroom, Mariann was perched on the edge of the bed, her feet suspended above the floor like a child's. I took her the pills and fixed her a glass of ice water.

"You should eat something with this medication," I said. "Otherwise, you're likely to get nauseous."

"I've taken it before. I'll have room service send something up."

I went to the living room and retrieved my bag, pulling out

Erik's journal. I returned to the bedroom and handed the journal to her.

"You said you wanted to know what he'd been going through," I said. "I found this a few days ago. In his dorm room."

She reached for it with one of her tiny, spidery hands, tears pooling in her one open eye.

"His last entry is from May of his freshman year," I said. "He doesn't mention hurting himself. It won't answer that question for either of us."

She looked up at me, fear furrowing her brow. I knew she was afraid of what she would find between those pages. "You've read it?"

I nodded. "I would have given it to you last night. I wasn't sure whether you would want to see it. It's a tough read."

"He mentions me?"

"Mostly his father," I said. "And his pain for you."

She gripped the book in both hands.

"Thank you, Dr. Foster. I'm so grateful."

I didn't know how long that gratitude would hold. Erik's journal clanged with reverberations from her choices.

We said our good-byes. I thanked her again for talking to me and then let myself out, leaving her sitting alone on the edge of the bed.

28

~

As I left the Four Seasons, the sky coloring itself in the flaming oranges of a pollution-tinted sunset, I began to think for the first time that day about the night ahead of me. It dawned on me that I had no place to stay. I'd checked out of the Best Mid-Western earlier that afternoon. Once again, I was operating in a plan-free zone.

I couldn't shake the urge to get out of Chicago entirely. It was Thursday evening. I'd planned on leaving for home Friday afternoon anyway. I didn't want to check into another hotel. The Neon's bucket seats sounded like a pretty terrible option, especially on the streets of Chicago. I'd already had more trouble than I could handle in this town. I wanted to go home.

A quick phone call to American Airlines brought good news. The last run to Dallas tonight had seats available. I changed my ticket, biting the bullet on the transfer fee.

I'd promised Christine Zocci I'd try to see her tomorrow. I called her instead. We had a brief, Punkin-like conversation.

"Why?" she asked.

"I need to go back to where I live."

"But why?"

"I miss sleeping in my own house."

"Where is it?"

"Dallas."

"Is Dallas like Mexico?"

I smiled. "Not exactly. More like Chicago. But without the lake."

"When are you coming back?"

"I don't know, sweetie."

"Will you bring me a present?"

"I'm going to be gone for a really long time, honey. But I'll send you a present. I promise."

"Okay."

"Can I talk to your mommy?"

"Okay."

"Christine?"

"What?"

"Don't forget to pray for me."

"Okay." She dropped the phone with a clatter and shouted, "Mommy!"

I was crazy about that kid.

Liz and I had a short conversation. I suggested she check on Mariann tomorrow morning.

"She was in a lot of pain," I said. "Do you know how long she's been taking pain medication?"

"I have no idea. Why?"

"She had a refill prescription, for a very high dose of narcotic. Usually indicates tolerance for the drug built up over time."

"Maybe she's sustained some chronic injuries from Joe," she suggested.

"That could be it. Has anyone heard from him?"

"Andy's going to try to talk to him tomorrow. Try to get him to drop the charges against you."

"Mariann said she would speak to the police in the morning and clear my name. I don't think they can prosecute me if she refuses to press charges."

"All the same, someone needs to call Joe off."

"Wish Andy luck, then. And thank him for me. Maybe you should have Christine put in a good word for him with her angel."

"That's not a bad idea," she said, laughing.

"Listen, I wanted to ask you...do you know anything about how Joe and Mariann's first son died?"

"Not a thing. Only that it was an accident of some sort. No, no, honey. Don't put your finger in there."

Put my finger in where? It took me a minute to realize she was talking to one of the kids.

"No one in this family talks about anything," she said to me.

"Have you ever asked Andy about it?"

"I don't think we've ever talked about it directly, no. Andy's a Zocci, remember? Why?"

"I'm just curious. Would you mind asking him if he knows anything about it?"

"I'll ask him," she said. "He's pretty tender, though. Especially since he just lost another brother. He's the only one left, you know. But I'll ask him."

"One more thing. Do you happen to know if Andy ever saw an autopsy report on Erik?"

"I'm certain he didn't. He would have mentioned it to me."

"Okay. Thanks, Liz."

"Be safe, Dylan."

"I will. And Liz?"

"Yes?"

"I really don't know how to thank you."

"Don't jump bail," she said, cracking herself up. "That will be thanks enough."

"I won't. I'll call you tomorrow from Dallas and check in."

The facade of the Vendome loomed in front of me, daring me to come in. I don't know what I was thinking, marching myself back in there on my way out of town, risking arrest and who knew what else? I'd heard Joseph Zocci instruct Sam Molina to alert hotel security. Knowing Zocci, he'd locked the place up with restraining orders and private security guards as well. But I was hoping no one had circulated a photo of me. Most of the staff, I reasoned, were likely to know me by name only, not by sight.

And I was motivated. I was on the hunt for Mariann Zocci's secret. I was convinced Joseph Zocci had been responsible somehow for the deaths of both sons. That he'd pushed them both, either literally or figuratively, to their deaths. And I was closing in on the final piece of the puzzle. Someone was about to hand me the gavel so I could pronounce judgment on this vicious, horrible man.

So in I went. And this time I went in with a plan.

I bustled through the lobby and headed straight for the elevators behind the concierge desk. The ones that had brought me up from the catacombs.

After riding the elevator down alone, I wandered around the basement for a while, as I'd done before, this time passing numerous black-uniformed hotel staff. I'd brought a notebook. I held it like a badge and tried to look official so no one would stop me and question what I was doing there.

The area I was looking for was fairly deserted, I knew, so I just headed away from the crowd, feeling myself getting closer as the people thinned out. At last, I came upon the right office suite and tried the door.

The suite was locked. I'd figured it would be since Sam Molina had used a security card to gain entry. Molina, I knew, was a day manager. He would be gone by now.

The lights in the suite were on, but it was unpopulated, with the exception of one woman, who looked like she was packing up to leave for the day.

I knocked on the window and waved, a huge, friendly and of course fake, smile on my face.

The woman buzzed me in.

She had a pucker on her like she'd been sucking a lemon. Or, more likely, like her lips had recently been collagen-enhanced. With her stiff helmet of brown hair and a manufactured British accent, she was all business.

"How may I help?" she asked cordially.

"I have an appointment with Sam Molina." I started my mental lie tally. That was one.

"I'm sorry, he's gone for the day. And you are?"

I held out my hand, which she took gingerly. "Darla. Darla Jackson." That was two.

She didn't introduce herself.

"Rats," I said. "I'm so disappointed. Maybe I got my times mixed up."

"Perhaps you should call him in the morning and reschedule," she said.

"Listen, maybe you could help me out. I'm a freelance writer"—three for three—"working on an article about historic downtown hotels. I was supposed to interview Mr. Molina. But you'd probably be able to answer even more of my questions than he would. You're probably the one that really runs the place." I winked at her.

No response.

"You don't happen to have a few minutes to talk with me, do you?" I said. "I know it's an imposition and you're very busy, but it would really help me out. I'm working on a deadline."

She looked at her watch. "I suppose I could spare a moment."

She seated herself behind her desk, indicating I should take one of the wing chairs opposite her.

"I'm doing some background on longtime hotel employees," I said. "You have a porter here, an elderly black gentleman. His first name is Earl. Do you happen to know how long he's been with the Vendome?"

Her brow almost furrowed, but not quite. Botox.

"I don't recall a porter by that name. Are you certain he's with the Vendome? Perhaps one of the other hotels you've researched."

"I think it was the Vendome," I said.

"I'm afraid you must be mistaken. We have no porters on our staff who match your description. Unless he was hired recently."

"No. He's a longtime employee."

"I'm sorry. I don't believe he's with the Vendome," she said.

"Must be my mistake." I could tell I was losing her. "Maybe you could tell me something. You're obviously very professional, very polished. Great at your job."

"Yes?" Her botoxed eyebrows almost raised again.

"What's it like working in management for an iconic hotel like the Vendome? It's gotta be a lot of pressure." I nodded and furrowed my non-botoxed and prematurely aging brow, as though I was sympathetic to the crushing burdens of her job.

"It is an awesome responsibility," she said, nodding her head vigorously. "The entire hotel, every minute detail, from ash trays to zinnias…it all boils down to the manager. He, or she as the case may be, is the captain of the ship."

She'd obviously given this speech before.

"Wow. That's gotta be tough," I said.

"Not if you're properly trained."

"How does that happen? The training, I mean? Do you start out at some other position and then work up?"

"The Vendome is a destination hire," she said. "You come to the Vendome after you've been trained elsewhere. The Vendome is not a hotel where one *learns* one's job. The Vendome is where one *does* one's job."

"Wow." I nodded some more. "How long has Mr. Molina been here?"

"Going on ten years."

"Wow. Long time. As a destination hire, is the Vendome management position one that you keep for a long time?"

"Most people do."

"How about you? How long have you been here?"

"Going on six years."

"And how's it been?"

"Wonderful," she said grandly. "I have no complaints."

"I saw the photos. Past managers?" I gestured behind me at the waiting area. "Can I take a look?"

"Certainly."

She ushered me out, no doubt grateful to get me out of her office. I perused the photos. There were no dates.

"Quite a hall of fame," I said, as if I recognized the names. I chose the one whose photo appeared to have been taken in the Nixon era. Thick-framed glasses, fat polyester tie. The one dressed sort of like Bob Newhart.

"I've heard of this one. McMillan. Wasn't he here just forever?"

"You've done your homework," she said. "Charles McMillan. He was here almost thirty years."

"Ending?"

"1993. The year Sam Molina arrived, as a matter of fact."

"He's sort of legendary," I said, as though I had a clue what I was talking about. I'd lost track of my lies at that point. "Do you happen to know what became of him? Is he still around?"

"He's in a nursing home, I believe."

"Do you happen to know how I could get in touch with him? I'd love to pick his brain."

"Really, Ms…?"

I couldn't remember the name I'd given her. Some presidential name. "Johnson."

Lucky for me, she didn't seem to remember either.

"Ms. Johnson. I wouldn't have any idea. He retired from the Vendome years ago. It's not as though we're socially acquainted."

"Okay. Sure, I understand," I said, making my way toward the exit. I held out my hand. "I really appreciate your time. Thanks so much for talking to me. You've been a big help."

"Certainly," she said.

I bolted out of there, running around madly in the basement maze before I found my elevators.

I left the Vendome for the last time armed with two valuable pieces of information. No, make that three.

One: Earl no more worked at the Vendome than I did. Which made me wonder if angels got a pass on lying, in some sort of sin-free way. Maybe he never told me he worked at the Vendome, but he sure implied it.

Two: Earl was probably Christine's angel. That could be nothing but good news, since he'd cut me a couple of breaks already.

And three: I had learned the name of the man who managed

the Vendome in 1972, the year Joseph Jr. fell from the twelfth-floor balcony.

All I needed to do was find the right Charles McMillan. In three hours. In a city of eight million people.

How hard could that be?

29

WHAT I NEEDED NOW was a good library. I went back to the Loyola campus since I knew where it was, making a beeline toward the reference desk. I skipped the computer station and went straight to the librarian. He was paunchy and balding and looked bored—three facts that could only work in my favor.

"Hi. I'm a visiting scholar"—sort of a lie, but maybe it would pass the Earl test—"and I'm in a hurry trying to meet a deadline. I have a weird little problem I'm hoping you could help me with."

He picked up a pen and pad of paper. "Shoot," he said.

"Guy named Charles McMillan. Manager of the Vendome in 1972. Need to find him. I think he's in a nursing home now."

He scribbled all this down. "M–c or M–a–c?"

"M–c."

"Let's start with the phone book."

He led me toward the bank of computers.

"But he's in a nursing home. He won't have a listing."

"If he's old enough to be in a nursing home, he's probably got a wife whose phone is still listed under Mr. and Mrs. Or her name will be Gladys or something."

"Genius man."

"Thank you."

He tapped out a white pages search and came up with seven Mr. and Mrs. McMillans, one Shirley, one Edna, and a Pearl. And, to my surprise, only one Charles.

"What year did you say?"

"1972."

He scanned the addresses, pointing at the screen. "These two are in the grandma-house areas of town. Old houses, little. Built in the 1950s when the war brides were having their babies and no one minded five people sharing one bathroom. I'd start with those."

He printed the page for me.

"No cell phone use in the library. Phone booths in the lobby."

I was in awe. And feeling lucky. The entire search had taken two minutes.

I snatched the paper from his hand. "Thanks," I said, already turning for the lobby.

"No problem," he said.

I hadn't turned on my cell phone in twenty-four hours. They'd taken it away from me in jail, of course, and since then I just hadn't wanted to deal with it. Every time that phone rang, it seemed to bring bad news.

Sure enough, when I turned it on, the little voice mail icon beeped immediately. I didn't even want to contemplate the contents of those messages. I would deal with that later.

It was supper time, so I felt I had a good chance of catching these folks at home. I dialed the numbers, one by one, and got a hit on call number four.

"Why yes," she answered. She actually sounded delighted to be asked. "He was manager there. For almost thirty years."

I could barely contain my excitement. I told my lie about being a freelance writer and asked if she minded if I tracked him down at the nursing home.

"Oh, he would be so excited," she said. "He loves talking about his work. It's one of the few things that gives him pleasure."

"I don't know quite how to ask this, but what sort of shape is he in? I mean, will he be able to answer my questions?"

"Well, honey, it depends on the time of day. He's better in the morning."

"I was thinking of tonight."

"That depends on the pudding."

"Pardon?"

"If they have tapioca pudding, he seems to settle down. He loves his tapioca."

"So tapioca pudding makes him more lucid?" I'd never heard of the healing qualities of tapioca. Someone should alert the media.

"I think it just gives him a little something to look forward to. Seems to ease him."

She gave me the name and address of the nursing home.

"Could you send me a copy of the article when you've finished it?" she asked.

What a sweet woman. I hate lying to sweet people.

"Sure," I said, feeling like a heel. "I'd be glad to. But there's a chance it won't get published."

"Well, either way, I'd just like to see it. Charles was very proud of his work at the Vendome."

"I'll see to it that you get a copy."

What sort of person was I, anyway? I should have just told her the truth. She would have helped me. But of course, I couldn't have known that when she answered the phone. And it was far too late to do a take back. I'd have to write her a note and confess after I got home.

It took me a while to get my bearings, but I found the neighborhood without too much trouble, about twenty minutes away from Loyola. I stopped at the grocery store and bought four lunch-box servings of tapioca pudding.

The unmistakable smell of urine greeted me as I stepped into the doorway of the Meadowood Elderly Care Facility, which was neither in a meadow nor near a wood. Actually, come to think of it, the nursing home smelled just like Cook County lockup. The inmates were nicer here, and most of them were in wheelchairs or wandering around in bathrobes, but it had basically the same smell. And the same distinct feel of incarceration.

I found Charles McMillan in room seven. Lucky number seven. Wearing a plaid bathrobe and playing a game of gin rummy. Alone.

"Mr. McMillan?"

"He's not here," he growled.

I checked the name on the door.

"You're not Charles McMillan?"

"Who wants to know?"

"I do, sir."

He looked up. "Who in tarnation are you?"

His wife hadn't warned me about this part. I'd assumed the man had dementia. Instead, he just seemed pathologically cranky.

"Dylan Foster," I said. "I'd like to talk to you about the Vendome hotel."

He hesitated.

"And I brought some tapioca pudding."

"You talked to Pearl, didn't you?"

"Yes, sir, I did. May I come in?"

"Only if you bring a spoon."

I went back to the nurse's station and rustled up a spoon, popping the top on the tapioca as I sat down opposite Charles McMillan.

He took a bite, which seemed to pacify him considerably.

"What do you want?" he said, without looking up.

"I want to ask you about a day in 1972," I said. "The day the little boy fell off the balcony."

He looked up, his denim-blue eyes seeming to focus on me at last.

"Joey Zocci," he said to me.

"Yes. You remember."

"Course I remember. Kid went flying off a balcony in my hotel. While I was on duty. I felt responsible. You have no idea."

I did, actually.

"Who are you?" he snapped.

"I'm a psychologist. His brother was a patient of mine. He jumped off a twelfth-floor balcony at the Vendome three weeks ago."

He swore and put his pudding down.

"Do you remember the room number?" I asked him.

"1220," he said, without hesitating.

I felt a chill start at my scalp and race down my spine.

"How do you remember the number so clearly?" I asked. "Just because it was such a traumatic event?"

"Fool family stayed in that room for twenty more years after that. The rest of the time I was at the Vendome. Probably still do." He gestured with his spoon. "Not all the time. They didn't live there, mind you. Some people do. After Joe Zocci made his money, they had some big estate in the country. But every time they came to the Vendome they stayed there. Same room."

"Why do you think they did that?" I asked.

"Joe Zocci, that's why." He stabbed at the pudding.

"Meaning?"

"Man's a tyrant. He did it to punish her. That's what I think. That's what I've always thought."

Her? My puzzle was falling apart. I wanted to blame Joe.

"Punish whom?"

"His wife. That Mariann."

"For what?"

He kept his eyes on his pudding and continued stabbing at it.

"No one has ever asked about this. And I've never talked about it. Never said a word to anyone."

He got up and shuffled around the room in his slippers, an arthritic version of pacing. "You see everything in the hotel business. Every little quirk these people have. They ask for raspberry Jell-O at 4:00 a.m. They need down pillows or feather pillows or those dang hypo allergy ones. They drink too much whiskey and throw up on the floor or leave their dirty underwear behind or watch smut on that dang cable they would never watch in their own homes."

He sat back down. "People do things when they're away from home they don't want anyone to know about. They are their worst selves. Absolutely their worst selves. And you don't talk about it. You never say a word about any of it to anyone. You just don't." He jabbed his spoon in my direction. "No one has ever asked me about this."

"Asked what? About Mariann? Did she kill the little boy?"

"No one knows what happened to that little boy," he snapped.

"Punish her for what then? Was she supposed to be watching him? Did he blame her for the accident?"

"Have you met Joe Zocci?" He was almost shouting now.

"Yes," I said. "He's a cruel man."

"Where was he on October 2, 1972? You ever ask him that?"

"I assumed he was there. At the Vendome."

"Man's a war hero."

And then it dawned on me. I'd read it in the newspaper articles in the Zoccis' library that evening. Zocci had been shot down in Vietnam. In 1971. He'd spent the next two years chained to a wall in a prison in Hanoi.

"He wasn't at the Vendome that day, was he?"

"No."

"Was Mariann alone?"

"No."

"Was she with another man?"

He didn't say anything.

"Mr. McMillan?"

"I've never talked about it."

So that was it. Mariann Zocci had checked into the Vendome in 1972 with another man. While her husband was in prison in Vietnam. Their son had died that day. And Joseph Zocci had punished her for it for the rest of her life.

"Who was it?"

He didn't say anything.

"Mr. McMillan?"

"Garret," he said finally. "Name's Garret."

30

~

MARIANN HAD CHECKED into the Vendome alone, but had spent that weekend in 1972 with a man named Sheldon Garret, a New York businessman who had made his fortune in men's clothing. That was all he knew, McMillan told me. He had neither seen nor heard from Garret since the day the little boy died.

Garret's name had never appeared on the hotel's register. As far as McMillan knew, the police had not even known of his existence. No mention of him had ever appeared in the media.

Mariann had never been accused of killing the boy. Or of neglect leading to his death. The investigation had wrapped up quickly, the death ruled an accident.

Apparently, neither Mariann nor Garret had noticed Joey Zocci wander out onto the hotel balcony. The toddler had squeezed himself through the bars of the railing to retrieve a toy car that had rolled past the railing, and had then fallen twelve floors to his death.

The Vendome had replaced all its balcony railings after the accident, closing the gap in the wrought iron to four inches from six.

I thanked Mr. McMillan for his time and honesty and said my good-byes.

"Next time bring whiskey," was all he said to me as I left.

I had no time to look for Sheldon Garret. But I had a hunch that if I tracked down Garret Industries, I would find him. I drove straight for the airport, surrendered my car, and then endured a marathon of security check-in procedures before falling asleep in the waiting area at my gate.

The loudspeaker woke me up as they called my flight. I prayed for a safe return home as I boarded.

The late run to Dallas from Chicago was surprisingly full, populated with hapless travelers like myself who would rather be anywhere but on a plane at 12:15 in the morning.

I found myself in a middle seat—no doubt a consequence of my late ticket purchase—squeezed between a snoring teenager with truly astonishing body odor and a man at least twice my body weight. He made no pretense of cramming himself into his own seat. He shoved the armrest up and lapped over onto me, his seatbelt popping off each time he tried to latch it. I got not so much as an "excuse me" out of the jerk for the entire two-and-a-half-hour flight. He just sat there taking up my space, daring me to say something.

How could Jesus stand us, I wondered? We were an obnoxious lot.

I'd fought enough battles for the time being, so I conceded wordlessly to the man, squeezing my elbows to my side and scooting over into about two-thirds of my seat in order to reclaim my thigh from his. I spent the flight reading the research that Cynthia, the reference librarian at SMU, had done on Garret Industries, which I hadn't looked at until now. I discovered that many pieces of the puzzle had been in my possession the entire time. I just hadn't known what I was looking for.

Garret Industries, Inc., was founded in 1968, the year Joe and Mariann had married, a joint venture between MAZco, Incorporated, and Sheldon Garret. MAZco, I was guessing, was owned by Joseph Zocci and, I suspected, named after Mariann Zocci. Which meant Joe Zocci had named his company after his wife, who had later, while he was in prison in Vietnam, had an affair with his business partner.

The two men seemed to have a knack for sniffing out potential for profit and then going in for the kill. Garret Industries had a number of interests, all seemingly unrelated to one another. It owned a fleet of cattle trucks in New Mexico and Colorado, hotels in Hawaii, and lumber mills in the Pacific Northwest, as well as a chain of clothing stores in the Midwest.

Garret Industries had most recently, it seemed, developed an interest in drilling for oil in the Gulf states and in the Gulf of Mexico. That branch of Garret's business had begun seven years ago, I gathered around the time Andy Zocci started his company.

I flipped through the file, fascinated with the strange politics of the Zocci marriage. How had Mariann tolerated her husband's staying in business with Sheldon Garret? It must have been a constant, daily reminder of her sin and of the terrible loss of her boy. The two men had obviously been business partners, perhaps even friends, before Zocci left for Vietnam. Had Mariann and Garret been involved in a prolonged affair? Had it ended the day Joey died? Did Joe Zocci ever find out that Garret was with her at the Vendome that day?

My mind reeled with questions. But the questions would have to wait, because the plane was landing at last. I could not wait to get to my clean little house, throw myself into the tub, and then burrow under my high-thread-count sheets and my quilt. I'd probably be too excited to sleep.

At the gate, the man next to me heaved himself out of the

seat and walked away without a glance in my direction. I grabbed my carry-ons and made my way up the jetway, out of the airport, and back to my truck, which was waiting for me, all rusty and rumbly and familiar. The door opened silently, a welcome little surprise—I'd forgotten about the WD-40—and I drove through the Dallas night to my house, nodding with exhaustion as I went.

My porch light was off. I couldn't see a thing as I hauled my bags out of the truck and dropped them onto the porch. I stubbed my toe on something heavy and immovable as I unlocked the front door, swinging the door open and gasping, repulsed.

The smell that greeted me was beyond foul. It was deviled eggs times ten thousand. Rotten deviled eggs. And old shoes. And the BO from the kid on the plane.

Something buzzed past me as I flipped on the light. I didn't need to get a look at it to know what it was.

I covered my mouth and stepped into the house, leaving my bags on the porch and turning lights on as I went. Flies dotted the walls; a strange, pulsing, buzzing wallpaper, an occasional scout taking flight and humming through the nasty air around me. Their corpses were scattered over every surface. My normally spotless floors, tabletops, counters were all covered with little pepper-black flecks, their nasty wings to the ground, hairy little insect-legs pointed at the ceiling.

Peter Terry had thrown a temper tantrum.

I walked through my trashed house, doing a quick inventory and determining that nothing was missing, though the glass on every picture of my mother or myself had been broken. I unlocked the buffet in the front room and found my mother's ring, still in its little velvet pouch. The necklace had been in Chicago with me.

Nothing was out of place. Not a single thing.

Except my peace of mind. I wasn't at peace in my own home. Peter Terry had seen to that.

I couldn't see him, but I could sense his presence everywhere. It was as palpable as the smell. I could feel him watching me, feel him enjoy my revulsion, almost hear his laughter.

I was beginning to know him. Peter Terry was impulsive, rageful, mischievous. And cruelly calculating and deceitful. He had the whacked-out emotional capacity of a two-year-old on acid and the predatory mind of a serial killer. He had lied to my mother, seducing her into believing that he was just a fellow traveler, someone who would listen to her and who needed her advice. And he had lied to Erik Zocci, convincing the poor boy he was worthless. Nothing. That his life had no value. Now he was lying to Gavin. And he had set out, for some reason I might never understand, to destroy me.

But he was absolutely not going to succeed. Not tonight. Not on my turf. I remembered Tony DeStefano's words once again. As a child of the King, I was entitled to protection.

I was exhausted, but there was no sleeping now. I couldn't sleep in the house like this, and I had nowhere to go at nearly 2:00 a.m. I ran around the house, tossing out prayers as I went, throwing open all the doors and windows, airing the place out.

I vacuumed and swept and mopped and dusted until I had rid my home of every last dead fly. I emptied two cans of bug spray killing flies. I broke my flyswatter, I swatted so many. I turned all my ceiling fans onto helicopter speed, creating a wind tunnel in that house that made it impossible for anything but a jet airplane to alight in there.

By the time I was finished, the sun was coming up. The egg smell was almost gone, replaced by Pine-Sol and Windex and

Lemon Pledge. The washing machine was humming with the third load of sheets. I had decided to wash everything in the house. I'd be doing laundry for days, probably.

I was consecrating my home. Setting it apart for myself. Taking it back from the demon. He couldn't have it. It was mine.

I fixed myself a cup of tea, took a few aspirin, and settled down on my porch swing to rest. My eyes fell on the boxes my dad had shipped to me. My mother's estate records, which had almost broken my toe in the dark six hours earlier. I hauled the boxes inside and stacked them in the corner of my dining room. I'd go through them this afternoon if I had the energy. I'd told my dad I'd call him about them before the weekend.

All the fight went out of me as I sat back down on the porch swing and set my cup of tea on the porch railing beside me. The birds were singing their morning song, the sun heating up the day, and I was wilting. Not in defeat, but from fatigue.

I laid myself down on the swing, my back flat on the wooden slats and my foot on the porch, rocking myself.

I must have slept, and slept hard, because when I woke up, my face was sunburned and the sun was two hours higher in the sky. It had to be at least nine o'clock. I went back inside and washed my teacup in the sink.

All the flies were gone, as was the smell. And I had the feeling they would not be back. Maybe taking a stand against Peter Terry had liberated me. Maybe God had just decided to win the battle for me, as long as I was willing to show up and fight. I wasn't sure. But my radar was quiet. Peter Terry wasn't around. I was positive. He'd packed up and gone somewhere else.

Even with all my pending legal problems, with my job hanging by a frayed piece of thread, my professional reputation on the line, and facing prosecution in the state of Illinois, I felt safe for the first time in days. Something had happened that had granted me, for however long, a thorough sense of peace.

Once I realized I could stop moving for now, I discovered how truly exhausted I was. I felt like I could sleep for a week. I took a bath, fixed myself a peanut butter sandwich, and then snuggled myself into bed. With the drapes pulled tight, it was dark enough in my bedroom to sleep even in midday.

I made it four hours. The phone woke me up at two o'clock in the afternoon.

It was Liz Zocci.

"Did I wake you?" she asked.

"It's okay. I was up all night."

"I'm sorry. I have some bad news."

I thought I'd won a reprieve from bad news.

"What is it?"

"Mariann is dead."

I was wide awake now.

"Oh, Liz. What happened?"

"She was dead in her hotel room this morning. In her bed. She had a plastic bag tied over her head."

"Liz, I'm so sorry."

I listened as she choked back tears. "She had a hard life," she said at last.

"I know."

She pulled herself back together. "Mariann called the police after you left last night. Detective Thornton. Who seems like a really good guy. He'll probably be calling you today."

"Okay."

"She told him everything. She told him about all the years of abuse from Joe. How he'd beaten her and the kids. She gave him Erik's journal. I guess you'd given it to her."

"Yeah. I found it in his dorm room."

"She read it. I think it made an impression on her. I think that's what motivated her to call the detective. To stand up to Joe at last. Erik's words. From the grave, I guess."

"You talked to Thornton, then?"

"I spent the morning with him. I was the one who found her."

I pictured Liz walking into the room and finding her mother-in-law, still bruised from that beating, blue-faced underneath a collapsed plastic bag.

"Was her pill bottle still beside her bed?" I asked.

"Yes. It was about half full. I told him you had seen it there the night before."

"It had at least twenty pills in it when I left. Maybe she took them to get up the nerve to…" I let my voice trail off.

"Thornton doesn't think it's suicide," Liz said.

"What else could it be?"

"Joe's been arrested."

"They think Joe killed her?"

"And maybe Erik too."

I was too stunned to respond.

"You'd asked me about Erik's autopsy," Liz was saying. "No one in the family ever saw it, it turns out. Maybe Joe had it suppressed or something. He's so powerful. Who knows? But it was inconclusive. Erik died of trauma to the head and massive internal injuries. They never determined whether the head injuries were a result of his fall. Now they're thinking Joe might have hit him. And then tossed him over the rail to cover it up. Thornton told me he thinks that could be why Joe was trying to blame Erik's death on you."

"But why?"

"In a scuffle, maybe. Joe is a violent man. Maybe Erik confronted him. Everyone else was afraid to."

My mind went back to the journal, to Erik's agony over his mother's passivity. His musings that he might eventually need to do what she would not.

Liz continued. "Since the police didn't know about Joe's history, they never suspected foul play. But with Mariann telling her story to Thornton last night, and then turning up dead, he arrested Joe and charged him with her assault. They haven't charged him yet with murder. And Erik's case has been reopened."

"Wow."

"Yeah. Wow."

"So Joe's in jail?"

"I'm sure he won't be for long. He'll buy his way out of this. He'll hire the best attorneys money can buy. Probably already has. And he'll win. He always does."

"So Thornton's not coming after me? I'm the one they charged with her assault. And I was with her the night she died."

"Mariann exonerated you of the assault charge. She gave Thornton dates going back three decades of doctor's visits and hospitalizations and everything else and signed releases for all her medical records. And all the kids have come forward to confirm her accounts. She gave him more than enough evidence to convince him that Joe was the one who had beaten her, not you. The charges against you have been dropped."

"How's Andy?"

"Relieved, in an odd way. Mariann's been gone a long time. She was such a shell of a woman. Maybe she's at peace now. And maybe Joe will get what he deserves."

"I'm really sorry, Liz."

"I know. Me too."

"When's the funeral?"

"Monday or Tuesday. After the autopsy."

"Your family's had a lot of loss."

"Too much," she said.

"How's Christine?"

"She's sad. But she told me this morning before I left for the Four Seasons that Earl came by last night to tell her that Grandma says good-bye. I didn't know what she meant until I got to the hotel."

"Wow."

"Yeah. Wow."

We sat silently for a minute, neither of us knowing what to say.

"Can you come for the funeral?" she asked. "I think Mariann would want you there."

"Sure," I said, wondering where I was going to get the money.

"Andy and I would like to fly you up. We have free passes on Eagle Wing."

"Yeah, I guess you would, wouldn't you? I'd really appreciate that."

We agreed to talk later.

I cried after I hung up the phone. Cried mostly, I think, for the wreckage of the Zocci family. Two children dead and now their mother gone, after a lifetime of violence and secrets. And now the family patriarch jailed, accused of murdering his wife and son.

It was a cruel end to a terrible story. I was relieved on my own behalf, of course. And many of my questions still remained. I'd probably never get answers to most of them. But the answers themselves had lost meaning in the face of such catastrophic loss.

It wasn't a puzzle anymore. It was a massacre.

31

~

THE REST OF THE AFTERNOON passed quietly for me. I cried for the Zoccis and prayed for them. I prayed for myself. I prayed for Gavin. And I cried for my mother, whose involvement in this entire affair still mystified me. But it didn't matter, really. I missed her. I put her wedding ring on my finger, tucked myself back into bed, and slept until evening.

At six o'clock, I roused myself, ate a quick supper, and then went to visit Gavin at Green Oaks. I found him sitting with Tony DeStefano on a stone bench in the tree-shaded courtyard, the bucolic setting belying the true nature of the facility. If you didn't know to look for the locked gates and the medical charts and to listen for the misery, you'd think you were in a park somewhere. And that the boy sitting on the park bench was happy and free. Like a twenty-year-old should be.

"Hey, Gavin," I said as I walked up.

"Dr. Foster," he said. "I'm glad you came."

"I'll give you guys a minute," Tony said. He stood and walked into the cafeteria. I saw him fix himself a cup of coffee and find another spot in the courtyard. It was a nice evening to sit outside.

"How're you doing?" I said to Gavin.

"Better."

"You look good."

And he did. His eyes were clear. He was alert. He seemed lucid and fairly lively, considering what he'd been through.

"Tough week, huh?" I said.

"I heard yours wasn't too good either."

"You don't know the half of it." I could almost laugh about it now. "Tony doesn't even know this yet. I ended up in jail in Chicago."

"For what?"

"Something I didn't do. It's all over now. I'll tell you the whole story sometime. Maybe after you graduate."

"If they let me. I've missed a week."

"I think we can work that out, Gavin. When are you getting out? Have they said?"

"My shrink said tomorrow. Maybe the day after. They want to make sure I'm not going to jump off a bridge or something."

"Are you?"

"What?"

"Going to jump off a bridge or something?"

"No," he said, his face becoming somber.

"What was that about, Gavin? Why did you try to kill yourself?"

"I wish I could explain it," he said. "It's like I was in this hole. This dark, horrible, scary place. And somehow I'd convinced myself there was no getting out of it. That I was going to be in there forever. And the only way out was to die. I convinced myself it was the only option. The only solution."

"It sounds awful."

"It was. And then it was like I couldn't find myself anymore. Like I was gone. I couldn't seem to get myself out of this fog. I was seeing things. Hearing things."

"You said Peter Terry was your roommate."

"He was. I swear. That was real. He lived in that bed next to me for three days."

"The nurse told me you didn't have a roommate."

"She told me the same thing. Diane. She's nice. She's a good nurse."

"So what do you think? About Peter Terry?"

"I think I believe in demons."

"I think you do too."

"Tony says as a child of the King, I'm entitled to protection."

"He's right about that," I said.

"Good. Because that Peter Terry dude is bad news."

I laughed. What an understatement. "You are right about that."

A psych tech was gathering patients for evening group. I said good-bye to Gavin and walked over and sat next to Tony. We sat there for a while without saying anything, listening to the birds sing and to the occasional plane fly overhead.

"I wonder what else is flying around this courtyard?" I asked.

"More than either of us wants to know, I think," Tony said. "Sometimes I wonder what it would be like. To see them all."

"I think we're better off blind."

"I do too."

"You're back," he said.

"I got back last night. Late."

"You look awful."

"Thanks. I feel awful. It's been a long week."

"Gavin's better."

"Yeah. He seems good, doesn't he?"

"How long do you think they'll keep him?" Tony asked.

"A day or two. Until they're sure he's stable. He's in pretty fragile shape psychologically. He's recovering from psychotic symptoms and a suicide attempt. Obviously. You know that better than I do. They won't send him home until they're positive he's out of danger."

"He's doing well spiritually. Just seems more at peace. A little wacky still, but more at peace. Said the white guy moved out of his room."

"He moved out of mine, too, I think."

"How'd you manage that?" he asked.

"I didn't go down without a fight, I guess. I spent the entire night swatting flies."

"That's disgusting."

"Tell me about it."

"What'd you find out in Chicago?"

"It's a long story," I said. "And it doesn't have an ending yet. What I still can't figure out is, why is this all happening to me?"

"Who said it's all happening to you?"

"I'm the one in the target zone. You told me that yourself."

"Yeah, but you're not the only one. And who's to say how it's going to turn out for everyone? Gavin, for one, is better off now than he was before."

"How do you figure that?" I said, incredulous. "The kid's in a psych hospital in a town in which he knows no one but you and me. He tried to hang himself from your shower curtain. How does that make him better off?"

"He became a believer," he said simply. "Peter Terry scared him right into the arms of God."

"You think that's what this whole thing was about? Salvation for Gavin? Or did he just have the misfortune of living in a dorm room inhabited by a demon? Maybe he just got caught in the middle."

"No idea. Doesn't matter, really," he said. "Those are things you can ask Jesus one day. I got a list going myself. Until then, we don't get to know the mind of God."

"I met another angel...I mean besides the fallen one." I told him about Earl.

"See?" Tony said. "Perfect example."

"I don't follow."

"You know for sure there are two forces at work here, right? One good, one bad."

"And?"

"Which is responsible? Did God put you in this situation? Or did Satan? Did Peter Terry orchestrate all this? Or Earl?"

"Satan. Peter Terry. Whoever."

"How do you know?"

"It's obvious."

"How? How do you know?"

"Look at what's happened."

"I'm looking," he said. "Tell me what you see."

"Well, starting at the beginning, or at least at my beginning with this mess, all my colleagues think I'm nuts. They think I sent them all personalized anonymous gifts and that I'm hitting on Loser John Mulvaney."

"And what has been the result of that?"

"I'm losing my professional credibility!" I was beginning to think Tony was insane. "Surely you're not suggesting that any good could come of that."

"Why not? Maybe you're not supposed to be in that job forever. Maybe God has other work for you. Who knows? Maybe John Mulvaney needed an ego boost. Plus, you got a great necklace out of it, and you got your mother's wedding ring back."

"This entire mess has cost me a fortune," I said. "I *paid* for that necklace. And for John Mulvaney's stupid Day-timer."

"Who ordered the gifts?"

"Peter Terry," I said firmly.

"How do you know?"

"It had to be supernatural. I don't know how anyone could have known what each person would have wanted. It had to be him," I said.

"Maybe it was Earl," he said. "I love that name, by the way. Who knew there were angels named Earl?"

"Why would Earl want to get me in trouble like that?"

"Maybe he had some other purpose for it. Angels aren't omniscient, you know. They don't know the future. Maybe he took a shot and it backfired."

"You're insane."

"I'm in the right place," he said, laughing. "I think there's a therapy group starting now that we can both catch."

I thought through the week's events. It was true, as Tony said, that I couldn't pinpoint the source of most of this mess. Other than the obvious stuff. Joe Zocci had beaten his wife, for instance. That much was not up for grabs. But the spiritual layers were thicker, more opaque. I didn't have the discernment, the clarity of vision, to see through them. I wondered if I ever would.

"Let's get out of here," Tony said, standing up.

"Right behind you."

We walked to the parking lot together.

"Want to come over for dinner?" Tony asked. "Jenny's got spaghetti and meatballs."

"I'll take a rain check. I'm going to spend the evening alone. In my flyless, demon-free house, enjoying the smell of cleaning solutions and chemicals. I'm pretty excited about it."

"Let me know if you hear from Gavin before we do," he said.

"We can come pick him up if you want. Or if you get the call, you can just drop him by."

"You're going to let him stay with you? After all this?"

"Why not?" Tony said. "Kid's going through a rough time is all. Besides, he's a rookie now. He might need a little help along."

"You're a nice man, Tony DeStefano."

"Tell that to my in-laws. They still haven't forgiven me for taking Jenny off to the mission field."

"Well, you're home for a while now, right? They ought to be happy."

"We're both getting the itch already. We got a year of hard time in this cesspool," he gestured around him. "And then we're out of here."

"Where to?"

"No idea. Someplace with roaches, probably. That's what Jenny keeps telling me. I go where the roaches are."

"Better than flies, though, huh?"

Tony shook his head. "You haven't seen these roaches."

We said good-bye and I headed home. My house, as I'd predicted, remained free of flies and egg smells.

I spent the rest of the evening on the front porch returning phone calls.

My father and I agreed to talk next week after I'd had a chance to go over my mother's files. I'd set aside some time to look them over this weekend.

My brother had called. He'd heard Dad was having trouble tracking me down and wanted to know if I was okay.

Helene had called. The Pink Ice Queen lawyer had phoned her to schedule the Monday noon meeting I'd requested. I told Helene I was heading back to Chicago Monday. She agreed to call the Ice Queen for me. We made plans to meet in the morning, Helene and I, so I could tell her all about Chicago. I told her to fasten her seat belt and get ready for a strange ride. She sounded appropriately wary.

My last call was to David Shykovsky.

"David. Dylan," I said.

"You're standing me up."

"Why would you say that?"

"A woman never calls a man a day before their first date unless she's going to break the date."

"Is this written down somewhere? I've never heard that."

"It's true. It's a fact."

"I'm standing you up."

"I knew it."

"I'm sorry. I've had the worst possible week. I just can't go out dancing tomorrow night. I don't have the heart for it."

"Why don't we go do something else then? We don't have to go dancing."

"Like what?" I said. "Do you have an alternative proposal?"

"Never use the word *proposal* so early in a relationship."

"Never use the word *relationship* so early in a relationship," I said.

"I stand corrected."

"So. What do you think?"

"How about a quiet dinner? At the restaurant of your choice. Someplace with cloth napkins."

"That sounds perfect." I suggested a tiny, quiet place with a great wine list and no eggs anywhere on the menu.

"How was your trip, by the way?"

"Rough," I said. "I'll tell you about it tomorrow night. And I have to go back to Chicago Monday, I think."

"World traveler. What for?"

"A funeral."

"Oh. Want company?"

"You're inviting yourself to Chicago with me to go to a funeral? You don't even know who died."

"What does it matter? Dead people all look alike to me."

"I bet they do."

"You should take me up on this. I can be very comforting in the face of the tragic loss of a loved one."

"You're being sarcastic."

"Only partially. But I would be happy to go if you need the company. I'll stay at an entirely different hotel. No hanky-panky, I promise."

"Let's see how our first date goes before we plan our first trip together."

"I'm going to sweep you off your feet, Dylan Foster."

"We'll see."

32

~

I SPENT THE WEEKEND REGROUPING, taping my life back together, reorienting myself. I did mounds of laundry, washing every item in my linen closet and every item of clothing that I owned. I washed all my dishes, running my dishwasher constantly.

I began my attempts to launder my career, meeting with Helene Saturday morning and telling her the entire sordid story.

We agreed to postpone our meeting with the Ice Queen until I'd had a chance to talk to Detective Thornton in Chicago. I was hoping my legal woes would take care of themselves, since Joseph Zocci had been arrested for Erik's murder. If the boy had been murdered, it stood to reason that I couldn't be held responsible for his suicide. Maybe I wouldn't have to meet with the Ice Queen at all.

I spent Saturday afternoon at my dining room table, the legacy of my mother's generosity stacked in piles around me.

I fought off twinges of resentment as I pored over my mother's financial records. As my father had said, she had indeed left a sizable estate. My brother and I had each received modest trusts when she died, which, I now realized, represented a very small portion of her estate.

I had never touched a dime of mine. It wasn't that much to begin with, and it was all in stocks she had chosen as investments long before she died. I'd probably liquidate some now to get myself out of my financial hole, but I felt a little guilty about doing even that. My mother had specified that the money wasn't meant "to pay the electric bill." It was for my future, she had said.

I wondered now why she couldn't have been a little bit more interested in my future, given what she'd had to work with.

Though most of the estate's giving was left to the discretion of the trustee, who was now me, my mother's will named various charities as beneficiaries. Some of them I knew about. She'd always donated her time to a homeless shelter in downtown Houston, fixing meatloaf sandwiches once a month and handing them out to shuffling lines of lost-looking men. She had left the shelter some cash.

In the last years of her life, she'd also done some work in adult literacy, teaching classes for folks who somehow had managed to make it through their entire lives without learning to read. She'd left some money to a Houston adult literacy program.

My mother had always had a heart for these types of causes. She always sought out the people who had fallen through the cracks. The ones, as she used to say, "who have no shot in this mean world."

Halfway through the second box, I saw a name I recognized. Rosa Guevera. I couldn't place where I'd heard it. Her name was on a list of loan recipients who had received money from a nonprofit my mother supported. The organization gave small business loans—microscopic by U.S. standards—to help women in impoverished countries get on their feet. Rosa Guevera was part of a women's cooperative in South America that had received such a gift. Each of the five women in the co-op had received a grand total of five hundred dollars.

It took me the rest of the day to dredge the name from my memory.

Rosa Guevera had made my necklace. I'd learned her name in the gift shop of the Vendome. Each piece was one-of-a-kind, the man had said. Handmade.

I went to my bedroom dresser, where I had casually tossed the necklace into a jewelry box, and picked it up, feeling once again that my mother was with me. Here in my room. Reminding me of the importance of her work. Somewhere in Guatemala, Rosa Guevera was making a living because my mother had sent her five hundred dollars. A tiny, slight little sliver of my mother's estate.

I sat on my bed, holding that necklace, and cried.

Had my mother sent it to me? I'd never believed it was possible for a person to reach beyond the grave. Had Earl sent it? Perhaps he had been her messenger. *Angelos* means messenger in Greek, after all. Perhaps my mother had wanted me to understand fully the weight of her gift. Wanted me to know what five hundred dollars could do.

Or had Peter Terry sent it? Had he tried to frighten me away from finishing my mother's work? Was that why he had broken the glass in her photos and later in mine? Who had retrieved her wedding ring?

Was the gift of the necklace intended to spook me away from following my mother's lead? Or to entice me to follow it?

I didn't know. But I sat there that night, crying for my mother, grateful that she had left that five hundred bucks to Rosa Guevera rather than to me. Up until that moment, sitting on my bed with that handmade necklace in my hand, the money would have been wasted on me. I never would have understood the reach of her intentions. I vowed to myself to steward her legacy well.

I wore the necklace that night on my date with David Shykovsky. He didn't comment on it, and I didn't mention anything about Rosa Guevera or the necklace or my mother. It was almost too private. A whispered gift from my mother to me.

33

~

I WENT TO CHICAGO ALONE on Monday, David Shykovsky's offer notwithstanding. Liz and Andy had made arrangements for me to fly, first class, on Eagle Wing Air. The airline staff must have known I was flying as a guest of the Zoccis. They treated me as though I were royalty, waiting on me so attentively that I didn't want to get off the plane.

Liz and Christine picked me up at the airport.

I got another "Miss Dylan!" from Christine, which sent my heart soaring. She tackled me by the knees again and asked me if I'd brought her a present.

I produced a gaudy fake diamond tiara, complete with an enormous fake pink diamond in the center. Christine seemed delighted.

Liz turned to me. "Thanks a lot. You know she's going to want to wear that to the funeral."

"I don't think Mariann will mind."

"Probably not."

We drove straight to the funeral, which was at St. Patrick's Cathedral in downtown Chicago, and which was attended, I'm certain, by every last citizen of that city. We got there an hour early, and it was already standing room only.

I would have been standing like everyone else had it not been for the generosity of the Zocci clan. They seated me in a reserved section behind the family, which gave me a perfect vantage point to observe them.

They were a beautiful bunch. The girls, the oldest twenty-eight and the youngest just eighteen (I knew all their names from my research), were stunning. Black raven hair on all of them, their father's sharp good looks and their mother's quiet dignity. The two oldest were married, and each had two fussy children with them, whom they shushed throughout the somber service.

Andy and Liz were there with their three, Andy poised and somber as the only remaining Zocci son. He sat on the end of the first row, in the patriarch's position, his father's absence palpable and rigorously unmentioned.

Joseph Zocci, of course, did not attend. He had been denied bail. I tried to squelch my private satisfaction when I heard this—I, after all, had made bail—by praying for him. But I was lying to myself. I could offer neither grace nor mercy to this man. Only God could do that.

And though I knew God wanted me to do the same, He would have to change my heart. Because the truth is, I felt Joe Zocci was getting what he deserved. I pictured Mariann's battered face, and then Joe in his six-by-ten cell at Cook County, watching him pace the room in my mind, and I was glad. Glad he was no longer terrorizing his family.

After the funeral, at which no mention was made of how Mariann Zocci had died or of the violence that had marred her troubled life, the family and their close friends gathered at the Zocci mansion on Lakeside.

It was strange to set foot on the Zocci estate under such

radically altered circumstances. I had been there before as a fugitive of sorts, an interloper. As one who had been accused of harming this poster-perfect family.

But now, of course, I knew they were not perfect at all. That in fact their lovely appearance clashed against the putrid reality of their secrets. And the discordance was astounding.

The mood at the wake was light if not quite happy. No one seemed terribly sad to me. No one spoke of Joe. It was almost as though he had never existed. A strange silence surrounded his absence, made even more odd by the fact that he had wielded such a powerful presence.

I remarked on the lightheartedness of the event, over a plate of smoked salmon and cream cheese, to Liz.

"We're all glad for her, I think," Liz said. "That she's out of her misery. She's in a better place now."

"Do you believe that?" I asked.

"Of course. Don't you?"

"I guess it's never been quite so real to me. To think that, literally, she's better off. It's a strange idea. Heaven always seemed to me a consolation prize for having to leave earth. It always sounded boring to me."

"I think Mariann is experiencing her first true joy in decades. Maybe in her entire life," Liz said. "I hope she is, anyway. What a waste if not."

Andy walked up and offered his hand. We hadn't yet been formally introduced.

"I'm really sorry," I said. "About all of it—Erik, your mom, your dad. I don't even know where to begin."

"There really is no place to begin," he said. "Or to end, I guess. You just get back on the train and ride it out."

"What will happen now?" I asked. "To the airline, I mean?

Was your dad involved in daily operations? Will it fold without him?"

"I doubt it. No company can easily survive the loss of its founder. Or at least the loss of his reputation, at this point. But a company that big has an infrastructure far beyond one man. It'll take a hit, I think. The smaller businesses are the ones that will suffer."

"Like Garret Industries?" I asked.

"Possibly." Andy raised his glass. "To my father. The most vindictive man I've ever known."

I raised my glass as well, not sure how to respond to such a toast.

Liz raised her glass. "To your mother. I'm going to miss her."

"So am I," Andy said. He turned to me. "How do you know about Garret Industries?"

"I ran across it in my research about a gift I received. I didn't know at the time your father owned the company. Your father and a business partner, right?"

He nodded. "Sheldon Garret." He said the name without flinching. My guess was he didn't know his mother's secret. "Actually, Mother owned MAZco."

"Pardon?"

"Mother. She was the owner of MAZco Incorporated, which owns Garret Industries."

"She used Garret to try to put you out of business?"

"No, my father did."

"Come again? I don't get it."

"MAZco is named for my mother. Obviously. She and my father started the business in '69 or '70-something, I forget, with money from her family. Right after they got married. The charter specifies that all the profits be held in my mother's name. I guess because of where the money came from. Technically she was the owner of the company, but he ran it. Every last decision down to the paper clips. She had no power...or at least she never wielded any."

"So she ended up profiting from your father's efforts to put you out of business?"

"Yep. Sick, huh?"

"Very." I let it sink in. "What did she do with the money?"

"Gave it away. Every penny. All the grandkids have huge trusts, though I hope to God they never know it. Talk about the kiss of death. And she provided for us all in other ways. Covert ways. She financed the purchase of our house, mine and Liz's. There's an apartment in Chicago that everyone seems to rotate in and out of. Stuff like that."

"What's Angel Wing Air?" I asked. "One of her charities?"

He nodded. "She founded it with MAZco money. It's basically a worldwide airline, made up of small single-engine planes whose sole purpose is to support humanitarian and charity work in remote areas. Angel Wing planes bring supplies and support into areas, all over the world, that are otherwise inaccessible. There are missionaries all over Africa, for instance, who have water and antibiotics because of my mother."

And because of your father, I thought. Who could have anticipated that his cruelty would yield, in the end, such a beautiful legacy?

"Who will run MAZco now?" I asked.

"You're looking at him. Mother passed ownership to me. It's written in the company's charter that she can choose her successor. And that the new owner will have power to run the business."

"And Angel Wing?"

"One and the same," he said.

"I guess Garret Industries is going out of business. As of today," I said.

"Actually, no. My company, A&E Oil, and Garret will probably merge. Much better solution. Works out well for everyone."

"Will Sheldon Garret agree to that?"

"Sheldon Garret died six years ago."

"But I thought he was a co-owner of Garret Industries."

"He was, when it was founded."

"So you knew him?"

"I did. Really nice guy. Decent. Never understood why he went into business with my father."

I had my suspicions about that, of course, but whatever the truth of it was, Mariann Zocci had taken it with her to her grave. And I suspected Joseph Zocci would never tell.

"Guess who named the airline? Angel Wing, I mean?"

I smiled at him. "Christine?"

He nodded to the corner of the room. "Look at her."

Christine was twirling around in circles, her dress flying up around her, that gaudy tiara still sparkling on her head.

"That kid is the joy of my existence," he said. "The other two, those hoodlums," he laughed and nodded at his boys, who were banging on the grand piano, "will be the death of me. But that one, she's got my heart."

"Mine too," I said.

My cab arrived to take me to my suite at the Vendome. Liz and Andy had paid for the room, insisting I have a suite. Not on the twelfth floor, and not even on the same end of the hall as the suite where the Zocci boys died, thank goodness.

"But it is the best," they had said to me. "Just relax and try to enjoy it. You'll see what we mean."

I'd never stayed in such a nice place. I scheduled myself a massage and a pedicure for the morning—rare and wildly extravagant treats for me. I was due for an interview with

Detective Thornton at noon, to wrap up loose ends before I headed home.

I spent the rest of that evening taking a bubble bath and sitting around in my fluffy white bathrobe, ordering room service and thinking of Mariann Zocci. And of my mother. And of Rosa Guevera. And of Tony and Jenny DeStefano and their kids, toughing it out on the mission field in Haiti and Guatemala.

My mother's estate didn't have near the resources that the Zocci clan did. But I had learned recently what even five hundred bucks could do to change a life.

After I finished my supper, beautifully prepared and presented by the crack staff at the Vendome, I sat down and, on Vendome stationery, began to make my own list of missions, my mother's ring on my finger and her purpose in my heart.

34

~

ON THE WEDNESDAY MORNING after Mariann Zocci's funeral, I received a hand-written note in the mail, on stationery from the Chicago Four Seasons Hotel.

Dear Dr. Foster,

I have read my son's words and they have broken my heart. I believe that his death is mine to answer for. I cannot live the rest of my days wondering what would have been different for my children if I had never caused the terrible anger that their father felt toward me.

I have never told anyone about that day at the Vendome. Never spoken of it. You shall be my father confessor.

I was with another man the day Joey died. It was my neglect that led to Joey's death. My husband spent the rest of his life punishing me for this terrible mistake. I tried all my life to put it behind me, but my life was full of daily reminders of my sin.

By now you know my choice. I believe that no heaven waits for me. I will die in sin as I lived in sin. I hope I leave peace behind me. Without me to hate, maybe Erik's father will learn to love.

Bless me, Father, for I have sinned. It has been thirty-four years since my last confession.

—Mariann

I fought with myself briefly about whether I should have given Mariann Erik's journal. His words seemed to be the final exhibit in her long litigation of liability. The evidence with which she finally convicted herself. But I knew, even as I felt my own twinges of guilt, that Mariann's choices had ultimately been her own. Erik's pain, and certainly the pain of her other children, could not have been a surprise.

They were prisoners of war, all of them. Guilt, hard and unyielding, for a sin committed more than thirty years before had imprisoned them all.

I wasn't immediately sure what to do with the letter. Mariann had obviously meant for it to be read only by me. But my indecision lasted only a moment. My thoughts turned to Joe Zocci, who was sitting in jail in Chicago. He surely deserved, by my measure at least, punishment for his own heinous sins. He had inflicted years of horrific violence on his family, and may have murdered his own son. But of this crime he was not guilty. Joe Zocci had not killed his wife. Though I had so eagerly searched for the gavel to convict him with, I now held his exoneration, for this offense at least, in my hand.

I reached for the phone and dialed Detective Thornton. I was, after all, in no position to withhold truth. God had demonstrated ample sovereignty. He would know what to do with Joe Zocci in the end.

I grieved for the emptiness of life without grace. The Zoccis' had been a marriage of punishment, not of mercy. They had never known forgiveness. Never exchanged healing words. Mariann, I knew, had never sought forgiveness even from herself, nor had she asked it of God. Not, at least, until the last terrible moments of her life.

I hoped that Liz was right in guessing that Mariann was finally free to experience joy, that she had accepted the grace of the cross at last. The grace that had been hers the entire time, had she only known to look for it.